Bully

By

A J Kirby

A Wild Wolf Publication

Published by Wild Wolf Publishing in 2009

Copyright © 2009 A J Kirby

ISBN: 978-0-9562114-5-3

www.wildwolfpublishing.com

Cover Art by Nick Button

www.nickbutton.co.uk

"For John,
The spirit of Elvis lived in you,
You'll be sorely missed."

Chapter One

"Singin', this'll be the day that I die."

Books and film tell me that at this very moment I should be enveloped in a great shining white light. They tell me that I'll kind of mellow out the pain and simply settle into being guided down that conveyor belt into nothingness. Maybe books and film tell us this so we don't simply scream the place down in rage and fear. Maybe they don't want to turn us into dribbling wrecks at the thought of what death really is...

I can't see any white light. I don't feel mellow. Instead, my sensory perception is almost overwhelmed by the agonising pain in my chest. And it is represented by the colour purple. Angry, hopeless purple. It feels as though I've had a spear driven into the very folds of my heart and some mischievous demon is wiggling it about, tearing at the wound. I don't think that I've blacked out at any point in the last few moments since it happened. My body won't let me. It won't let me surrender or enjoy any of it.

Some people around me look as though they're enjoying it. The guy next to me has this big shit-eating grin on his face as he revels in the loss of control and responsibility. I think he could be Sergeant Davis, a man I'd once thought too serious to be taken seriously. And now look at him. Despite my own pain, I feel Davis's shit seeping out of his fatigue pants; hell, its being sieved out of his pants so I get the pure unadulterated core of it, right on my face. I can't move my arms to shield myself.

Someone's murmuring something somewhere. Somebody else is screaming. They could be privates that were under my command, but I can't tell any more. My own throat feels as though it has been cut. I can't gulp back the swimming pool of saliva which is in my mouth, and for a moment, I really believe that spit is going to be the ultimate cause of my death.

But spit is just a bi-product. The real cause of the excruciating last chapter of my life is the damn explosion which ripped through the supposedly secured building; the explosion which is still ringing in my ears.

It feels as though the explosion is still in progress. Metal and concrete tear and whine against each other. The floor I'm lying on feels insecure; as though at any moment, it will give way. I've experienced earthquakes before, and this feels like an aftershock.

But it hasn't been caused naturally. The still-sane part of me knows that. Us grunts *knew* this place was a Taliban hideaway before we set foot in here; they always look like this; a typically low-slung grey building which would be hard to pick out from the air on fly-bys, and easy to mistake for an agricultural building even if it was spotted. It's the tyre tracks in the dust that really give these places away though, like they've been goddamn parking lots in a former life. There'd been reports of miscellaneous activity – training perhaps – radioed through to our unit. Whispers from the Comms Zone that large lorries were coming in the dead of night and loading up with suspiciously-shaped objects. But, as with all such reports, we always seemed too far behind the action. When we arrived there, all we expected to find was an abandoned building, the Taliban long gone.

The low-slung building was set in a gully about five or six clicks away from a small, dilapidated town which seemed to be pretty much carved out of the lunar landscape. We all asked ourselves how the hell the locals could stand it to live in a place like that. On arrival, we handed out the odd bit of scran to them, doing our humanitarian duty like good little boys before asking them about their friendly neighbours down in the gully. And, of course, we were met with that shifty-eyed look and sudden inability to speak English, despite the fact that seconds earlier, they'd been practically climbing up our packs, shouting 'chocolate, chocolate' or 'water'.

It was always the same in Helmand – or Mayo as we called it, in homage to the most famous manufacturers of that particular foodstuff - always this uneasiness between us and the locals. Lots of the other grunts found it difficult to cope with situations like that, but I knew all about inward-looking towns and I knew all about how communicating with outsiders wasn't so much frowned upon but a hanging offence. So I suppose that's why the CO's had my lads and I stay down in the town for a while, just to see whether I could find out anything else, while Sergeant Davis and his lot went down to the gully to act as the recon squad. Apparently there'd be some men from another regiment already there waiting for them waiting to fill them in on the latest intelligence on the site.

So there were five of us that remained in the town, and everywhere we went, we were followed at a safe distance by teems of small children. They looked so helpless that we had to keep reminding ourselves of how dangerous they actually were. Hell, some of the little bastards had probably been trained right up at the gully and had remained behind as some kind of intelligence operative or something.

Nothing moved in the town apart from our little Pied Piper procession. Most of the windows were boarded up, most of the vehicles looked to have been so overcome by dust and rubble of destroyed buildings that they'd never move again. It was like a version of one of those old American Wild West towns in the films where some bandit-group has come in and killed the sheriff and made off with the loot. We were stepping into the aftermath.

As our boots crunched across the loose gravel, we didn't see many males over the age of about sixteen, but those we did – those wrinkled old specimens that sat mournfully on the roadsides – looked so immobile that they'd become a part of the landscape. And it may sound funny, but some of these men's faces were so stained by war that they'd turned purple, or so it seemed in the harsh sunlight. Some of them practically *radiated* purple so that it seemed a kind of aura around their heads. Of course, I said nothing of my strange visions to any of my men. It doesn't pay to sound like a glophead when you're Lance Corporal in the Kingsmen; it's the kind of thing that could end up as a permanent, if unspoken, destroyer of trust. And we were nothing if not a *tight* unit... So instead, we walked in silence – you get used to it here, you really do – and performed our hopeless task. Eventually, we were called up to the gully-building and we couldn't get out of that dead end town fast enough.

We're known as one of the most mobile of all of the infantry units, trained in dealing with the most demanding environments, but Mayo, Afghanistan, the heart of opium country sometimes asked us too much. Two of the younger grunts that I looked after were already struggling on our walk around town; now, in the open land where there was no shield from the blazing sun, they were starting to miss beats. I saw one of the lads – Selly from Preston – almost go down. Only his SA80, which he held in a trembling hand, stopped him from going over.

But I pushed them, despite the aching of my own legs. I pushed them because we were the Kingsmen, with over three hundred years of tradition behind us. I pushed them because Sergeant Davis would most likely complain if I took any longer than the time *he* thought necessary to cross the open land. Most of all I pushed them because it was part of me now, this machine-like intensity. And by pushing to the physical limits, I didn't ever have to go to the mental limits. I didn't have to think about why the hell I was in the arsehole of the world in the first place.

Occasionally, I did think, but only to vaguely wonder what the other men thought about when we trouped through the dustbowl. Were they, like me, staring off into the distance searching for single points of reference which were not tinted with the same sepia tones as everything else seemed to be; something that was not doused in the same dishwater brown-grey used in the credits of old episodes of *The Waltons*.

What was Reynolds possibly thinking about? With his wiry frame and his dead-shot eyes he was destined to be a good soldier, but at only a year my junior, was he frustrated by his lack of progress up the chain of command? Was he plotting, cursing his luck or simply not thinking at all? And what about Smith, the young lad with the archetypal British name; a name which should have brought him the obvious nickname of Smit or Smitty, but who, because of his Chinese

10

heritage was known as '28' after the number of a dish on a takeaway menu? Was Smith disappointed or angry with his lot? He certainly never seemed to be. In fact he never seemed to be much of anything. Most of the time I wasn't even sure if he ever listened to what anybody said. Certainly, he never made much of a response, save his oddly Mancunian grunt of 'yessir' or 'can I have a snout?'

How about Delaney, the only one of us that was married with children; did he spend his time thinking about when he'd next see them again or did he block them out of his mind completely? I knew he carried their photographs around with him, but that was common. Some men were so determined to have *someone* back home that I suspected their photos were downloaded from websites or cut out from magazines. Delaney was known as Diva because he was always moaning; he even moaned about the nickname that had been dished out to him, which of course simply reinforced the fact that the rest of the grunts had chosen wisely.

And then there was Selly, the youngster that I'd had no bones about making my favourite. Did he realise how much he relied upon the rest of us? Did he realise that even as he walked, Reynolds and Smith often mocked him? Poor Selly reminded everyone of a puppy-dog. He had huge feet and hands which he looked as though he still needed to grow into properly; sandy hair which became mop-like when he didn't shave it. Selly had the most nicknames of anyone I knew. Reynolds liked to call him 'Dulux'; Delaney liked to call him 'Chubs'; Smith, when he could bring himself to speak to the big daft lump, referred to him as 'Forrest', as in Gump.

But bullying like this was par for the course and I let it go, even joined in if the mood took me. The powers-that-be in the forces actively encouraged it; it was their stock in trade to belittle the shit out of a man and then build him back up into the machine that they wanted him to be. That I'd actually been promoted in my time meant that I was already on the way to being half-Terminator.

To my left, Selly had started to whine again: 'Why couldn't they leave one of the Landies for us to take? Why do we always have to walk everywhere?'

'Are we nearly there yet?' mocked Reynolds.

Delaney snorted with laughter.

Smith plodded.

'Shut up Selly,' I said, letting him walk past and then planting a gentle kick up his arse. Just to be friendly, like. He staggered forward a little. For a moment I thought he was going arse –over-tit, but he managed to correct himself. Then he started to walk on a little ahead of the rest of us, sulking.

'The little arse-wipe,' sneered Reynolds, 'he's just like a little rug-rat.' And for one dangerous moment, he reminded me of someone in my past. Another shark that could scent the blood of a weaker animal from so many miles away. I had to bite back the urge to crack him one, but I also had to bite back the urge to join in with him. Because although Selly was my favourite, I also hated him for his weakness. And sometimes it paid to let people know that you knew *exactly* how weak they were.

'This dust gets everywhere,' moaned Delaney, and then all of us launched into him instead, knowing that he could take it.

Presently, Selly returned to the main group. He already looked to have got over his sulk; even looked excited about something.

'I can see where they are,' he panted, 'the sarge and them…' He paused to get his breath, gesturing towards a slight ridge in the distance. I shielded my eyes and peered off into the nothingness and then finally saw what looked to be a collection of medium-sized vehicles and a large group of men.

'Nice one, Sells,' I said, by way of thanks, apology and whatever else he wanted it to be. And there was a new spring to our step as we picked our way across the shit-tip towards Davis and whatever other regiment were there to offer reinforcements.

Now we could actually see our destination, the going was better. It seemed somehow less hot. But something was still concerning me. When Selly had first pointed out the camp on top of the ridge, all I'd seen at first was a mass of dazzling purple light, flickering like a fire shot through a purple lens on a camera. Only after screwing up my eyes had I picked out the individual figures and vehicles. Only after I'd convinced myself that it was a trick of the light or of the desert or of dehydration. Nevertheless, it worried me. It seemed like some kind of a sign that things were not as they seemed; not easy. The whole thing was making me uneasy, especially after I'd seen virtually the same light display in the faces of the old men by the roadside in the town. I gave an involuntary shudder and then furtively looked around the grunts to check whether they'd noticed. It wouldn't do to be caught shivering out here in the scorched desert; it was a sign of weakness.

As we approached, I saw that there were about fifty men, arranged haphazardly across the ridge at the top of the gully in between five or six Wolf Land Rovers and a Challenger. Sergeant Davis and the man I took to be the sarge from the other regiment were the only ones standing; they were having an animated discussion. I didn't envy the other sarge; Davis was one boring fucker at the best of times. The worst of times was generally when you first got to meet him; when he was trying to impress his iron will upon you like it was a job interview or something.

'Look at them lounging about like they're catching some rays,' said Delaney. 'They're worse than the Septics, this lot.'

It always riled our boys that whenever we were engaged in some heavy menial task or other, Davis's men or the Yanks or men in other regiments weren't. He took it as a personal affront. What he didn't ever seem to get through his thick skull was the fact that when *we* were on a bit of R & R, generally it would be Davis's men or the Yanks or men in other regiments that were working, or policing the war-torn streets, or dealing with the civilians. Still, Davis's grunts *were* resting. Leaning against their packs and smoking snouts. Looking for all the world as though they were in the middle of enjoying a nice, comfortable walk in the British countryside and they'd only stopped for a bite to eat. Only the fact that each man still wore their helmet and had one hand clamped on his SA80 told me that they were in any way concerned; but that, I suppose, is the monotony of fear. Something you get more than used to in the Kingsmen.

'Have a rest yourselves boys,' I said, 'I need to go over and talk to the sarge and see what the plan is.'

My lads jumped at the opportunity and moved over to lean against one of the three Wolf Land Rovers and regain their breath. I noticed that they stood *as a four*, slightly away from the other grunts. Despite their personal differences, they still recognised the importance of standing tight as a group, especially when other eyes were on us.

'Anything from the town?' Davis barked over at me as he saw me approach.

'Nothing, sarge' I confirmed. 'As per usual.'

I waited patiently for Davis to introduce me to the other sergeant, wondering whether he'd bother; wondering whether he'd yet again try to reinforce his own position by undermining everyone else's.

'So are we all set to go now, Davis?' asked the other man. 'The Second Yorkshire's have been ready for twenty minutes now…'

They really were two peas in a pod. Apparently my duty was done and neither of them had thought it necessary to tell a grunt like me what we were planning to do. As I walked away, I heard them start to talk again. Something about the building being abandoned as suspected. Something about being on the lookout for trip-wires. Something about there being no need for snipers.

I walked back to my lads and nodded to them. I took a pull of water offered by Smith – which tasted overwhelmingly of cigarettes of course, but anything was better than the taste of the water purifier tablets - and wiped some sweat off my brow.

'So what's the plan, Lance Corporal Bull?' asked Selly. And in that moment, he became my favourite again. He had seemed to sense the need to reassert my authority after the shambolic chat with the two sergeants, and yet he was as thick as two short planks which had been gradually whittled down into ashtrays. Through pure, numb luck rather than judgement, he always seemed to pull me right out of my bad moods. But then, whatever life you walk, it's always comforting to know that there's someone, somewhere that's far, far worse off than you.

'Fuck off, Selly,' I said, already feeling back to my best. 'You don't need to know that at this stage of the game.'

14

I watched him flop back down by the Wolf and start to fiddle with the cap of his water bottle. Sand and dust would get in there if he continued the way he was going, but he didn't seem to care. Reynolds flicked a bit of cigarette ash onto the lad's lowered head, but Selly didn't even notice because of the helmet. But there was something else too; he was lost in his own world; probably one in which big Dulux dogs like him frolicked in the sun and were rubbed on the stomach once in a while by their owners and betters; people like me.

One of the doors of the landie was open, and from the inside, the low, tinny sound of music could be heard. I tried to place the song. Knew I'd heard it before somewhere in the deep mists of time. I listened hard to try to pick out the lyrics which were fuzzy at best. But it was only when Private Smith started humming along that I realised what it was; Don McLean's 'American Pie'. Somehow, it seemed wildly out of place for him to be singing it here. But maybe that was because the song once meant so much to me; reminded me of long, hot summers back home. There was a reason I'd not listened to it for a while though, wasn't there. And I didn't want to think of that now; this could well be the day our music died.

Soon, the men were called to assemble and we started to walk down into the gully, picking our way through assorted debris and over sharp-looking rocks. It didn't make for easy-marching. Again, I felt that uneasy feeling creaking up within me, only now we were coming so close to the building, it was starting to transform itself into dread. And so, when Sergeant Davis started walking alongside me, it took me a while to notice.

'Lost in your own world, Lance Corporal?' he asked, with this nasty little smile on his face. I could barely bring myself to look at him. He was a big man and he still wore a moustache, despite the fact that he probably knew all about how the privates ripped him for it behind his back. He had this annoyingly superior way about him as though he thought he knew everything in the world and it was his solemn duty to impart it to country-bumpkins such as me.

'Sorry sarge,' I muttered.

He waved away my apology and grunted as he climbed over a particularly large piece of rusted machinery. Why he couldn't have stepped around it was beyond my comprehension.

'This gully was most likely made by a tributary of the Helmand River that's long since dried up,' said Davis as he rejoined my path. Sometimes, I wished he could just lighten-up a little. This wasn't a damn geography test. We weren't supposed to think; not too much. 'That's maybe why we can't see any opium fields round here... Or much of anything really.'

I grunted by way of response. What with the way that my scalp was itching so much from the pressure-cooker helmet, and the steepness of the slope down the gully, it was all I could do to stop myself from saying something I'd later regret. But sometimes, just sometimes, I thought about how delightful it would be if Davis wasn't around any more. If I didn't have to subject myself to his looming presence and his stony-faced disapproval of the way I handled the four men under me.

Stony was pretty much a good description of Davis, in fact. He was like a massive boulder that got in the way of all my plans. A man so set in his ways it was as though concrete had been set in his blood. Sometimes, I thought I could hear the rumbling of his joints when he walked with me.

'Good terrain for training,' he said. 'The Taliban picked well. And even the Landies couldn't get down to the building from this direction...'

'We could have gone round the other way,' I muttered. 'Taken a Wolf.'

Davis looked at me sternly, shook his head and said: 'But that would have taken away from the element of surprise.'

Dread was setting in strong now. Who was he hoping to surprise? What was he hoping to surprise? I thought he said the building was abandoned...

Soon, he started to sense my mood and my unwillingness to talk and he stepped up his pace to join another of the Lance Corporals – a renowned arse-licker that seemed to *just love* Davis's geographical

16

lectures - and I was again left with my only own thoughts for company, despite being surrounded by fifty men.

Thankfully, we reached flatter ground in time, and soon could pick out the low-slung building, which was in fact *two* buildings, separated by a small courtyard which was filled with overflowing bins and leftover equipment. Silence had crept up behind us and taken over us all, and now all we could hear was the lazy rattling of one of the shutters in the light breeze and the occasional heavy clump of someone's boots on the turf. Even Selly didn't feel the need to speak, for once. I watched him as he followed *exactly* in Private Smith's footsteps as though it were some kind of superstitious game, like a child trying not to step on the cracks in the pavement. Perhaps it was his way of trying to waylay death; perhaps it was his way of trying to sneak *around* death and out the other side, into his own little world of Dulux dogs. Or maybe he was worried about landmines? For about the first fortnight he was here, he walked everywhere like a cat on a griddle-pan. Only after numerous complaints from the rest of the lads did I set him straight.

But here there were no landmines. They'd swept the area, hadn't they? There were other worries though. We were in full view of the building now, but surely if there was some sniper inside, he'd have started to pick us off by now. There were lots of little cracks in the concrete walls through which an AK47 could have been poked, and yet there was no fire. I began to agree with the sarge; the place was dead; abandoned. We'd find nothing here just like they'd found nothing in so many similar places across the province.

I wasn't scared of death, not then. But I suppose that I was scared of what would come next. What would be waiting for me afterwards. I knew I was going to hell, but then, what was this place if it wasn't hell already? And it was these thoughts that *made* my stubborn legs keep going as we crossed a fence and into the scrubland out front of the buildings. And yet, still nothing.

In the courtyard, we stepped over feral cats that could barely even muster up the energy to glimp up at us. It was so hot that we could almost see them cooking as they lounged. I braced myself for the sight of Selly reaching down to stroke one of them, but he kept to his task wearing a pale mask of concentration that probably matched my own.

Davis took the lead, frantically gesturing for various divisions to approach the building in several different directions. There seemed to be four or five entrances – broken-down stable doors and the like – and apparently he wanted all of them covered. Which made sense, I suppose.

I led my men to the furthest entrance; one which was partially blocked by a large, rusting piece of corrugated iron. We slipped quietly along the concrete walls, just as we'd been trained. We kept low, but mobile; even Selly. When we reached the entrance, I looked each of my men in the eye. Somehow, I knew that it was important that I did this. Reynolds looked typically dead-eyed and keen to get on with it; Smith looked typically non-plussed by the whole situation; Delaney looked a little sulky. But Selly; Selly wore this look that scared the shit out of me. His face, which had been so pale on the approach, was now blazing hot. His cheeks looked almost purple.

And that look at Selly made my decision for me. Without another moment's thought, I pushed the corrugated iron away from the door and we stepped into the building. The smell of decay was everywhere; nobody, it seemed, had been here in a long time.

And they hadn't. Only, bombs can sleep for a long time before they go off. They don't really care how long they have to stay awake. And depending on how well they are made, they can still be alert long after even the hardiest of soldiers would have lost patience. And Davis's recon squad never noticed the bomb that the Taliban had left behind at the low-slung building. And when Davis or Selly or any of the other men stepped through the door, it was primed and waiting for them.

Hello boys. I wondered what had taken so long...

So now, as I try to think about what I would have done differently; as I try to make whatever deal will stick with whoever ultimately controls the universe – *if* there is anyone – a sense of regret mixes with the pain. If I hadn't got so ratty with Davis as we traipsed down the slope. If I hadn't wished him dead at one point. If I'd checked for bombs myself... If only I'd paid attention to the warnings I'd had; the purple.

But none of it will do any good. If a second blast occurs, I won't be as lucky. I won't be able to run. I'm stuck under one of the displaced room beams. Some other thing has come down from there and pinned me right against the floor by the chest. There is no escape. I'm a sitting duck.

I can't even remember the explosion itself. It's like a massive mental block, like my head-loss. One minute I was stepping through that door, the next I was laying on the floor. I try to close my eyes; close out the pain. Death is coming to be now. Death is closing in and I don't know what to do about it. In fact, the only thing I can do is to try to hasten its ill-effects by *making* my life flash before my eyes.

I try to remember the faces of those that are closest to me; my old dad, my fiancée Jane, my brother, Selly, Reynolds, Smith, Delaney... But for some reason – maybe the wiring to my brain's gone to pot – all I can think of is the faces of some of the boys from back in Newton Mills. That was a long time ago, almost in another life.

I can't even remember the last time I thought of Newton Mills properly, let alone the people. The guy wedged above me in this train-wreck of a building has been with me for the past few months on this mission and yet I can't even remember why I hated him so much. The guys from Newton Mills - Tommy Peaker in particular - have been buried under the rubble of the rest of my life for so long now that it is almost scary to think of them now, and at a time like this. I've tried to put them out of my mind. And yet today I heard 'American Pie' again. Today I was painfully reminded of one of the boys back there through the cruelty of one of my men. And now, I almost believe that if I reach out, I could touch them.

Newton Mills; I wince in pain at the thought. I remember the line from *Godfather III:* 'Just when I thought I was out, they pull me back in...' Maybe after all, I'm being punished for the things that happened back there. Maybe I'm being punished by the restless spirit of the kid we bullied into the grave... That's a chapter of my life that I want buried beneath everything else by the way, if anyone's listening. And if that means that I have to die right here, right now, then so be it. So be it.

From above, ceiling tiles start to rain down on us once again. Then come the clouds of dust, and probably asbestos too, although now's probably not the time to be worrying about minor health and safety fears like that. From somewhere else, perhaps my own pocket, I hear a radio crackling pointlessly. I hear urgent barked enquiries from HQ. I groan in response, which in turn causes my throat to constrict yet more and the spear in my chest to twist in complaint.

And suddenly, silence sweeps the building. Everything stops creaking and groaning; people, walls, *everything*. It is a snapshot moment of absolute peace which must be something like what death is really like; just eternal nothing. I know exactly what is going to happen next. This moment of calm is like the building taking a final sucked breath before it suddenly gives up altogether and collapses.

I've taken a deep breath too; steeling myself for what is to come. My nostrils take in gallons of dust, the scent of shit, the stench of fear. They also take in another smell; one that I'd not noticed before. It smells strangely familiar but in amongst everything else I find it hard to place. It is a tangy, salty kind of smell. It's out of place, here.

'It's too early for you,' says a voice in my ear, scaring the shit out of me. *'This is not your time.'*

'What?' My eyes try to scan the room for the source of the voice. It is difficult because I can't really move my head at all, but I'm pretty sure that it's not any of the men from the mission. It's not Selly or Davis, Reynolds or Smith. They are all stuck inside their own private hells, I know it.

'Not your time,' repeats the voice, tickling my ear with its closeness. I am now absolutely sure that the voice is not coming from any of the other men, but also that it's not the outward projection of a voice in my head; I'm not totally mad yet... That smell has grown strong now too, and suddenly I know what it is. It's the rich sweaty aroma of fish.

I feel something touch my arm; icy fingers crawl under my armpit. I feel myself being jerked upright and away from the grip of the roof-beam. I feel myself being spirited up off the ground and collected-up into the arms of something powerful. It's as though my weight is as irrelevant as that of a very small child...

The last thing I hear before I finally black out is the second explosion, and by this time, I know that I'm already, miraculously, outside the building and back in the courtyard. In the distance, I can hear one of the feral cats meowing in fear or pain or victory.

Chapter Two

"Dirges in the dark"

I couldn't remember the last time I dreamed about school. Could you? There was a time, once, when I had near-nightly panic attacks about being late for an exam or walking naked along the familiar black and white chessboard tiles of the corridors. Even after I had long finished with my education, the dreams continued on a regular basis. Some people on the mission claimed that they still had them; these dreams. Perhaps it was on account of the fact that the routine and regularity of the army was so similar to school-life. But I seemed to have finally buried them when I started being posted abroad, and my dreams, when I had them, were populated by fragrant-smelling foreign women. Most of the time, I hardly dreamed at all; the booze saw to that.

Nevertheless, as I came to, I felt the air thick with the Newton Mills smell; a mixture of the aromas from the toffee works and the undertone of faraway muck-spreading from the surrounding farmlands. I could also pick out the claggy scent of cigarettes and a vague texture of stale beer. *That* had been the Newton Mills I knew once, and I was so convinced of the reality of it that it took me a good while to work out that I had been dreaming, or whatever they call that recurring flick-show of images that revolve around your head when you're dead to the world. For a fleeting moment, I thought that all I needed to do was reach out and I'd be able to touch the reassuring bulk of Cross-Eyed Lion or feel the rap of a deck of Twinnie's cards on my knuckles. Or maybe Tommy; maybe Tommy…

When I opened my eyes, my dream quickly slipped away. I was clearly *not* in Newton Mills at all. And the new reality slipped over me like a comforting blanket; I could hear the cicadas croaking outside;

could feel the parched heat on my skin; could smell foreign spices; could still feel grains of dust and sand on me in places where they surely couldn't have hoped to have infiltrated. I wasn't even in the same country as Newton Mills; I puffed out my cheeks in relief.

My behaviour must have given the rest of the inhabitants of this new room much amusement. For it's not many people that wake up in a military hospital and look so delighted to be there. Or come to think of it; perhaps my reaction was a completely ordinary one. I'd swapped one hell for another, but at least I was alive. And fully intact too. A swiftly gathered inventory of my body parts confirmed that no part of me had been blown off in the blast. Sure I couldn't move properly, but I was all there; physically at least. What had happened to that spear which had been sticking out of my chest?

The room was much as you'd expect from a makeshift hospital in the back of beyond; some farm building which had been quickly commandeered for that use. You could still see the holes in the corrugated iron ceiling and a light spattering of stars in the sky. Behind the pale blue medical curtains, you could see that the paint on the walls was peeling. Underneath the smell of cooking and of disinfectant, there was the unmistakeable smell of cow-shit.

There were six beds in the room, arranged into three rows of two like the starting grid for a grand prix. Indeed, the metal struts at the head and foot of each bed did a good impression of the grill at the front of a car. Only the 'passengers' spoiled the illusion. Three of the beds were unoccupied, but the one next to me contained the broken body of a man that had fared much worse than me. His face was destroyed, as were his legs. Occasionally, he would let out a growl, much like an old dog at the vets that knows he's about to be put down. It wasn't a growl of rage at the fact that he was surely going to die, but rather a growl which said, *why the fuck don't you just get on with it?*

I wondered if the man in that bed would turn out to be Selly, and his puppy-like yelping over the past few weeks had finally crossed over into full, doggy adulthood. Or perhaps it would be Smith, or Reynolds. And would they still be gasping for a cigarette despite the fact that we'd all come so close to death? Would the fact that this person didn't even have a face any more act to finally make them

23

knock the old ciggies on the head? I knew it wouldn't be Diva Delaney. He would have been moaning far more than this poor guy was; he'd have been screaming the place down, bringing the corrugated iron roof crashing down on our heads like another, much later aftershock.

But even thinking about Selly, Smith, Delaney and Reynolds made me feel light-headed. I was responsible for those men. Somehow, I already knew that the three of us in that room were the only survivors of the blast. Which meant that two of them had already departed; which meant that I would have to inform the parents; which meant that I was the one that would have to feel guilty for the rest of my life.

It's a funny thing, guilt. Well, actually, it isn't; it's not funny at all. I know what feeling guilty can do to a person. How it can empty them; leave them nothing but a shell of what they once were. In a way, it would be better if the destroyed man next to me was Sergeant Davis, here with his punishment for what had come to pass; ready to discuss the geography of the region at length to his captive audience; me.

I sighed, wheezing like an old man would. Screwed my eyes tightly shut and tried to numb myself to the mental limits of pain.

'Nice place, huh?' said a voice from the other occupied bed. It came so suddenly that I felt my heart creak in complaint. My vision was still blurry so I couldn't make out his condition, but judging by the sound of his voice, he wasn't as badly off as the other man.

I tried to sit up in bed, but felt an overwhelming pain as I tried to use my arms. They felt as though they'd been dragged out of their sockets by some unnatural force. Although they weren't broken, they were perhaps dislocated. I gasped, tried to grit my teeth. I felt the overwhelming urge to cough, but somehow knew that if I did, it would send more wracking pain through me.

'Don't move, lad,' said the voice. 'You'll only aggravate your injuries.'

The voice was strong, with a hint of a broad Yorkshire accent. Not Tyke though; that had a more street-wise manner to it. This man's voice was rich and also rather slow. Probably, the owner of the voice was from uppermost North Yorkshire; probably he was a country boy like me.

After meeting so many folk from so many different places, I'd become pretty adept at reading accents. I was a bonafide cunning linguist, if truth be told. Some part of me wanted to laugh at the thought. *Cunning linguist;* I wanted to screech with unrestrained laughter just like when I used to feel that same urge to laugh in funerals. You just know that you can't do it; that it would be the most disgraceful thing in the world, and somehow that makes it all the more funny. And infectious, like someone farting in assembly or making jokes about the girl in the year below that only has a few sickly weeks to live. A spluttering half-cough, half-laugh erupted in the back of my throat.

'What you laughing at?' snapped the man in the bed.

'Nothing,' I muttered, trying to rein this gust of childish freedom which had somehow blustered into my head. I'd always been a bit sick in the head; easily led astray. And although I tried my hardest to keep myself on the straight and narrow – like by joining-up – I found it hard not to give way to the *head-loss.* That's what I'd come to know it as; a wind-wild head-loss which made me just join in with whatever terrible scheme somebody else had dreamed up until it reached its logical and terrible conclusion. And then I felt guilty. *Ah! There's that guilt again,* I'd think, and I'd welcome it like an old friend.

'Sorry,' I muttered. 'I just can't get my head around it… I can't remember everything…'

I could remember the aftermath of the blast all right and most of what happened before, too. I was buying myself time. I could remember everything but the point of impact, and that was the truly scary thing. *Those arms grabbing me… That voice in my head…*

'You don't wanna remember everything,' said the Yorkie.

Again, I tried to train my eyes to see again. In the flickering artificial light, it wasn't easy, but eventually I made him out, or at least, I made out his form on the bed and the terrible fact that although one leg was being held by a hoist, there was no corresponding *other* leg underneath the starched sheets. I slumped back down onto the pillows and felt bad for laughing. But in truth it was the shock what did it, your honour. People that have been through what I've been through are liable to behave like loons for a while, if not for the whole rest of their lives; I suppose it's the knowledge you have about death, the fact that it's still waiting, tapping its staff with impatience. And you know too that what he'll do to you won't be pretty. Oh, it won't be pretty at all.

'What won't be pretty?' asked the Yorkie, a new slyness creeping into his voice. I hadn't realised that I'd been speaking aloud. I'd thought that the thoughts were spinning around my head, crashing into one another like bumper cars, but apparently I'd been speaking after all, like an old drunk that's got so used to the company of the voices in his whacked-out Ice-Dragon head that they just mumble along without caring.

'If you're worried about your injuries,' he continued, 'then don't. You'll still be a pretty-boy. In comparison to us two, you got out of there with hardly a scratch on you at all,' he said. Then he whispered something which made my blood run cold: 'People are saying that you got yourself some kinda guardian angel, son. Someone that pulled you out that building when all hope was lost. Everyone else in that building was fucked, and I mean fucked; but you?'

'Got lucky,' I whimpered.

There was a long silence. Uncomfortable; we listened to the injustice in the other bed; the unfairness of that man's life being chosen instead of mine.

'Don't feel guilty for getting out of there alive,' said the Yorkie. 'That's the last thing you wanna do. I been lying here a good few days listening to you talk to yourself and him groaning, and all I thought was that he lost his body but you lost your head. *I* felt guilty... It ain't a nice feeling... What's your name?'

'Lance Corporal Bull,' I replied, shifting uncomfortably in the sheets. 'Kingsmen...'

'Ah, the Duke of Lancaster's Regiment,' he said, 'so you're from the red rose county then, eh?'

'I am, mate,' I said.

'White rose through and through, myself. I'm in... I was Corporal in the Second Yorkshires...'

I suddenly felt thoroughly sick of all of the formalities. Here we were, blasted to fuck in some godforsaken country that most of our relatives back home couldn't even locate on a map, and all we could talk about was our proud regiments. The same proud regiments that had got us blasted to fuck in the first place. And it wasn't just the fact that he ranked higher than me that rankled; something about the fact that his injuries were far worse than me rankled too. Hell, he'd probably be up for at least one blag rag for getting so badly injured.

'Look,' I interrupted, 'call me Gaz. Gaz Bull.'

'Good name that; sounds kinda like a footballer's name,' said the Yorkie, sounding more convivial than he had before. 'What's your dad's name? Terry?'

I'd heard it all before; dad called Terry-Bull, mum called Una-Bull... Most of my friends just called me Bully; always had, always would. I knew that this stranger would end up calling me by the same name; Bully by name, bully by nature. Maybe it was in my genes to be this way. Maybe, no matter how hard I tried, there was no other way that I'd have turned out.

'What do they call you?' I asked. Gradually, my eyesight was starting to return. I could make out the Yorkie's thick dark hair and his unshaven chops. I could see his jutting forehead, like the overhang of a cliff, and reckoned that he would have been adept at the head-butt. Hell, he probably made the head-butt his special-move.

'Dean,' he said, creasing up his heavy forehead with concentration, as though it was a struggle to remember his own name. 'Dean Howitt. Or Do-Nowt to me pals.'

I chuckled to myself; in his soft country accent, Dean Howitt did sound a bit like 'do-nowt.' I wondered if he was similarly cursed by his name. Had his name caused him to be a lazy bastard that couldn't be bothered to do much of anything? Probably not, I concluded, on account of the fact that like me, he was stuck in this military hospital. People don't just get their legs blown off for no reason. He must have been doing *something* to cause it. Perhaps his name was one of those ironic names.

'Sorry about your leg, Dean,' I said, trying to take all emotion out of my voice; trying to sound sympathetic as most people would have done in this kind of situation. Or perhaps 'most people' wouldn't have even mentioned the leg at all. He fixed me with his bloodshot blue eyes for a heavy moment and then gave me a reassuring smile. Evidently surviving an incident like we had allows you to say just what the hell you want and people just oblige.

'So am I,' he said, making this grimace as though to show how hard he was. 'But to tell you the truth, I was sick of being out here, and this means I can go back and do-nowt for the rest of my days. Sit down the pub and not have to worry 'bout work. It'll take some getting used to, but I'll do it... They used to call injuries like this one a *blighty one* back in the old days. Me dad told me about it.'

'How did you get out?' I asked.

'Me an' Bolton there was hanging back, you know, in case of anything unexpected coming up from the rear. Tell you the truth, I was glad about it when our sarge told us... There was something about that building...'

I knew exactly what he meant. Wondered whether he'd seen the strange purple light that day too.

'Once that first blast went off, it went awful quiet,' said Do-Nowt. 'Then, after a few seconds, we could hear all the shouts and screams from the men we'd been with for the best part of our lives, and they sounded like babies or something. It were horrible. Horrible. He couldn't hack it, could Bolton. He just went charging in there, mad-like. I tried to stop him; I could kinda sense there'd be another one. I could feel it in the dust, like. And I suppose that was how he got done so bad when the second one went off like that, worse than the first... And by that time, I'd got too close an' all.'

'Shit,' I commented. It was about the only response I could formulate.

'Shit is right,' said Do-Nowt. And for a while, we were quiet. Remembering.

The silence soon became too painful for me though. I had to change the subject again.

'Does it itch, the leg?' I said, remembering some story I'd heard or seen once about missing 'ghost' limbs; it must have been one of those awful horror flicks that Twinnie used to rent down at M and S Video Supplies. *Fuck:* why was I remembering Twinnie at a time like this?

Do-Nowt sighed, as though having lost a leg for – what was it; five? six? days – suddenly made him the word-leading authority on the subject. 'You know sometimes and you're drunk and trying to watch porn and you feel all light headed and think about having a wank and then you look down and your poor old dick is just lying there, numb. That's what it feels like; like I've sat on it too long or something and that if I just give it some care and attention, everything'll be okay.'

'You've not…' Even I couldn't bring myself to ask the next question.

'No!' snapped Do-Nowt, almost too quickly. 'And if you'd have seen some of the nurses, you'd know *how* I know that!'

Ah! It had started already. Here we were, lucky to be alive, and already we were making up brag-stories in our scratchers. Give it a couple of hours, and I would have convinced this guy that while he was asleep, I had this amazing threesome with two buxom nurses… Even now, we have to talk-up our masculinity. Legless, he had even more reason to talk about his third-leg, I supposed.

Suddenly, we heard sounds of movement from what must have been a neighbouring building. Only when we heard the sound of the creaking door and the scrunch of footsteps upon gravel did we realise how eerily silent it had been, apart from our stupid voices of course. Immediately, I felt the fear creeping up inside me, slivering like a parasitic animal into my bowels. *What if it was the enemy? What if they were coming to finish us off?*

What if it was whatever had pulled me out of the building?

The thoughts that I'd been trying not to acknowledge gathered around me and clung to me like cobwebs. Deep down, I knew that whatever it was that had touched me was not human. And deep down, I knew that it had plans for me. My survivor's-guilt told me that; my dreams told me that.

Finally, we heard the door to our building being unbolted. We heard the rattling of keys and the slight sound of breathing. Like a baby, I pulled the sheet up higher. I pulled it up until it was almost covering my face, ignoring the pain which was ringing out from my arms.

And then I heard the chuckle from Do-Nowt's bed and smelled the unmistakeable smell of a woman – one of the nurses surely – as she entered.

'Good evening, Dean,' sing-songed a posh, Southern voice. It sounded like the best voice I'd heard in my life. 'And how are you feeling today?'

Already, I could picture her from the voice. She was probably early-thirties; experienced enough not to sound as though she was going to faint at the sight of blood but using that kind of disassociating voice in order to distance herself from the full reality of the situation. She was probably not much of a looker, despite Do-Nowt's earlier protestations; most likely she was the tom-boy outdoorsy-type that usually volunteer for these thankless jobs in thankless places.

'He's awake,' I heard Do-Nowt say to her. Then I heard her clip-clop sensible shoes crossing the room until she reached my bed. Gingerly, I lowered the sheet from my face.

'Welcome back to the land of the living, Lance Corporal Bull,' she said, smiling broadly as our eyes met. She was an uncommonly tall woman, I saw, with deep red hair which was almost spilling out of an elastic band. She was wearing faded blue jeans and a tight black T-Shirt; in all, she was nothing like the Florence Nightingale that I'd expected.

'Um... hello,' I said, my voice sounding weaker than I'd meant it to.

'Not still feeling sorry for yourself, are you?' she asked, hands-on-hips in a pose just like one of my old teachers used to have when they confronted me about another terrible excuse for not doing my homework.

I was taken-aback. I'd been expecting her to be cooing over me and fussing with the sheets and pillows. I'd been expecting her to at least show some sympathy for my predicament. Evidently, she didn't have time for sympathy.

'You've been yammering and moaning away through the night since you got here,' she said. 'Nice to see that you've finally agreed to allow your fellow patients a little bit of rest.'

Then she started to walk away, back to Do-Nowt.

'Um… Do you not need to do tests on me and stuff?' I asked.

She turned and again looked at me as though I was a disobedient child. 'Tests on *what*, Lance Corporal Bull? You are in pretty good shape, physically. If you are talking about *mental* tests, then I can get in Dr. Fisher…'

'My arms!' I blurted. 'I can hardly move them.'

She tutted. Unbelievably, she tutted at me. 'Lance Corporal Bull; a lot of people pull muscles in their arms in everyday, normal situations. You dragged yourself out of a building that was about to blow-up. I think you can expect a little strain.'

'Meet Nurse Thomas,' laughed Do-Nowt. 'She's a fuckin' proper trooper!'

Nurse Thomas narrowed her eyes at Do-Nowt: 'That's enough of that language in here,' she chided, but from the way she said it, I could tell that she didn't mean it. I watched her apply soothing lotion to Do-Nowt's stump out of the corner of my eye. It felt like I was intruding on some private ritual. And all the while, I started to wonder whether what she'd said had been in fact what had happened. Had I dragged myself out of that building?

When she finally left, Do-Nowt seemed to want to talk some more. He didn't seem to sense my extreme anxiety. And indeed, what he said next chilled my blood:

'Do you know the weird thing, Gaz?' he asked. 'Bolton was only by the door when the explosion went off, and even though me leg were fucked, I managed to drag him away, like. But once I put that call in over the radio, I laid down next to him. And I swear there was nobody else in that courtyard. Not one of us Second Yorkshires; none of you Kingsmen, neither. Exactly *when* did you pull yourself out?'

Chapter Three

"Bad news on the doorstep"

My sleep had been ragged again, full of tortuous dreams and memories which I'd thought long-forgotten. When I woke up, there was a fishy smell in the air and for a while, I was sure that I was in the presence of somebody from the old days; somebody long buried for fear that he might haunt the rest of my years: Tommy Peaker. Why was I being assaulted with such recollections now, of all times? Why was that name uppermost in my thoughts?

Psychologically-speaking, I suppose that it may have come from my worries about what might have happened to Selly and the rest of the lads back in that building in the gully. But there was something else too. Something even darker which lurked in the past, and now it seemed to be sharpening its fangs and preparing to bite me on the arse.

In my dream there'd been the usual group of us – Twinnie, Cross-Eyed Lion, Dick and I – arranged in a circle around the smaller boy, Tommy. Tommy was curled up into this foetal comma and had snot trailing out of his nose. He was whimpering something under his breath that might have been a prayer. We were taking it in turns to kick him in the kidneys. Eventually, we kicked him so many times that he pissed himself. And I laughed so hard that I thought I'd burst my appendix.

'Tommy Squeaker's pissed himself, pissed himself, pissed himself,' chanted Dick, to the tune of *London Bridge is Falling Down*, 'Tommy Squeaker's pissed himself. What a fanny.'

The excitement of seeing Tommy's collapse had given us the blood lust. We all lost our heads a little. Part of me wanted to *keep on* inflicting this misery on him. I wanted to see his little freckled face destroyed. Because through the tears, snot and piss, for some reason Tommy was smiling that gap-toothed, *not-all-there* smile of his; it must have been the nerves, shot to hell.

'You little scrubber,' I yelled. 'What the fuck have you got to smile about?'

He turned his face into the loose gravel of the playground and kind of tried to slither away from us a little. He left a trail of blood behind him like in some horror movie.

'We should stop now,' said Cross-Eyed Lion, the biggest of all of us, but also the one least enamoured by the intoxicating violence which we habitually doled out. But as I watched, Twinnie carried on. He took it too far. He started kicking little Tommy in the face. He mashed up his nose badly and knocked out a few teeth but he kept going. The rest of us were now standing in silence. Before we'd been laughing and shouting, but now... Now Twinnie had taken it too far. And with every new connection that his spanking white Nike's made with Tommy's head, this great big crack started to appear. Parts of Tommy's brain started to seep out and blood; oceans of blood. It soaked into Twinnie's Nikes, but he didn't care. He kept going. Tommy wasn't making a sound at all now, but Twinnie still kept going. In the end we had to drag him away. In the end, Lion had to smack him one, just so's he'd stop screaming and foaming at the mouth like a rabid dog. In the end, Tommy didn't come back to school for a good few weeks.

I tried to shake off the clinging remnants of the dream and my guilt. I was always going to feel this way, I knew it; trying so hard to make up for what we'd all done to that poor kid. But the debt was too great. No matter how many things I added to my plus column, the negative column was always going to tot up to something far, far weightier.

Outside the makeshift hospital, the wind howled ominously and rattled against what I imagined were old, rusting pieces of farm machinery, or perhaps the old pens for the animals. In the bed next to me, the broken man that I now knew as Bolton still refused to die, despite the overwhelming stench of death and rot that was seeping out from his every pore. He was well-cooked, like a burger that had been left on the barbecue for too long. In the other bed, Do-Nowt moaned gently in his sleep.

Why me? Why had I been the one chosen to survive the explosion at the building? Why, when both of the other men had - as I'd seen in the photos on the bedside tables - families? I was a waste of space; a black hole into which I pulled everyone around me. I infected them all with my negative energy, and especially Tommy; little Tommy Peaker. I could recall his eternally youthful face even after all those intervening years; the messy hair and the jug-ears; the gap-toothed grin and the freckles. He'd been dealt a poor hand with virtually every feature, and he couldn't even make up for it with height or weight. He was a whelp; the runt of the litter; the youngest and smallest of four, all of whom were from different fathers.

We'd been round to his house a few times and it never ceased to amaze us how a place could stink so badly of piss, but none of its residents seemed to notice. His was the worst house on the estate; the one which always had stray dogs sleeping in the garden and barking at the overflowing rubbish bins. His was the house which had feral cats fucking in the front room in front of the television and the one in which screaming arguments would be played out twenty-four seven, three-six-five.

I used to deliver the Sunday papers there when I was much younger, and it would be a hard job not to step in dog-shit on his front path. Then his mum would come to the door, dressed in nothing but a towelling dressing gown, showing off her unshaven legs and most of her tits. She was the local nutter, and it was said that she'd do anything for a bottle of white cider. That Tommy even had clothes to put on in the morning or water for an occasional shower was a minor miracle. He was grateful when we 'took him under our wing' because it meant that he could walk down his street or through those chessboard corridors at school without fear of anyone else attacking him.

The four of us were what was termed 'cocks of the school'. Long ago, it seemed, we'd proved our physical toughness through some stunt or dare that I couldn't even remember, and as such we were allowed to pretty much lord it over the rest of our school with impunity. The title wasn't without danger; sometimes you'd get a young upstart trying to take your crown when you were least expecting it, but usually we were allowed to barge our way to the front of any queue, be it for the dinners, a crack at the prettiest birds or to get on the back seat of the coach en route to some shit-hole place where we'd have to go on school trips.

Being cock of the school was like being big boss man on a prison wing or leader of a mafia clan or something. Nothing could ever go down without our say-so. And because of that, we always had all these terrible hangers-on. Now these would be the ones that would get it probably worse than anyone else. We'd get them to do all kinds of awful stuff for us just so they could prove their loyalty. Their choice, I suppose, was to subject themselves to *known* attacks, instead of forever watching their backs in case of a surprise attack like the rest of the no-marks at school. Tommy was our favourite hanger-on and hence got the best of the titbits that we threw from our kingly table, but he also incurred the worst of the beatings. Because he was always around – like a bad smell – one of us would always end up cracking him one or stealing his cigarettes or getting him to go and rob Burt's shop.

Poor Tommy.

In the darkness, Do-Nowt moaned in his sleep again. I heard the broken Bolton trying to suck air into his burnt-out lungs. Time was catching up with him; with each wheezing inhalation of breath he edged closer to the end. There was no way that I was going to be able to get back to sleep. Not with him in the room. Not with death waiting outside, ever-alert to the moment that I would shut my eyelids. Some part of me felt that I kinda owed it to Bolton, and to Do-Nowt, to keep watch over them.

Occasionally, I heard the frantic scratches of small, rodent feet upon the stone floor, going about their business. Far away, I thought I could hear the hum of conversation from a group of people – the medical staff perhaps – in their own building. Even further away, the echo of gunfire and explosions reverberated back to me. I couldn't be sure whether this was real, or just my mind playing tricks on me. Perhaps something terrible had happened to my ears; perhaps I'd always hear the ringing of a bomb blast. And so, when I heard that louder, closer sound, it took me some time to acknowledge it.

Tap, tap, tap.

From where I was lying, it sounded as though somebody was knocking at the front door. I felt the urge to pull the sheet up over my head again but resisted after the embarrassment of being caught like that by Nurse Thomas.

Tap, tap, tap.

This time, the knocking was unmistakeable. My voice rasped as I whispered across at Do-Nowt's sleeping form: 'Did you hear that?' But the poor Yorkie only rattled his remaining leg by way of response. Closer, I heard the rustling from more rodents. I heard them as they passed under my bed. There were quite a large number of them and they all seemed to be moving with a common purpose, as though called by a piper. A quick look over the edge of my bed confirmed that a thin carpet of vermin was swimming across the floor towards a crack in the wall and escape.

Tap, tap, tap.

Why would one of the nurses be knocking at the door? Wouldn't they just unlock the door and walk in? And surely, none of them expected us to hobble up out of bed and one-leggedly, with flaking, burned skin, *answer* the door did they?

Tap, tap, tap.

Bullies, they say, only behave in that way because deep down they are insecure. Over the years, I'd laughed at that notion; I hadn't felt very insecure when I was kicking Tommy in the kidneys had I? But now... Now I felt as though I was completely exposed. Whatever was outside that door could do whatever they wanted with me... Even the rats had deserted.

Before I realised what I was doing, I swung a leg out from under the sheet. Before I understood what was happening, I felt the cold of the stone floor on my feet. Before I could stop myself, I was grasping at the metal bed-head and pushing myself upright. As though in a trance, I walked to the door. And outside, it was as though whatever was there was simply waiting, arms-folded, for me to come; the knocking stopped.

I shivered; I was wearing only a vest and boxer shorts, I realised. As my eyes quickly scanned my once familiar body, I saw that my legs had started to waste away from the lack of exercise. I looked thin and reedy like an old man. Around my knees, the spare flesh had started to knot and wrinkle. I staggered forward, in no fit state to meet my doom.

I almost fell as I passed the broken Bolton's bedside table and its sad collection of memories of the life that he'd once lived. My flailing arm knocked into a photograph of his family on a long gone summer day. It landed face down amongst a jangling collection of pill bottles and coins and dog-tags. Once I'd steadied myself, I thought about picking the photograph back up again, but something inside told me not to. Something inside told me that I didn't want the family in the photograph to have to see what was outside that door. And something inside told me that I couldn't let the thing outside see the photograph. Ignorance is bliss, I thought as I made those final weary steps to the door.

As I'd half expected in this surreal night, the door was unlocked. My trembling fingers closed around the bolt and I felt it give in easily, as though it *wanted* to be opened. Outside, I heard the unmistakeable sound of somebody – something – clearing their throat. Numbly, I pulled open the door and stepped backwards.

A large man-shaped shadow almost filled the doorway, shrouded in darkness so black it was almost purple. He had big, hulking shoulders, over which was draped a long, dark cloak. He stood on the threshold, clutching this misshapen stick or cane, and *towered* over me breathing heavily, as though the rapping on the door had been an effort. With each exhalation, it released more of that salty-fishy smell that had haunted me for the past few days. Despite the contrary evidence provided by my eyes, I knew that this mysterious visitor was a ghost from my past.

We stood stock-still for a moment and stared at each other. I felt his glassy eyes creeping under my skin, seeking out the core of me with their poison. They seethed with animosity. They were deep pools which reflected nothingness back at me. I felt myself falling under his spell...

Then, without any warning, he banged his cane on the stone floor. I jumped still further away from him. *'Hello Bully,'* he said, in a deep booming voice. *'Feeling better, are we?'*

I felt my legs giving way under me and reached for the solidity of the wall. It felt strangely pliant to the touch, as though at any moment I might simply slip *through* the wall and into whatever alternative reality that this creature – this blast from the past – inhabited. I closed my eyes.

You're seeing things, I told myself, not really believing it. *Just close your eyes and all of this will go away. It's a vision; some kind of side-effect of the bomb blast.*

The reality of the strong hand that gripped my shoulder immediately told me that I wasn't seeing things. I felt claw-like fingernails sinking into my naked flesh and the overwhelming stink of fish almost choked me. I tried to lift my head to suck at the cleaner air towards the ceiling, but the stranger was so tall, so overpowering that he'd taken over the whole atmosphere of the place just like a black hole.

Gingerly, I opened my eyes again, dreading what I would see. In the darkness, his eyes shone bright with devilish light but the rest of his face was shrouded in shadow. The bulk of him was unmistakeable though, and darker somehow than everything else in the room.

'You're not Tommy,' I breathed. 'You can't be.'

The thing increased the pressure on my shoulder. It now felt as though my arms were on fire, about to break off like charred twigs. And then he laughed and it was like he sucked all of the remaining hope out of the room; the blue medical curtains fluttered in alarm. As he laughed, his bright eyes widened, and for a horrific moment cast unwelcome light on his features... or what were once his features. For his whole face was so slumped, so devoid of any usual point of understanding, that I couldn't get a proper handle on what I was looking at. His face seemed to be dripping like a melting candle. As he laughed again, I saw sharp teeth in there somewhere within the folds of flesh. I saw cracked bone poking through the waxy skin. I even thought that I saw brain.

The light dulled, thankfully, but the thing kept his hand clamped onto my shoulder. He showed me his cane. I now realised that it was actually made of metal; it looked like one of those twisted spears that reinforce concrete. It was badly bent in the middle and had a horribly jagged edge at one end as though the thing had simply torn it out of the ground using brute force.

'*Remember this, Bully?*' he said, somewhat proudly. '*This was what I pulled out of you in that building.*'

All at once, the crippling pain in my chest returned. I remembered how it felt to wish for oblivion.

'Now you comprehend the true nature of death and of pain,' boomed the creature. 'Now you know that horror awaits us all. Now you are scared.'

Too right I was scared. It felt as though my heart was being ripped out. I stared at the shadow, slack-jawed. *You're not Tommy*, was all I could think, or hope, or pray.

'*Now the fun and games can begin,*' he continued. '*Now you'll be able to get your mind around what it feels like to be tormented by a bully.*'

'I'm sorry!' I yelled, through the pain. 'I'm sorry, I'm sorry, I'm sorry.'

'*Sorry won't change what you did; you and your fucking tyrant friends. And speaking of your friends...*'

'They aren't my friends any more,' I begged.

'*That may be true, but they were your friends, weren't they? And that is the point. You all brought about that situation in the graveyard, Bully. And you will all pay. There's a Lion I need to tame; Crossett first,*' he said, gravely.

'But... but...'

Tommy released his grip on my shoulder finally and started to move back out of the door. As soon as he let me go, my heart started to beat properly again and I was left with only the memory of the pain. I gasped with relief and sunk to my knees. Tommy must have heard me because he paused in the doorframe, silhouetted by the moon and fixed me once more with those terrible eyes.

'*I will be watching you,*' he said. '*I will be waiting. Death is coming, Bully. And there's nothing that you or anybody else can do about it.*'

He slammed the door behind him. It felt like the closing of a tomb.

Chapter Four

"And do you have faith in God above, if the Bible tells you so?"

My hands were still trembling as I rooted under my bed for my old pack and clothes. It took me two attempts to pull my boots out because the laces kept getting caught on something. Although the thing – Tommy – had gone, I still felt his presence in the room. I felt his hatred of me pouring out from the walls. I had to get out. I had to follow the rats. I had to desert this sinking ship and get as far away as possible. Only, as I already knew, I couldn't run away from myself.

So this is what it feels like to be hunted, I thought. I remembered an old wildlife documentary that I watched once; some poor young wildebeest which was being tracked by a lion. The wildebeest had sensed that he was being stalked by something much bigger and more powerful than him and had simply flopped onto the ground and given up, allowing himself to succumb to death's embrace. At the time, I'd been exhilarated by watching the kill; I'd been rooting for the lion. Now I knew just how that young wildebeest had felt. My every nerve and sinew wanted to simply let things wash over me and give up. Sighing, I pulled on my boots and completed a final check of my pack.

Do-Nowt must have heard me. 'What are you doing?' he whispered, sounding annoyed. 'If you're not carrying-on in your sleep you're fiddling around...'

'Sorry,' I muttered.

'What was all that shouting and yelling a few minutes ago?'

'Nothing... Bad dream,' I said, and then thought better of it. Questions would be asked come the morning and come the discovery of my empty bed. It would be better for Do-Nowt if I at least gave him the heads-up. 'Look; I have to get out of here… Something's happened and…'

'What can possibly have happened in here?' asked Do-Nowt. I heard the creak of wire against metal as he changed position and his leg dragged in the hoist. 'Are you crazy?'

He must have heard the panic in my voice… And if he had heard my mad shouting from earlier, then he had every right to think me insane. But then a thought struck me; if he *had* heard me earlier, why hadn't he remarked on the fact that there was clearly another person's voice in the room? Why hadn't he commented on that deep, booming voice of the new Tommy? That would have been the first thing I would have mentioned.

'Not crazy,' I said, although some part of me felt like laughing like a loon again. 'I'm worried… I think there's trouble back home. I need to get back there before it gets really bad.'

'Can you smell it?' asked Do-Nowt, ignoring me.

'Smell what?'

'That smell of death in the room. The air is thick with it; I can hardly breathe. I think Bolton may have finally passed-on. Will you check him for me?'

I had to agree. I bit back my disgust and leaned over the broken body of the B. Bolton. His face resembled Tommy's; it was devoid of most of the skin and the tissue underneath had crusted up into a lunar landscape of peaks and troughs. Most of his hair had burned away but odd patches sprung up here and there like sad little oases in this parched desert.

I forced myself lower and tried to listen for breathing. Hearing nothing I placed a hand under what was left of his nose. Still nothing. I placed a reluctant hand on his brow and felt it cold to the touch; bone cold. Somehow I knew then that when Tommy had left, he had taken the broken man back with him to whatever afterlife he came from.

'He's gone,' I confirmed.

Suddenly, Do-Nowt let out this long, low groan. 'Don't leave me in here on my own,' he said finally. 'I don't want to die.' I could hear him choking back the sobs and for once was glad of the cover of darkness. To see that great brute of a man reduced to a snivelling wreck would have been too much to bear. As it was, I collected up my pack and stepped out of the hospital. Like the rats, I deserted that sinking ship.

Cold air on my face felt strange and uncomfortable. Although I hadn't been seriously injured by the blast, my skin still felt too new, too raw; I could feel every speck of dust, every grain of sand grating against me and wearing me down. If I had stood there forever, I would have eventually have been ground down into tiny particles myself. Parts of me would have been carried far away on the breeze and I would have been free.

Behind me, the hospital door rattled and creaked, swinging in the breeze as though it were as light as a sheet on a washing line. It was hanging off one hinge now; Tommy must have damaged it by slamming it so hard. I reached for a large stone in order to wedge it closed. I couldn't let Do-Nowt face the night completely unguarded.

Stealthily, I moved away from the door, searching for cover. I took in my surroundings as I went. We were indeed housed in one of a circle of low, one-storey farm buildings surrounded by a high fence. In the middle of the circle was a trampled area of gravel and dirt and a few pieces of rusted machinery. Outside the circle was nothing, just sand, the odd scattering of rubble and the occasional half-dead plant or tree. It looked like the landscape of hell; it was immediately obvious why the buildings had been arranged in such a way. They wanted to close out this nothingness. They wanted to ward off whatever evil lay out there. I'd seen documentaries about the inhabitants of primitive villages that used to keep their animals inside such circles in order to stop the predators from getting in. This was eerily familiar.

I moved into the shadow of one of the buildings and weighed up my next move. I listened, as I'd been trained to do. I made calculations based on the noises that I heard. The majority of the buildings sounded empty, but I'd heard faint sounds from two of the buildings close to the main gateway through the fence. These were not, I decided, the sounds of more vermin, but were made by something bigger - human beings. There was bound to be somebody keeping watch. Only problem was, where were they?

43

Most likely they'd be keeping watch over the key strategic elements of the camp, I decided. And that didn't mean wounded soldiers; that meant something else. Outside the fence, underneath tarpaulins, I could see the obvious shapes of vehicles; Land Rover Wolves and Defenders, probably. Perhaps there'd be a Warrior in there too. Because of the nature of the terrain, these vehicles were a lifeline. Without them, we might as well have been buried in a sandpit.

What I had to try and work out was how this night watchman would react if they were to see me emerging out of the gloom. Would they shoot me on sight or would they know me as one of the patients and hence use caution? In the end, I decided that whatever happened, even if I happened to be mown down in a rain of bullets like Butch Cassidy as I stepped into the open, it was still preferable to what awaited me with Tommy.

I took a deep breath and stepped into the shaft of moonlight which intersected the first two of the buildings. The crunch of gravel as my feet touched the floor made me wince. But I needed to move quickly, while I still had the element of surprise on my side, so I pressed on. Still nothing moved. I kept imagining that at any moment, I was going to trip some heretofore unseen wire and alert the whole hospital camp to my escape, but it seemed that camp security *within* the perimeter fence wasn't a high priority. I was pretty much allowed to move wherever I chose. Perhaps they didn't really expect any of the patients, and especially the ones that had survived the blast, to be making any such bold moves.

Grimly, I clutched onto the strap on my pack and tried to stop it from rubbing on my shoulder, where Tommy had touched me. His fingernail-claws had left deep scores in my flesh there, but there'd been no blood, strangely enough. It was as though his deathly touch had started the decomposition process within me. The constant thought of Tommy kept me going. It guided me over the marshy ground behind the second of the buildings and over the broken pipes which crashed out of the third as though they were a knot of dead snakes. I felt my booted feet sinking into years and years of animal droppings, although where all the animals were now, I could barely even contemplate. The smell was almost unbearable.

44

As I approached the last of the buildings, I began to discern signs of the humanity contained within; the low buzz of a radio, the slight tang of cigarette smoke in the air, and the flickering light which shone out from the gap underneath the door. Part of me longed to step inside, to feel warmth and companionship again, but they'd only send me back to my own building, wouldn't they? They'd think my sudden panic a sign of madness and probably subject me to all kinds of psychological testing. They'd find out about Tommy and what we did to him...

I slunk past the windows keeping low to the ground. Retching at the smell, at the fact that my bare hands were now wallowing in the years of sewage, I crawled towards the gate and my freedom. Every creaking, stinking, filthy bit of progress that I made was accompanied by a throb of pain from my shoulders and chest. On all-fours like a dog, I crept towards my destiny.

Suddenly, just as I began to believe that my hands were about to touch the wire of the fence, two dazzling lights fizzed into life. They were perched like sentry birds on top of the gate and had clearly sensed my approach; so much for my theories of no security detail. I was frozen in the glare of the spotlights, like road-kill. I kept expecting the exploding pain of a Browning bullet, ripping into my back. I kept expecting the enraged shout of the night watchman or sniper. Nothing happened.

Finally, I allowed myself to climb to my feet. Despite the pain in my shoulder, I lifted both hands above my head in surrender and still nothing happened.

'What the fuck?' I heard myself ask.

There hadn't been the slightest movement from the nearest building. There hadn't been even a crackle of gunfire. I edged towards the building, keeping my head bowed in submission and my arms aloft. Still nothing happened. I placed my hand on the gnarled wood of the door. I felt the reality of it, so strangely juxtaposed alongside the dreamlike quality of the whole situation; the emptiness.

I opened the door, not quite daring to wonder what I'd see within. But there was nobody there, not even Nurse Thomas. I let out a breath that I'd clearly been holding for some time and scanned the room. Four beds; medical equipment stacked neatly over to one side; a lopsided shelf containing weighty tomes which were probably medical textbooks; a gaslight burning away on the wall. Otherwise, it was decorated much like our ward; only the briefest personal touches made me believe that there'd been anyone in here at all. Above one of the unmade beds, there was tacked a picture of cows and green fields and rising hills in the background; England. On one of the bedside tables, there was a picture of a small red-haired boy. I wondered if this might be Nurse Thomas's son. The portable radio that I'd heard was hanging from a hook in the ceiling, as though it could achieve better reception up there. Where was everybody?

Suddenly, I became aware of the smell of cigarettes. In an ashtray on an old desk which had been pushed against the back wall, a lone cigarette end burned away into nothing. Whoever had left it there had only left it there a matter of minutes ago, perhaps as I was stalking the perimeter. I had the sinking feeling that as well as Bolton, Tommy might have visited the doctors and nurses. Perhaps he'd pied-pipered them all out of there... What other reasonable explanation was there for the Mary Celeste-like state of their room? Where else could they have gone?

Madly, I dashed from bed to bed, stripping back the sheets to look for bloodstains. I pulled down curtains, kicked away rugs and trampled through piles of dirty clothes but I found none. Where was everybody?

I thought back to the moment I'd first stepped out of our building. I'd listened to the sounds of the night then; I was sure that I'd heard people. But now they'd simply disappeared into thin air. Or not into thin air at all; into the thick fish-smelling air of Tommy's afterlife, perhaps.

'Help me,' I croaked, to nobody in particular. I had never believed in God or in some divine creator, but if I believed in Tommy and the hellish afterlife that he advertised, then surely I could believe in Him?

My voice echoed back off the bare walls. It echoed back off the salt-flats and the desert. It echoed back off the lonely rocks and the deserted buildings. It felt as though I was the last person alive on the planet. Not for the first time, I asked my favourite question; why me? Nobody in this post-apocalyptic world could give me an answer, but I did strain to hear whether the creaking of the corrugated iron roof was actually Tommy's laughter.

Do-Nowt! I remembered Do-Nowt, and finally I had a purpose again. I had to get him out of there and maybe somehow, in doing so, I'd redeem myself a little. I crashed out of the building and back into the shit-heap central courtyard. I ran headlong through the middle of it, no longer caring that I'd be seen. In fact, I was *hoping* that I'd be seen. Hell, the smash of a bullet rifling into my back would be welcome compared to the lonely agony I felt. Like the broken man's old dog act, I was now pleading to be put out of my misery.

I ran so fast that my breath burned in my throat and my legs wheezed and buckled in complaint.

'Dean!' I yelled, choking back snot and vomit and fear. 'Do-Nowt!'

I don't quite know what I expected him to do if he heard my cries. In his state, he couldn't exactly make ready to leave, could he? He was bed-ridden, legless; another broken man. But then so was I, wasn't I?

It took me a moment to remember that I'd had to wedge the front door to our building shut with a large stone. In that moment, I pulled at the door handle as though none other than Tommy Peaker were on the other side, pulling against me. Cursing, I kicked the stone away and entered my worst nightmare. Not only was the body of Bolton now gone, but Do-Nowt was now nowhere to be seen. It felt like the cruellest practical joke in the world. Even then, I believed that everybody was going to jump out of some concealed door and burst out laughing. Do-Nowt would be back on two-legs, the broken man holding some kind of mask that he'd been wearing to fool me. Even Tommy would be there, holding up some stilts and a wad of tissues that he'd stuffed down his jumper to make himself seem bulkier.

I started to laugh; quietly at first, but rising into a crescendo which could best be described as a howl. Why was this happening to me? Why was I being tormented so? Ah, who was I kidding? I knew exactly why, didn't I? It was a little dead boy's sick revenge fantasy and I'd blundered straight into it. I laughed again, and cried, and laughed again. I slumped down onto the stone floor and rested my forehead against its coldness. I waited for death to come take me. I gave up. Now I really was that wildebeest on the African plain. I felt death's teeth start to clamp around my ankle, ripping into the flesh. I carried on laughing hysterically.

I came to with a nagging coldness around my groin area. It felt like an old familiar friend, that clammy wetness, so it took me a while to figure out just what it was. When I did, I was disgusted; I'd pissed myself. Somewhere amid all the laugh-crying and the wailing and the giving up, I'd just let my bladder give way and then I'd slept in it. I wrinkled my nose and took in the smell. The hospital now smelled like Tommy's house back in Newton Mills. It *reeked* of piss, as though not only had I pissed in my combat trousers, I'd also showered all of the empty beds with it, and the blue medical curtains. Some awful voice in the back of my head reminded me that this was exactly the sort of humiliation we'd heaped upon Tommy that day in the playground when Twinnie had kept kicking and kicking until we feared there'd be nothing of the lad left. Absently, I wondered whether Tommy had pissed himself in the grave that we'd put him in and I concluded that he probably had. There was nowhere else that he could have gone.

I felt something start to nibble at my ankle again as though my awakening had reminded death that it still had a job to do. It gnawed at my cartilage and sinew. I heard the screech of sharp teeth against bone. I felt fresh blood starting to seep out, beginning to take consciousness with it. I hardly dared look down for fear that I'd see Tommy's new bright eyes staring glassily back at me. But then something crawled across my face; a rat. And it didn't crawl quickly as though it was scared. In fact, it stopped to wash its blood-coated paws right on my chin. Flecks of the thing's saliva flew into my open mouth. Summoning energy that I never knew I possessed, I flung out an arm and knocked it onto the floor where it scurried away giving a prolonged indignant squeak. It would come back, it told me. It would come back and with greater numbers.

Finally I looked down at my leg and saw the one remaining rat still chewing at my flesh. It had now removed a good portion of the top half of my boot, sock and foot. Underneath all of the blood, I could see either the tongue of the boot or a large flap of skin within the rat's jaws. He was pulling and pulling at it; trying to tear it loose. I looked at it with vaguely confused eyes. Was that really my foot dribbling through the shiny black leather? It certainly didn't *feel* as though any damage had been done and yet veins spilled out of the mess and mixed with the shoelaces to form a bloody portion of overcooked spaghetti.

All I could feel was a slight tingle, like pins and needles. When I tried to kick the rat away, something snapped and my foot started to hang loose like the front door on its one hinge. The rat darted back away from me but not too far. Not far enough to convince me that he wouldn't be back for more too. And I swear that as I looked at him, his chops collapsed into this deathly grin. His bared teeth were covered in my blood.

Then I decided that I'd probably seen enough to warrant a scream. Then I decided that it didn't matter if I screamed so loud that I made my head explode. Mine was the scream of a victim, of somebody that is constantly and consistently tortured until they cannot bear it any more. Mine was the scream of somebody that has been bullied to within an inch of their life.

'Kill me!' I screamed. 'Or let me die!'

This time when the corrugated iron creaked in response, I *knew* that it was Tommy's laughter, Tommy's revenge. All I could think about was his not-quite-all-there gap-toothed grin; his freckly face and pathetic floppy ears. I felt the anger starting to creep up within me. Suddenly, I wanted to smash his face in. Suddenly, I wanted to inflict great pain.

I used the anger to crawl over to the bed. It wasn't easy, not with one leg trailing behind me like a piece of heavy wood, but I made it through gritted-teeth- perseverance and anger. I smashed one hand down onto the bed head and tried to pull myself up with it. In the corner of my eye, I saw rats streaming through the crack in the wall. Some rats were even plucking up the courage to follow my trail of blood, and once they had that taste, courage became secondary. Blood-lust was all for them.

Sweat pissed down my forehead. My arm threatened to give up the ghost entirely, but somehow, I managed to drag myself upright. I loomed over the rats and sneered. Some started to back away from me, but when they saw my near-collapse when I tried to put weight on my mangled foot, when they saw the spray of blood that erupted from within me, they came back at me.

And then I saw it; the piece of metal that Tommy had been using as a cane was leaning against the wall by the door. If I could just make it to the cane, I could somehow limp my way out of there.

Slowly, I started to move. I longed for a weapon with which I could hold back this accumulating black tide of rats; a flame-thrower perhaps, or a carefully-flighted grenade. Goddamn it, I would have taken an A-Bomb right then, if it meant that those fucking rats would get a taste of their own medicine. In my final moments, I would have seen *their* paws and furry limbs being ripped to shreds as well as my own.

The tidal wave of my own anger was the thing that carried me through those terrible moments. It numbed me against the pain in my foot. It allowed me to finally gain the door and to grab at the metal cane. Sure, it made me linger longer than I should have done at the door as I beat the cane down onto the heads of the nearest rats, but eventually it dragged me out of there and into the open air.

I was surprised to see that it had become light during my time back in our building. It was as though, upon seeing myself being eaten alive, I'd automatically assumed that I'd never see sunlight again. But anger had seen me through, and it continued to be my friend as I crossed the centre of the courtyard and made directly for the gate.

Only after I'd thrown off the tarpaulin and gunned the engine of the Red Cross jeep did I allow that little whimper to escape from the knot of sustained terror which gripped my heart. Only then did I understand that Tommy's revenge was not some terrible practical joke, but was actually something which looked a lot like hell on earth.

Chapter Five

"Can you teach me how to dance real slow?"

Dr. Montaffian told me, in that typically forthright manner of his, that when they found me they virtually had to peel what was left of my ruined foot off the accelerator pedal of the Red Cross jeep. Apparently, I'd driven straight into the barrier at the military check-point. I'd lost so much blood that they thought I hadn't even seen the thing. I knew better. Even though I couldn't remember any of it, I knew that with death on my tail, I wouldn't have wanted to wait until the barrier lifted. Taking my foot off the pedal would have been tantamount to allowing Tommy in through the back door.

Yet again, I found myself in hospital, only this time it was a proper hospital; one run with military precision by the Americans. It had to be the Americans. Even accounting for my grogginess during my first meeting with the doctor - hell, even before then - I'd known. For this was a place which stunk of money, sparkled with efficiency and oozed confidence. Instead of the commandeered farm buildings of the British hospital, the Americans had built their own space and it was all gunmetal grey walls and proper sterility. Full of hushed voices reverberating along corridors and blazing lights on every ceiling, night and day. Like a proper hospital should be, if they ever expect any of the patients to survive.

Despite the fact that I was rigged up to all kinds of bleeping electronic equipment and had tubes sticking out of every available vein, I should have felt a strange kind of reassurance. And the fact that it looked like an episode of *ER,* rather than the goddamn *Texas Chainsaw Massacre* slaughterhouse I'd escaped from, should have had me thinking: 'Nothing but the best for a Kingsman.' But it didn't.

I cracked open my eyes, feeling the build-up of the mucus that mothers like to tell their children is called 'sleep' weighing heavily on the lids. I took another look around the small room which they had installed me in. There was no corrugated iron to be seen; no other patients either. Just me, the big comfortable bed and the machines that were arranged around me ready to take care of my every bodily need. But what about my mental needs?

Almost without knowing I was doing it, I took furtive glances for shadows lurking in the corners of the room, but it was too light for that. I should have felt reassured… But I didn't. I felt my heart marching along far too quickly. It would stumble and fall like poor Selly if it continued like that.

I felt heaviness around my head like water. Pressing, pressing. Like there were hands there, forceful as a vice but soft too, so the fingers didn't even make an impression on my head. And now, as I looked back at the machinery, I realised that it actually looked like praying relatives collected around a death-bed. Waiting. Just waiting.

I looked for comfort somewhere, anywhere in the room and settled on the fact that although it was cold and impersonal, at least it felt secure; cell-like. And from the look of the weighty door, it did look as though they had me imprisoned, but then I wasn't worried about getting out, I was more worried about *something* getting in. In a space so sophisticated, some people better off than me could have readily believed that monsters didn't exist, but I knew better. I knew about Tommy Peaker and what he'd done to me. And almost as soon as I even *thought* his name, I was wracked with more excruciating pain from my foot, and from my shoulder and from my chest and I'd find it difficult not to scream.

Okay, I suppose I did scream. And then, shortly afterwards, I saw a face squashed up against the small grilled-window on the door, fogging up the glass with her breath. But presently, the figure slipped away back into the corridor instead of coming in again and administering me with the cure-all, forget-all drug which I so needed. They probably had me smacked up to the eyeballs on methadone or something, but in a country like Afghanistan, they could have got hold of some proper H for me. Hell, in Mayo province alone, they had more opium fields than in the whole of the world's second biggest heroin-producing *country*. Hell, they could have reached out into the hospital garden, if there was such a thing, and plucked out a few choice poppies for me.

Why weren't they coming in? Why weren't they telling me what was going on?

My mind tripped back to the horror videos I'd watched in my youth. All of the awful things they could do to you even in a hospital as professional-looking as this. I'd seen films about people being kidnapped for their organs. Some spooky surgeon would just cut out people's hearts without anaesthetic, on beds just like this one, and stick them in the chest of some rich guy that just had to carry on living. I'd seen films about body-snatchers lurking through wards. I'd seen films about... Oh why was I choosing to concentrate on thoughts like that?

I suppose it is part and parcel of bullying that the bullied develops this all-encompassing fear of *everything*. And in the end, they end up torturing themselves almost as badly as the torment which has been dished out by the bully. Tommy Peaker – whisper the name – hadn't needed to warn me that he would watch me. Some part of him was already inside me, meddling with the wiring of my brain.

And with that thought, I suppose I screamed again. And this time, as I watched through the glass, a figure appeared. And this time, the figure at the door passed an access badge along a reader. Heavy locks clicked back. The figure ran a hand through his hair, paused for a moment as though composing his thoughts, and then stepped into my cell.

'I'm, uh, sorry, Lance Corporal Bull,' he began, absently looking around the room for something; refusing to meet my wild eyes. 'I'm sorry we kept you waiting, only... Only I'm only just back from trying to scrape two of our own boys off a dirt track. These road-side bombs... Simply terrible.'

I grunted by way of response.

'Don't know if you remember me from yesterday, son,' he continued. 'I'm Dr. Montaffian and I'm apparently scheduled in to treat you today.'

Treatment? What were they planning to do to me? I studied his face carefully for any signs of what was to come. Dr. Montaffian was a grim-faced little Yankee with salt and pepper grey hair, a goatee beard and a big tattoo on his right arm. He didn't look like a doctor. He didn't *sound* like a doctor either. As he reached over to the foot of the bed and picked up a flip-chart which obviously contained my observation records, he began whistling that old Prince number, 'Purple Rain'.

If my foot was working properly, I'd have leaped off the bed and clocked him one. He could have at least shown me some respect, no matter that I wasn't one of 'his boys'. Instead, I concentrated on staring at him; hoping that my eyes would burn a hole in him. I watched him flip through a couple of pages before he abruptly stopped whistling. Now he started this annoying tutting, occasionally nodding his head, all the while stroking his stupid goatee beard. For some reason, I kept wondering why he was allowed to have a beard, being a doctor. Surely it was some kind of hygiene-risk. And all the time he was reading, I longed for him to start whistling again, because that would mean that I was all right, wouldn't it? That would mean that it was nothing serious…

Suddenly, he slapped the clip-board against the metal rung at the bottom of the bed and looked me full in the face for the first time as though only now remembering that I was still in the room.

'Where am I?' I gasped.

'You don't remember our conversation yesterday then?'

'Clearly I don't or else I wouldn't have fucking asked,' I seethed.

Dr. Montaffian strolled around the side of my bed, bumped one of the machines away with his thigh, and promptly took a seat, almost crushing my arm.

'Perfectly understandable that you're a little… wired,' he said in a new, softer voice. His face didn't look so grim any more now either. 'From what the nurses said, you had a rough night. But they checked on you round the clock.'

'Stuck their heads through the door… Or peered through the window more like,' I snapped. I wasn't getting sucked in by his doctor's smooth-talk. I'd seen it every week on *Casualty* when I was growing up. Smarmy, lying, untrustworthy sneaks, they are.

'Well, uh, Gary; they've actually been instructed that they are not to set foot in this room,' he said, quietly. Then, leaning over me so close that I could smell the onion on his breath, he added: 'Uh, military police instruction.'

'Military police?' I yelled.

Montaffian placed a remarkably small hand on my shoulder. I felt the warmth from it. Real human touch for the first time since... Nurse Thomas, back there. 'Uh, did you really think that you could just show up on a military base from outta nowhere, smash through our security gates and just get away with a stern ticking-off?'

I shook my head, like a good little boy.

'Well, uh, don't worry about it anyway, son. Not for now. While you are under my care, *they* have been instructed that they are not setting foot in this room either. You're safe here, son.'

I longed for him to say those words again: *you're safe*. In fact, I longed for Montaffian to simply keep talking. Once he got into the flow, his voice had a real soothing quality to them, like the kind of voice that you could listen to on one of them stupid relaxation tapes or something.

'Where's here though?' I asked.

'Well, let me see now, uh; how well up are you on the geography of Afghanistan?'

I wanted to laugh at the irony of it all; here was me that had a fucking near-geography teacher no less talking-talking in my ear all day long about Afghanistan in Sergeant Davis and yet I knew nothing really. I knew where we'd been one day, where we were going the next and that was it. But explaining that to an American –even one of Montaffian's obvious intelligence - would have been a difficult task. They don't get irony, do they?

'Fuck all,' I said.

'I'll make it simple then. Uh, we're in an American base close to the eastern edge of the Helmand province. To get here from virtually any direction you would have had to pass through hundreds of miles of unforgiving countryside, assuming that you are who you say you are; a soldier from the Duke of Lancaster's Regiment. We've looked at the briefings, and from what we can tell, your boys were last stationed way out west... If you'd got your bearing wrong by even a single degree, you would probably have ended up baked by the sun, dehydrated, run out of diesel, or stalked by some animal...'

'Shit,' I whistled, not sure whether I would have been more pleased to have simply died out there in the desert, sparing me the terrible knowledge of what was to come.

'You're very lucky, son,' continued Montaffian. 'Just remember how lucky you are...'

It was the second time in a matter of days that I'd been told I was lucky, or charmed. It didn't feel like it, not after everything I'd been through. In fact, if this was luck, give me *anything* else. I closed my eyes. The light was becoming too harsh. I needed to go to sleep. But Dr. Montaffian's hand started to shake my shoulder. There was something else he had to say. And suddenly I knew that it would be bad.

'Son, uh, I hate having to do this to young men like you, but it seems to be my lot in life to have to do it,' he said. Then he let out this long sigh, and I swear that right in the middle of it, his breath seemed to catch, like there was actual emotion in there somewhere and not just smarmy doctor-emotion. 'What I was saying earlier about you being lucky. I suppose you could say I did that in order to sweeten the pill. Because the next thing I'm going to have to tell you is that we can't save your foot. I'm sorry, but there's nothing we can do.'

For a moment I didn't say anything. All I could think of was poor Do-Nowt and his amputated leg. They were going to amputate my foot. They were going to amputate my foot!

'No,' I said, quietly. 'Let me out of here and I'll make my way back to...' 'There's no way I can let you out of here... Disease will spread from it if we do not act now,' he said. 'You won't survive.'

He probably expected me to fly off into a rage, because rather too quickly, he swung his legs round and climbed off the bed. But he hadn't reckoned with the fact that this wasn't the scariest thing I'd heard recently. Not by a long chalk. I closed my eyes yet again and breathed a heavy sigh.

'I'd like a second opinion,' I asked him calmly.

'Son, uh, son. I know that this must be a shock you... You can get angry; I'd understand,' he muttered. *He* was the one that didn't understand.

'Okay, I'll get angry,' I said in this awful monotone voice that came from somewhere deep within me – perhaps the Tommy part. 'I don't believe anyone so stupid-looking could ever have made it through seven years of med. school. So bring me someone that doesn't whistle fucking 'Purple Rain' while they read med. charts and I'll say no more about it.'

Of course, Montaffian took it all with a pinch of his salt and pepper hair; he showed me the x-rays and I couldn't really argue against that evidence. Yet still, he brought one of his colleagues to see me for the fabled 'second opinion'. The new guy was a tall, vampire-like man that simply looked at my foot and shook his head before leaving the room as though I'd really wasted his time. The lanky twat didn't even bother to speak to me; it reminded me of the two sergeants up on the ridge before we went down into the gully, before the building and before Tommy.

When he came to collect me to take me down to the operating theatre, Montaffian was flanked by two burly looking orderlies that looked as though they'd been through a spell in the marines. The doctor nodded to me as though acknowledging the absurdity of the situation; as if I was going to escape. In fact, he looked a little guilty about the whole state of affairs. Part of me wanted to tell him that it wasn't his fault, but I've never been that guy. I've never been the kind of person that will go out of his way to make another people feel better, I know that about myself. And I reckon that I'm pretty much excused any recriminations considering the fact that I was about to have my foot amputated.

It was strange the way that I couldn't seem to get properly angry about what was to happen to me. The old me would have kicked and screamed so much that they would have needed five or six of the big, mean orderlies to restrain me. But the old me hadn't had so many other things on his mind. Meekly, I allowed myself to be lifted onto a gurney and then wheeled out of the room. As we went through the door, the gurney jolted against the door jamb. Pain shot through my foot. I met the eyes of the meaner looking orderly and he gave me this revolting sneer as though he'd done it on purpose. I grinned back at him; he'd just given me the last feeling that I'd probably ever have in my foot.

I didn't feel sorrow or anger or even fear. Just numbness. As I was wheeled down the sterile corridors, I spotted the military police. There were four of them; all had their arms folded tightly across their chests and their chins jutting out. When they saw me, they stood up even straighter, if that were possible, and one of them tipped me a wink. *Later,* the wink said. *After the operation, your ass is ours.* At least, I thought that was what the wink said. It would probably have had an American accent after all.

I twisted my head and looked the other way. And I just so happened to see the black and white chequerboard tiles on the floor of the corridor. Just like at Newton Mills School. It had to be a sign from Tommy, it just had to be. And if he could infiltrate this place, then I had nothing to worry about from the damn military police. Assuming I wasn't just imagining the whole thing.

It was only when we reached the swinging double-doors that led directly to the operating theatres that I realised that it was really happening, and it was happening now. That it wasn't a dream; I really was going to lose my foot. That Tommy or no Tommy, something awful was happening. It wasn't just some faraway event like when the doctor broke the news to me, or even when the mean-looking orderly bashed the gurney against the door to my room... It was happening now.

Everything seemed to click into focus. It was as though, for the first time in my life, I realised that there was such a thing as consequence. Only in that moment had I realised that the world was turning; a spinning dance-floor of momentum from which I couldn't escape. For so long I'd been living in that one moment, head-lost. Now I understood that this terrible thing was going to happen to me and I would have to live with the physical consequences of it for the rest of my life. And although that life might not have been forever, it was still real. This moment was still real. More real now than in my most desperate moments of the previous sleepless night. More real now than even a few moments ago, as we passed the military police. Before, the situation was abstract. This *could* happen to you at some point in the future. Now, there was no avoiding the fact. My foot was going to be amputated. I would no longer be whole. I would forever be defined by what was missing. If there was to be forever. For now, what I had to worry about was the very real possibility that I would be fleeing Tommy Peaker a cripple.

I gripped onto the metal struts of the gurney with white-knuckled hands, started chanting in my head: *this can't be real. This can't be real.* But I couldn't convince myself. I knew. I knew.

'Is there no alternative?' I pleaded.

Montaffian solemnly shook his head. He looked tired. More tired than I'd seen him even yesterday after he'd had to scrape two Americans off the road. Big black saddlebags hung from his eyes. His beard looked more unkempt.

'No way we can delay it?' I begged.

Montaffian looked away for a moment. But then he looked back at me.

'Give us a moment, will you boys,' he said to the orderlies. And they immediately left us alone, clomping off down the corridor muttering between themselves.

'There's no going back, Gary,' he said, softly. 'You need to understand the reality of the situation. If you do not have this operation, you will die. And I know that, uh, in your current condition, you may believe that death is a viable alternative to this. After all, what fit and healthy young man could consider themselves an invalid… But at some point in the future, you will value life again. I promise you.'

I stared into his milky blue eyes. I both hated and loved him in that moment. Montaffian told me what I needed to know; which was unlike my experience with the rest of the medical profession. People who usually wanted to keep the cards close to their chests, not revealing anything of their hand until the very end, if at all. Dr. Montaffian told me his hand from the off. He also told me *my* hand. And when you're dealing with the devil, that's very important.

Our eyes still locked, Montaffian shouted back to the two orderlies.

'I think we're ready now.'

I nodded and succumbed to consequence.

At first there was darkness and I was not aware of anything. Not time, not space, not my mind or my body. In this time, I suppose I was floating. Drifting, like someone that's lost at sea. Next, a vague awareness washed over through me; not feelings per se, but rather the humming emergence of some kind of consciousness. Faraway sounds. Dappled light. Colours. Like falling from a great height. And at the bottom came more confusion.

I was drowning in an enclosed space filled with mud and leaves. I could sense the edges of my known universe, as though my mind was sending out distress signals and they were simply bouncing back to me off the walls. Somewhere else, voices became louder and more distinct. I felt that if only I had the strength, I could push on through to the other side. The walls weren't rigid at all. Somehow I knew this as a law of the universe before I knew much else. I knew I could get back. But I had no strength. I didn't know who 'me' was. But I knew that whoever this 'me' was had crossed over onto the wrong side of the fence. I wasn't supposed to be here. And deep within this new place, I knew that fear was my first reaction.

Nevertheless, voices became louder. Somewhere, faraway, dazzling lights were being shone through the walls, trying to reach me. But they wouldn't reach me. Not through all of the mud and leaves which teemed around me.

I'm here, I wanted to shout. *Just push through the walls and help me out.*

But the voices did not respond. The inane chatter continued. Somewhere in the distance, music was playing. Two records at the same time, blended into this awful cacophony. Past and future mingling into some discordant present that just didn't sound right.

And then my mind was finally clicked off stand-by. I clutched at the lifejacket of awareness and I tried to push. The voices finally sounded as though they were being directed towards me. I reached for the voices. I kicked up from the depths, not caring whether some kind of interstitial bends would render me half-senseless for the rest of my life. I had to get away. And I was getting away. I could feel this 'me' growing into the empty shell of my body. But just as I woke, I felt icy claws raking at my shoulders, trying to pull me back in. Just as I woke, my nostrils were filled with the overwhelming stink of fish.

At first, waking up felt as unnatural as snorkelling. Everything felt wrong, as though I shouldn't be able to breathe any more. When I tried to open my eyes, it was the *visual* equivalent of snorkelling. My body sensed that what it was doing was all wrong after so long on the other side and tried to reject this new place as dangerous too. They didn't want to see. They said: 'Better that place where it was simply nothing. Where there was no 'me' at all.'

But unwanted adrenaline was being pumped into my body. I started to feel things. I felt a hand on my arm. The sting and tear of another needle. The worrying numbness in my foot. An aching in my heart. I heard more distinctly now, too: whistling. The sound that I had mistaken for a song on the radio was whistling. And I even recognised the tune; some long dormant part of my brain informed me that I was listening to some interpretation of 'Purple Rain'.

With a great wrench, I opened my eyes. At first, it hurt with a breathtaking teary sting, but eventually they became accustomed to the light. Started to pick out indistinct shapes. Colours shifted lazily into focus. I saw white, first.

'Ah! Good evening , Lance Corporal Bull,' said a voice that I thought I recognised. 'Thank you so much for, uh, coming back to the land of the living. For a while there, I thought you preferred it over the other side... How are you feeling?'

I tried to focus, but could still only really see a white figure. It leaned over me and shone an even brighter light into my eyes. I tried to blink it away, but it was no good.

'Turn that fucking light off,' I croaked.

'That's more like it,' said the man that I now remembered to be Dr. Montaffian. And as soon as that realisation set in, a deeper, scarier thought quickly followed. Involuntarily, my eyes shot down to my foot. It was wrapped heavily in bandages, but I knew. I knew.

'You did it then,' I croaked again. And this time, it felt as though I'd strained a muscle in my vocal chords. Christ! How long had I been out?

'Your operation was a great success, uh, if that doesn't sound too patronising after what you've been through,' said Montaffian. I discovered that I could focus on him properly now. And if anything, he looked even more tired; his face was pallid and greasy-looking; his beard had become straggly now, like some Afghan goat-herder's; worse, the bags under his eyes now stretched over his bloody cheekbones. He'd clearly been waiting a long time for me to emerge from wherever I'd been.

'So, I'm footless and fancy free?' I asked, trying a bitter smile on for size.

'Only *half* footless,' he corrected. 'You'll be able to walk in time, given the right, uh, motivation.'

At that point, I thought I'd never meet this 'motivation' character ever again; certainly I'd never shake him by the hand; certainly I'd never *walk* with him. And with that thought, I suddenly felt overwhelmingly tired. My body felt as though it had been through several explosions again, as well as a mad flight across the Afghan countryside and a few rounds with Dr. Montaffian's chainsaw.

'Rest your eyes, Gary,' he soothed. 'Get your sleep while you can.'

And for a moment, I wanted to ask him exactly what he meant by that, but soon, I was plunging back down into that other place again, only this time the water felt warm and welcoming. No icy claws ripped at my body. I needed this...

As my mind clicked on to stand-by mode again, I heard Montaffian's low whistling begin. 'Purple Rain' *again;* I made a mental note to ask him about it. I wanted to know whether he even knew he was doing it, and why he always whistled that particular song. But then I decided that I wouldn't ask him; I didn't ever want him to stop whistling. It was a comfort.

And for once, my dreams were happy; I dreamed about Montaffian with his big un-doctorlike tattoo and his 'Purple Rain' fantasy. I dreamed of him sitting astride this great big motorbike like

Prince in the film of the same name, and just riding off into the sunset.
I suppose the dream gave me hope.

Chapter Six

"When the jester sang for the king and queen"

It was hopeless. I was a hopeless liar, I knew I was. And everything I told them seemed to contradict something that I'd previously said. One of the military policemen – the taller one with the look of Tommy Lee Jones about him – actually spluttered with laughter every time I told another of my 'fabrications' as they called them. He was leaning against the gunmetal grey back wall of my small room, squeezing his polystyrene coffee cup as though he wanted to strangle the life out of it if he couldn't do the same to me.

The other bad cop was even worse. He had pulled up a plastic chair right next to the bed and leaned forward on it so that his face was so close to mine, I could smell the cigarettes on his breath, despite the chewing gum which he was hammering away on.

'Come on, Bully,' he drawled. 'You don't expect us to believe that, do you? I believe that's what you limey Brits call a cock and bull story.'

'And you're both the cock and the bull, aren't you Bully?' snorted Tommy Lee Jones.

'Very funny,' I sneered.

Suddenly, I heard the high-pitched wail of the plastic chair scraping back on the concrete floor. And then Chewing-Gum Breath was on me, hands round my throat, an elbow slammed into my ribs. I tried to push him away, but I still hadn't regained my strength properly, despite the vigour of Montaffian's prescribed work-out sessions.

'Just tell us what we want to hear and then we can all fucking rest in peace,' he roared, his breath tickling my face. 'You think we like being in here amongst all the fucking invalids?'

'I told you the truth!' I gasped. 'How many more times?'

And now, Tommy Lee Jones was on me too, from the other side. Close-up, I could see the pock-marks on his skin.

'We know everything anyway,' he said, his hand touching one of the drips in my arm. Threatening. 'Just admit it.'

'You're a deserter; the lowest of the low,' added Chewing-Gum Breath. 'We know that already. Just tell us what went down at the Cock-up Mansion.'

Apparently, that was what the exploded building in the gully had now come to be known as. Cock-up Mansion, or C.U.M for short. The military loved abbreviations; so much of our language was made up of it. It made it kinda impenetrable to the outsider; special. But what wasn't special, according to Tommy Lee Jones and Chewing-Gum Breath (they'd never actually introduced themselves) was the potential bad publicity which would come off the back of the almighty disaster which the Second Yorkshires and the Kingsmen had caused. So far, the full story had been covered up, mainly because nobody *knew* the full story. But now there was an unaccounted-for survivor, that meant everyone was quaking in their clod-hoppers.

'I'm telling you the truth,' I gasped. 'I must have lost my mind or my bearings after the explosion and that's how I ended up here…'

'What about the red cross truck though?' demanded Tommy Lee Jones, starting to pull the tube out of my arm. 'Where'd you blag that from? There weren't none of those in the vehicle roster for the mission up at the C.U.M…'

Now I'm not usually one that's scared of the sight of blood or anything. But needles and tubes and things go right through me. And when Tommy Lee started pulling at that tube, I felt my head starting to go. And I mean really go. Way out west. Ushering reserves of strength that I never knew I had, I swung my arm upwards and connected with his pock-marked jaw, sending him reeling backwards and into one of the machines.

'Now you really didn't wanna do that,' said Chewing-Gum Breath from the other side, but I swung an elbow into his chest, winding him.

This would have been the point that any sane and able-bodied person would have chosen to exit the room, but I was neither of the above and so I just sat up in bed and watched the two predatory animals as they started circling the bed again, but a little further off now. They'd been bitten-back, hadn't they, and now they were less sure of themselves. Oh sure, the confidence would come back, and then everything would be worse, but for now, I thought I'd done enough.

Thing was, I could have quite easily put an end to all of the questions by telling them about the makeshift British hospital that I'd been taken to directly after the blast. This would have cleared my name from the deserter's list straight away. Only, when asked, I couldn't have located it on a map. Nor could I have explained the mysterious disappearance of all of the staff and patients. I couldn't have told them about – whisper the name – Tommy Peaker. Just mentioning that place would have opened up a whole shit-storm that I didn't want any part of. And so, I knowingly told the half-truths that these guys recognised as such almost as soon as I'd said them. We were at a stale mate and neither side was ready to back down.

'Tell us what happened to the men in your unit. How did you get off with just half a foot missing if the rest of them were all blown-up?' asked Tommy Lee. He was goading me now. Hoping that professional pride would make me admit to something.

'I don't know,' I said. 'Look; all I can tell you is this: somebody radioed in that the building had exploded. And that somebody wasn't me. Check with the records of our Comms HQ if you don't believe me.'

Chewing-Gum Breath narrowed his eyes, surveyed my face for tells.

'It's something,' said Tommy Lee, breathing heavily.

'Check it!' I cried. I hadn't wanted to mention Do-Nowt at all, but this small concession couldn't hurt, could it? And by telling them about Do-Nowt, I'd put the whole thing in doubt. If there was more than one body unaccounted for – as there would be – then clearly there was something more complicated at play. And if the military police hated anything it was complications. All I wanted to do was to push them in the direction of the cover-up. Get some of that heat off me.

Chewing-Gum Breath still wouldn't stop staring at me, waiting for me to wilt, but I stared him down. Eventually, he collected his coat from the back of the fallen plastic chair and started to walk away to the door. Tommy Lee followed, not speaking either. As he reached the door, he faced me once again. I half expected him to come out with the old Columbo line: 'Just one more thing,' but he didn't. Instead, he simply said: 'We'll be back tomorrow whether this checks out or not. So you'd better hope that it does...'

Dr. Montaffian wasn't actually supposed to be responsible for my physiotherapy. They had the big orderlies for that, as well as the actual trained physiotherapists. But he said he enjoyed it. Said it was therapeutic for him to spend time putting somebody back together rather than taking them apart all the time.

'Most of the wounds we get here are so bad that the only thing for it is amputation,' he said, allowing me to rest what must have been almost my full weight on his arm as I rested. 'And Dr. Prendergast usually does most of the operations to repair internal organs.'

'He the vampire-man?' I asked.

Montaffian laughed and nodded. 'Sounds like a joke, doesn't it? Which is worse: looking like a, uh, vampire or looking stupid?'

I felt my face flush red, remembering the insult.

Montaffian smiled a fatherly kinda smile: 'Don't worry 'bout it, Gary. I know you were hurting... And you know that I've told you before a hundred times your physiotherapy don't just have to be for your foot. We've got people here that can give your mind a bit of a work-out too, if you've a mind to meet them?'

'And I've told you a hundred times that I'm not interested,' I said, propelling myself forward again onto the long corridor. And although Montaffian still had a hold of my hand, I was able to put more weight on my half-foot than I'd ever done before. Maybe I'd finally met that character 'motivation' that the doc was always chuntering on about.

Walking without your toes is no mean feat, if you'll excuse the pun. I once saw this documentary where they said that if a man loses just his little toe, he's liable to lose balance completely. And with all the toes gone, my balance had simply gone to pot. It was getting my head around walking in a different way that was the problem. I'd do two or three good steps and then simply revert to auto-pilot, try to press down with the front of my foot, forgetting that it wasn't there... Only Dr. Montaffian's close presence meant that I didn't cause myself some serious damage. In the olden days, back in Newton Mills, if I'd have seen a man staggering along in the fashion I was, I'd have given him no end of shit for it. But now the boot was on the other foot. Now it wasn't half as funny.

But the reality of the situation meant that I dug in. I was determined to get away from the hospital, from the close attentions of the military police and from Afghanistan *full stop,* and if that meant that I had to work extra hard, then I was used to it, wasn't I?

I felt as though I was a new-born, staggering down that corridor, wobbling like a goddamn weeble. I was tottering like a toddler but my face must have been contorted into a very adult grimace as I took a second and third steps and tried to remember the age-old system which is setting one foot in front of the other. From behind me, I heard Montaffian's breath starting to race, like he was the proud father capturing the image of his son's first steps for the old memory bank. I ignored him. Pressed on, feeling the memory of a million steps already marched in my aching knees and wasted thighs.

Somehow, I reached a seating area, about twenty metres down the corridor. Mustering up all the grace I could, I lowered myself into one of the plastic chairs and wiped the sleeve of my pyjama top across my forehead. Montaffian soon caught up:

'Fantastic, Gary,' he breathed. 'One, uh, small step for man, and all that...'

I looked up at him, caught that glittery look of approval in his eyes before he had a chance to extinguish it fully. And I suppose that in that moment, the little Yankee, saw me as some kind of hero.

But I knew that Montaffian also felt terribly, terribly sorry for me. He'd seen the way that I thrown myself into the physiotherapy and must have believed that I was somehow trying to make myself strong in order to fight again or something. He didn't know about the hold that Newton Mills and Tommy now had over me. For like a small moon, Newton Mills affected the tides of my emotions. I *had* to make myself strong enough to get back there. I dreamed about the place on a nightly basis. I dreamed about what nightmares were taking place before I'd even had the chance to warn any of them that it was coming.

After a while, I began to see the missing foot as an inconvenience. I cursed my stupidity in allowing myself to give up as I had in the British hospital, simply allowing those rats to gnaw at it. Sometimes, in the dead of night, I did feel an itch where the toes once were. In my mind's eye, I pictured the manky misshapen nail on my big toe; the one that had fallen off in my football boot once and had never grown back. Once, I'd been afraid to wear flip-flops as everyone else did when we were in mufti. I thought that the sight of my toenail would offend them. I'd now developed this kinda displaced attachment to that nail; I wished that I could see it again.

Now, when I steeled myself to look at my left foot, all I saw was a mess of candle-wax, almost like Tommy's face. They'd taken new skin from my thigh – taken two great strips in fact – and had kinda melted it over the edge, where they'd cut away just past the knuckle where the toes are. I couldn't imagine a woman ever even looking at my foot again, let alone giving me a foot-rub. Even I found it disgusting.

And it was getting in the way of my leaving. It was getting in the way of my return to Newton Mills. When the stern-faced military police returned, they noticed the change in me straight away. No longer was I the desperate *victim* that they'd interrogated earlier; now they could see the Kingsman that I'd once been. Some of my men were in danger, and I was prepared to do anything that I could to get back to them and lend a helping hand.

I'd not seen them for three, maybe four days since their last visit, when I'd clocked Tommy Lee Jones. But when Montaffian let them into my little room early that morning, I slap-bang knew straight away that something had changed in them as well as me. Chewing-

Gum Breath was wearing a freshly-pressed white shirt for the occasion. When he entered, he neglected to take up his usual position, on the plastic chair, threateningly close to the bed. Instead, he lingered by the wall, like Tommy Lee had done before. Tommy Lee himself seemed chastened; far less overbearing. Even his pock-marks seemed less goddamn angry. It was as though they didn't want to get close to me, somehow. I wondered what the hell they'd found out.

Evidently they didn't want to tell me straight away. For a while, we all maintained this stubborn silence until Tommy Lee could bear it no longer and he cleared his throat. 'Well, Bully,' he began, 'it looks like most of that cock and bull story you gave us checked out.'

They exchanged a mysterious look. Inside, I felt my heart leap, but I betrayed no outward sign of emotion. I hadn't expected to get away with things this easily. Surely the intel I'd given them about Do-Nowt's radio call hadn't changed everything *this* much. Or was there something else at play? Something more powerful than even the damn military police?

'The Brits have advised that they... They want us to let you go home,' muttered Chewing-Gum Breath, staring resolutely at the floor.

'No more questions asked,' continued Tommy Lee. 'How's that sound?'

'I thought you said there'd be no more questions,' I snapped, keeping my hands under my head despite the ferocious gleam which appeared in Chewing-Gum Breath's eyes. He wanted nothing more than to slam into my unguarded chest again. He wanted to shower me with punches. But something was holding him back.

'Of course, we'll be keeping your file open... should anything else crop up,' said Tommy Lee, trying to placate Chewing-Gum Breath as much as giving me the required information.

'Something *stinks* here,' snarled chewing gum breath.

I resisted the temptation to inform him that it was he that was the one doing all the smelling in that room.

'We know that, Chambers,' said Tommy Lee. '*He* knows that. But for now, there's nothing we can do. You heard the CO...'

'Well, I'd like to thank you boys for coming visiting me so often,' I said, grinning. 'Without your friendly little chats, I'd have had nothing to look forward to in here.'

Chewing-Gum Breath, or Chambers as I now knew him to be called, gritted his teeth. Tommy Lee cracked his knuckles. But neither of them said anything.

'I don't want to keep you boys from anything important though,' I continued. 'If there's some paperwork you can be doing or something, just go ahead and do it... sirs.'

'I'll wait for you outside,' muttered Chambers, and then he exited the room. I *think* he tried to slam the door after him, but because of the air-locking system, all that happened was it gave this muffled sound, like a *whump.*

Tommy Lee continued to stare at me a while. He made a big show of straightening his tie.

'My colleague might be a little hot-headed,' he said, softly. 'But he's a good soldier, despite what you may think. One of the very best. Don't think that your string-pulling is some kind of victory over us. You got lucky, is all.'

I didn't say anything. Continued to keep my hands clamped behind my head. After a while, I realised that this was what passed for an apology with those military police guys.

When it finally came to the time that I could leave the hospital, I wasn't sorry to see the back of any of it, apart from old Montaffian. He'd fought my corner all the way. He'd come down to the hospital foyer, still clutching my clip-board, still looking overwhelmingly tired, still my one and only ally in the place.

'The MPs won't come a-knockin' again,' he said, presenting me with a new set of crutches that he pulled from behind the reception desk. 'They've now officially listed you as a survivor of the explosion at the, uh, cock-up mansion. You'll be entitled to a full military pension, Gary.'

'I know,' I said. 'They came to see me a few days ago.'

'Well, that's good, isn't it? I thought you'd be over the moon.'

71

I wished that I could put my concerns into words, but it was impossible: 'It just seems so…'

'I know, I know,' soothed Montaffian. 'That's what's called survivor's guilt, what you're, uh, feelin' now. But you'll get over it, son. And remember, them military police were only doing their jobs… Mind you, it was funny the way they backed off so quickly. They were like a dog with a bone with you at first.'

I tried to suppress a wince as I stepped forward. *Oh sure*, I thought, *they'd been like a dog with a bone at first, but something had called them off. Something had caused them to trot off back to their corner, whimpering like scared puppies… And that something was surely not the British army. That something probably looked very much like my old friend Tommy Peaker. Now he was a man that could make things happen.*

Montaffian rested a hand on my shoulder. Looked into my eyes.

'I hope you do eventually, uh, find what you are looking for. And I hope you, uh, find happiness in your life,' he said. 'Just don't go looking for it in the wrong places, like the bottom of a bottle. I seen so many good guys like you go looking there after they've been signed out… Don't let it happen to you.'

'Don't worry about me, doc,' I sighed. 'I'm ready.'

Montaffian nodded, straightened up again and then started flicking through some more papers on the clip-board.

'We've got you on the supply plane which flies west to Egypt, and from Cairo, you're on a commercial flight back to Manchester, UK.'

Part of me loved the way that he said Manchester, UK, as though I was going to get that Manchester confused with the one in America. Part of me bristled at the idea; twenty-five kilometres from Manchester, nestling in the foothills of the Peak District, was Newton Mills. And it was waiting for me to fall into its clutches again. Now I was really going back, I was starting to have second thoughts. I'd already lost a foot, for Christ's sake.

'Thanks, doc,' I breathed.

His face brightened. 'We'll miss you, son. You've been an example to all of the other patients. We need more men like you out here. Men that are prepared to put their insecurities to one side.'

If only he knew, I thought. If only he knew.

Presently, Montaffian's name was called over the Tannoy. And as he walked away from me, he became the grim-faced doctor that I'd first encountered again. Suddenly, he stopped being like my father and became just another white coat fading away into the gunmetal grey background.

While I waited in the hospital foyer for the taxi to the airstrip, I caught sight of my sad reflection in the glass double-doors. My eyes had heavy, dark saddlebags under them, just like Montaffian's. They were watery-blue now, and had that faraway look in them that I always saw in the men that had been out in the desert for too long; too much time spent staring at the horizon. I'd also lost weight; quite a lot of it. My cheek bones, which had always been 'sculpted' or 'angled' as I'd once heard them described by some bird, were now too-prominent. And where once I'd been toned - the kinda guy that likes to wear tight tees just so that it looks like my muscles are going to break-on through the material like the Incredible Hulk – I was now more like a deflated balloon. But nobody would care about that any more. All they'd see was what was missing.

The taxi driver, when he finally arrived, gave me my first indication of what life would be like for me. He came right on through the double-doors and virtually carried me to his smelly Mercedes cab, talking to me as though I was mentally deficient all the way; as though he thought that I'd lost my brain as well as my foot. Before he allowed me in the cab, he put down plastic sheeting on the leather seats in the back.

'Just in case,' he said, winking.

I wanted to smash him in the face for his impudence. And why was he so proud of his fucking Merc? *Everybody* out here drove Mercs. They were like Peugeots in England. As I sat in the back and listened to him prattle on, I worked a hole into the back of his seat with my Swiss Army knife. As he talked about the hopes that he had for his son in this new country that the military were establishing on their behalf, I pulled some of the stuffing through the hole.

'In this place,' he said, 'we have too much awareness of death. The young people lack ambition because of it.'

Yeah, I thought, *and it was the height of your ambition to drive a fucking taxi, was it?* But I said nothing. Instead, I gazed dispassionately out of the window. I would not miss the place. Not because of the fighting and the pain and what had happened with Tommy, but simply because everything there was so undramatic. It was too sparse, over-cooked and limp. I wouldn't dream of the place as I did the embattled majesty of Newton Mills.

When I was deposited at the airstrip, we had a minor argument about my lack of a tip, as though the driver expected that his waffle about the geography and history of the place was some kind of paid-for service.

'I've spent enough time here to know all about the history and the geography,' I said, slamming the door. 'I didn't need no tour guide on my way home either.'

On the first flight, I was so whacked out on sleeping pills that I hardly even noticed time pass. Groggily, I was helped off the plane by another returning soldier who couldn't wait to tell me all about the 'foxy young thing' he was going back home to. In the end, to shut him up, I shared a few drinks with him in the departure lounge as we waited for our flights. It helped; the booze. It helped me come to terms with the naked stares of the Egyptians and the surreptitious glances from the English tourists. When one little boy came too close, I growled at him and he darted away, back to his mother in floods of tears.

The flight followed very much the same pattern. I was treated with an unholy mixture of concern, contempt and curiosity. Even the stewardesses were overly attentive with the contents of the bar, just so's they could get a better look at my footless state. When one of them asked my name, I told her I was Captain Joe Jackson, in reference to the former baseball great, 'Shoeless' Joe Jackson; the doc's hero, apparently. The poor woman didn't seem to get my joke.

As I downed the Lilliputian measures of Vodka and the dolls house bottles of whisky, I felt my mind starting to unravel again. I felt that stabbing pain in my chest, just to remind me that Tommy was there. I hammered my finger on the stewardess call-button constantly. I fiddled with the air-conditioning, trying to somehow stop myself from breaking out in a cold sweat. I twisted and turned in my seat and muttered and moaned to myself like a town drunk. In the end, when I fell asleep, it must have been blessed relief for my fellow passengers.

I was woken up by the air stewardess's shaking my shoulders. I still felt the old pain there where Tommy's claws had sunk in.

'Sir; are you all right?' she asked. 'You've been screaming in your sleep. You're scaring the other passengers. Would you like to come up to the front of the plane and sit with us for a while?'

Meekly, I allowed myself to be led up to the part of the plane that was curtained-off, where I was doused in strong black coffee and spoken to in the soft, reassuring manner that one would choose to speak to a poorly infant. What they couldn't stop me from doing, no matter how many itchy blankets they draped over my shoulders, was shivering. And when the captain's voice crackled over the Tannoy, telling us that we would soon be descending into Manchester, these shivers only became worse. I was going home; unavoidably, unquestionably, I was going home.

Chapter Seven

"Oh, and there we were all in one place,
A generation lost in space
With no time left to start again. "

The taxi driver from Manchester Airport back to Newton Mills couldn't have been more different from the one that dropped me at the air strip out there in the desert. This guy sat low in his seat and virtually drove the car with his huge beer belly, so much did it protrude onto the steering wheel. His car was the old Sarcophagus model; the colour purple, which I'd never seen on a car before. The interior stunk so much of cigarettes that I reckoned that he probably ignored the proliferation of 'no smoking' stickers which were plastered over every surface. Indeed, the man was so heroically impolite in his manner that I began to think that his behaviour was his own well-practiced routine for grabbing tips from his jet-lagged passengers.

My driver had perfected the art of looking unmoved by anything. He'd not said anything about my missing foot, but neither – a true rarity – had his eyes. He simply threw my pack in the boot and got on with his job, which appeared to involve driving to Newton Mills using the longest route possible, although he did seem to avoid nearly every traffic light, so careful were his manoeuvres around deserted council estates and down unused country lanes. For some reason, his silence made me want to talk. I wanted to tell him a horror story which would make him think twice about doing another airport run. I didn't. I simply stared out of the window and watched as we drew inexorably closer to Newton Mills.

There were a number of different ways to get to Newton Mills from Manchester, most of which I knew like the back of my hand. So it surprised me when he took a sharp right turn, apparently up someone's driveway, and ploughed up what was little more than a farmer's track up a steep hill.

'Umm... where are we going?' I asked, suddenly worried that this remarkably fat man might be some kind of agent that Tommy had employed in order to drive me off a cliff or something.

'Short cut,' he coughed. 'Over this hill's Grange Heights.'

Grange Heights; the memories flooded back thick and fast. And indeed, as we passed over the brow of the hill, there it was, in all its glory. It was an old viewing point. A bench had been erected there so idle ramblers could stop and take a lingering look over the panoramic view of the Peak District. A small, gravel car park had been laid in order that lazier sightseers could get up there too. But as the town of Newton Mills had grown, so less people had wanted to go up there to take a look. Newton Mills was not a pretty town. The youngsters hadn't minded though. Driving up to Grange Heights, up past the last of the pubs, you could gain the kind of freedom that you couldn't have anywhere else in the town. It was where we'd come to drink and smoke and where some had come to do something more, in the back of their rusting shit-can cars.

I felt a sudden yearning to experience the calmness which was Grange Heights in the day-time. It would allow me to collect my thoughts, and would, of course, delay the inevitable for a little longer.

'Would you mind dropping me here?' I asked, as the driver navigated around a particularly troublesome pothole.

Not at all sir; but sir, if you wouldn't mind me asking; how are you going to get down that hill with... well, no foot?

My driver didn't care. Instead of finding out how his crippled passenger planned to walk down to the town, he simply screeched to a halt, pulled down the sun-visor and pretended to stare at the knot of figures and fares which was sellotaped on the back. It was all for show; he already knew exactly how much he was going to charge me. I was obviously coming back from the war after all – my uniform and injury would have told him that – and would be full of money that I couldn't spend out there and the army *payout.*

'Twenty-five, fifty mate,' he said. And for some reason, the additional fifty pence annoyed the hell out of me. He'd simply tacked it on the end there so I'd be forced to give him thirty notes and then say keep the change while he fished around interminably in his big grey 'loot' bag.

I fished through my wallet for the exact change, forced to count up coppers in the end, but refusing to budge. As I handed it over, the driver sighed as though I'd short-changed him or asked for a discount. As I tried to climb out of the side door, I made sure that I allowed the edge of my crutch to clip him on the side of the head.

I hated the driver and everything he stood for, but as he drove away, scattering loose gravel into the grassy banks at the side of the narrow road, I almost wanted to call him back. For now he was gone, it was just Tommy and me; Tommy and me and Newton Mills.

I lurched across the car park and made for the bench. It was surrounded by flotsam and jetsam; ten years-worth of empty beer cans, white cider bottles and cigarette ends. I almost became nostalgic for some of the old names: Thunderbird, Mad-Dog Twenty-Twenty, and Ice Dragon. Some of these discarded bottles may have been drunk by the much younger, much prettier Gary Bull in his heyday.

I slumped onto the bench and allowed myself to see my town; the place that corrupted my bloodstream and gave me the desire to drink at the age of thirteen. I hated and loved the place. I knew I'd have been a completely different person if I'd been brought up somewhere else. I knew that I'd probably have had a far better life, but still, when I looked at it, and my own history inscribed into the landmarks, I couldn't help but smile. I cracked open a new deck of cigarettes, making sure that I didn't add any more litter to the site but instead crinkling up the cellophane wrapper and sticking it in my pocket.

The Dorchester and Grey felt strange between my lips. I'd long grown used to the army's standard brand and the cigarette felt thinner and more tightly packed somehow. But longer, always longer than standard cigarettes. I drank down the sulphurous smoke.

Newton Mills was built in the bottom of this deep gorge. That's how it got its name in the old days, on account of the river which ran through it and powered the massive cotton mills. Grange Heights overlooked all of this, and stood in judgement of the factories and the industrial estates which had started to spring up. The town was intersected by a railway; on the one side was the new town with its garish red brick, but on the other was the town I knew. In the old town, most of the houses were built from the local stone and when it rained, seemed to take on the water and darkened from light grey to almost black.

Now, Newton Mills was shadowed by threatening clouds and the place looked depressing; lifeless even. But I knew that life teemed within it; within the small dome of the school library which glistened with wetness and the corrugated metal sides of the new leisure centre and the main street and its countless pubs.

But more than anything else, what this aerial picture of Newton Mills showed me was the graveyards. Hell, even the damn taxi driver would have spotted the fact that there was a graveyard at the end of virtually every street. There were scores of them; grey gravestones pebbledashed the town. I remember when I first came up here and I felt this slight chill creeping up the back of my neck when I tried to count them all.

I don't know when I first noticed it. As a kid, you don't really go around comparing and contrasting towns. Measuring the number of shops or restaurants or houses and then coming to some kind of conclusion about the nature of the town was not really anything any of us ever paid any mind to. Newton Mills was simply home to us, and we wouldn't have had it any other way. It was a known quantity, a given. Even when changes occurred, such as when a shop came under new ownership or new houses were built, we never thought of it as change. It was on the periphery of our vision, and as long as the shop that changed hands wasn't Burt's sweet shop, and as long as the new residents of the new garish redbrick houses across the tracks were not going to be introduced into our classes and clubs, we simply didn't care.

But one day the understanding had washed over me. I suppose it was as though I'd finally given voice to that silent knowledge which I'd always known, deep down. Newton Mills had an unnatural amount of graveyards. And I mean there were a lot; miles more than such a town that size should have had.

'The Graveyards of Newton Mills' was the first school project that I ever aced. It was the first that I'd ever tried in. I suppose I was morbidly fascinated by them. I put together this lever-arch file full of photographs and maps, pencil rubbings of some of the gravestones. I even tried to draw some conclusions about why there were so many graveyards.

My dad loved that I was getting interested in history, and helped me out at the local library. We dug out loads of old books and newspapers. Gradually, he edged me towards his own conclusion about the graveyards. He suggested that working on the mills was a terrible, life-sucking existence and that most of the folk would die young. But because the farming industry was doing so badly, people kept coming into the town from the surrounding countryside, looking for work. He suggested, in his fiery working class hero way, that the mills were doing more than manufacturing cotton. They were cleansing the local area of the undesirables. They were *processing* the workers; depositing them straight into the graveyards at the end of the shift.

I stared out over the town and remembered. I remembered my dad and the way that he'd been a little obsessed with the graveyards; after my project, the teacher invited him in to talk to the class about them. Later, my friends gave me no end of crap for having a loony-tune dad. Nobody but nobody ever wanted their parents to come to the school, let alone if they came in and 'talked to the class.' That was the lowest of the low. But despite my embarrassment, I had found myself becoming interested in what my dad had to say. He was talking about the amount of different burial sites; there were some for the Protestants, some for the Catholics, some for the rich, and some for the poor. There were some that weren't affiliated to any church. In fact, he said, only two of the graveyards in the whole town came with your traditional church spire in the scene too. I'll always remember what he said at the end of that talk. It was like he'd shaped that voice in my head even further. He'd let me see the light.

'Newton Mills,' he said, 'is a town which has always been surrounded by an awareness of death. We're comfortable with it, even.

But we shouldn't be. We don't have to allow ourselves to simply sleep our way along the conveyor belt and succumb to our fate.'

Suddenly, I remembered the taxi driver that had dropped me off at the airstrip in the desert in Afghanistan. I remembered what he'd said about the 'awareness of death.' I also remembered that I now knew what death and pain really were, in the end. Involuntarily, I shuddered.

Dad wasn't invited back to the school again after the talk. I think the teacher thought that it wasn't his place to rant about stuff like that and put ideas like that in children's heads. The teacher was from out of town though, and probably hadn't grasped the fact that Newton Mills life was *exactly* how dad said it was. Most of us were surrounded by an awareness of death. We saw it in the heavy grey stone of the suffering houses. We saw it in the faces of the men and women that had grown up in the town.

As I stared out, I picked out some of the graveyards that I knew. And we did *know* some of the graveyards fairly well. Unconsciously, all of the lads I grew up with spent times in the graveyards. We were a little scared of them, of course, but what kids don't like doing things that are a little dangerous; a little close to the bone?

What we really liked were the old abandoned ones, like the one off Dye Lane, which I could pick out as it scarred across the land, running parallel to the river. Back then, we knew that we could play in the graveyards to our hearts' content and no adults would come asking questions or telling us to shove off. They were kind of like secret gardens or something. I didn't tell anyone, but I thought of them as magical places, like the plateau in *The Lost World.* I thought that time stood still in those places and that lurking in the dense bushes would be prehistoric creatures and mythical demons and the like.

As we got older, the yards had begun to mean less to us in terms of fright-value. Instead, they were places where you could go and let loose; rid yourself of the existential teenage angst by pushing over gravestones or writing other kid's names in the place where an old name had worn away. My friend Lee (Twinnie), the first of us to become sexually active (by a long way), chose the graveyard at the end of Cutter Street as the ideal place to lose his virginity to the local bike, Lisa Fletcher. In the end, she became his missus, and he told us that he loved nothing more than boning his bony missus in the bone-yards. Lee was right about his missus being bony; her face was downright skeletal and sometimes if you looked at her in the right/ wrong light you got to thinking that you could see right through her skin. I couldn't see the graveyard at the end of Cutter Street now; it had most likely been concreted over to act as a car park in the new industrial estate. But the knowledge that it had been there... well, it was enough.

Most of us had used the graveyards as a better place to go and smoke than up at Grange Heights. My dad used to call cigarettes 'coffin nails,' and I kind of liked the way that this image played out there amongst the real coffins and stuff. At fourteen, I was a hardened smoker. I puffed away about as much as the old mills would have done back in the day. Smoking helped me relax a little. I was always a bit nervous around other people and liked to hide away the fact that I was probably a lot more intelligent than the other lads I hung around with. I could hide behind a coffin nail and look as stupid as the rest of them.

We got our cigs from Burt's shop, which was just over the road-bridge on the river, and closest to the oldest of the graveyards on Dye Lane. At the start of the school day, the lads and I would pool together our pocket money and purchase ten cigs, or if we couldn't get enough, Burt would sell us individual cigarettes and a book of matches. I always wondered who the single cigarettes were aimed for if not schoolchildren. I mean, what right-minded working man would go and buy a single cig when they could buy the whole packet?

I suppose that was why we liked Burt's back in the day. It had an air of lawlessness about it which appealed to us. Two mouldy dogs wandered about the shop, in amongst the foodstuffs and the sweets, so if you ever bought a sandwich from there, you always had to check it first for stray black hairs. Towards the back of the shop, I remembered there being two old arcade machines which we could generally rob for a few extra coins if needs be.

Everything was old and decaying in the shop, and that included Burt. He was a big brute of a man, but he wasn't all there; half of his teeth were missing, the rest were little black gravestones which peeked

82

out of his rotten gums. He spat when he talked and always had all kinds of crap all over his fingers. It was as though he wiped his arse with his hand.

Burt pretended he hated all us lads. He'd shout at us for a while about messing up his shop every time we went in, as though he thought that was what behaviour was demanded of a shopkeeper, but eventually, one of us would always get him onto the subject of his army years, and then he'd drone on at us for hours and hours. The irony of the whole thing was that in a town where everyone died young, the oldest resident was probably the unhealthiest, angriest, and most undesirable of the whole lot. We all thought that Burt would live forever. I wondered if he was still alive now, but concluded that it was impossible.

My dad had once showed me a picture of the exterior of Burt's shop from a history book. It used to be a butchers shop, and right behind the windows you could see all these carcasses hanging up. The carcasses were the only thing that had changed in the seventy years from when that picture had been taken. It was still a grand old building, but one which looked as though it was halfway through being dismantled by a wrecking ball. It kinda leaned over to one side where the river had eaten away at the banks. Most of the walls were coated in a light covering of moss or mould.

We hadn't really cared what the place looked like as long as Burt would give us the coffin nails, and fair play to the old chancer, he never questioned our right to decide to die. And in a way, by living in Newton Mills and slipping into the same traps as most of the generations of lads that had come before us, we were kind of deciding to die. Or certainly, we were deciding that our *hopes* would die.

Not one of us even thought about the possibility of leaving the town. I had thought about it in the darkest hours, but I pretty much know for a fact that it simply wasn't an option for the rest of them.

'Them' was generally Paul Morton, Lee Crossett and Richard Featherstone, although none of them were ever referred to by their real names unless by teachers or by (unseen) parents. Paul was called 'Twinnie' by basically the whole town on account of the fact that he was born as one half of a set of twins. The fact that his brother Steven died at the age of two didn't seem to put anyone off calling him that. It was as though once you'd been through the rite of passage of being given a nickname in Newton Mills, nobody or nothing could change that. It was like your destiny.

And nicknames ran across generations too; Lee Crossett was called 'Clarence the Cross-Eyed Lion' or just 'Lion' for short, after some crap 1960s film that nobody of our age had ever heard of, let alone seen. But because his dad had been called 'Cross-Eyed Lion' back in the day, it was handed on like a baton which could not be dropped in the sprint relay which was life in the town. Richard Featherstone's nickname was less interesting; he was simply called Dick, and not in the affectionate *Famous Five* kind of way, which was numb to the very idea of a dick being a body part.

'Them' was the reason that I'd come back to Newton Mills, I supposed. One day we'd all done something that still made my blood run cold. Then we'd *started* something that was coming back to haunt us now. I suppose, looking out over Newton Mills and all of the *old* buildings and dilapidated houses and unsafe graveyards, it was an accident waiting to happen to anyone, but the fact that it happened around us four should have been no surprise.

I pulled my fatigue jacket close around my shoulders against the cold. The shivering had started again. I could delay my return no longer. Newton Mills waited.

It wasn't exactly a hero's return, my traipsing back into Newton Mills that morning. Once, men returning from war might have expected bunting hanging from the front of the shops on the main street; they might have expected an endless amount of free drinks lined up on the bar of the Royal Oak or the Mason's Arms. They'd certainly have expected the fluttering eyelashes of the local lovelies. Everyone loved a man in uniform.

Not any longer, it seemed. As I limped down Eaves Knoll Road and out of the thick cover of trees, I saw numerous curtains twitched and a few cars slowed to see if they could ascertain my business. Eaves Knoll Road took me down a steep slope which I found incredibly difficult to creak down, but nobody emerged from their dark houses in order to give the footless man a hand. Newton Mills was a town of hills; the land rises and falls with the old contours as set by the river. It was not ideal terrain for me.

When I finally gained Main Street, I was breathless and windswept and my hair, as I saw in a shop window, was matted against the sides of my head. More people were out on the streets here; old dears going about their daily shop; old men drinking on the promenade; truants drinking their leftovers. Still nobody spoke to me though. I began to feel like an invisible man. Until I saw Dick, that was.

I saw him first. It was unmistakeably him. Although he'd let his hair grow a little longer than he usually had it, I would have still recognised that bullet-head of his anywhere. As I would the leer which was constantly plastered across his mean face and the way that he always slouched when he moved anywhere, even now. He was backing out of the Main Street Caff, trying simultaneously to drag out a purple twin-seater pushchair, swig from a bottle of White Lightning and ward off the attentions of the café owner. The pushchair was too wide for the doorway and kept getting stuck. The owner of the café kept reaching over and trying to make a grab for Dick's bottle.

'You can't be drinking like this around kids,' he shouted, small-town knowitall that he was.

'Fuck off,' blared Dick. He'd never had any volume control, that one.

A crowd had started to develop now. Tutting young mothers and disapproving local businessmen shook their heads and secretly enjoyed the little break from the day to day mundanity of small-town life. I tried to melt into the background a little longer, just so's I could observe Dick in his natural state and surroundings, but he soon spotted me.

'What you lookin' at, soldier boy?' he roared. And then he tried his death-stare on me. And then, even through his drink-stained eyes, something sparked within him and he knew me.

'Gaz!' he shouted. 'Bully!'

He barged through the crowd, leaving his pushchair blocking the entrance to the shop. He was on me before I knew it; all daft, drunken-man bear-hugs and slaps on the back. As he reached to put his thick arm around me, he sloshed some of his cider onto my uniform.

'Soz, man,' he said, trying to wipe it away with the sleeve of his tracksuit top.

'Don't worry about it,' I said. 'Chill.'

And Dick certainly looked as though he needed to chill. He'd always been an edgy character, but now he seemed as though he was a walking time-bomb. His eyes constantly flickered from side to side. He masticated furiously on a piece of chewing gum; choddy, we used to call it. On close inspection, his face was deathly pale and covered with yellowy-green spots. He looked as though he was on something, and had been for a good while now. And whatever he was on, it was something harder than goddamn White Lightning.

'Come on. Let's go ferra pint,' he continued, mouth going ten to the dozen. He pointed at the Royal Oak, as though I wasn't aware that you could indeed buy a pint from a pub. 'There's something I need to tell you. Something bad…'

I narrowed my eyes and looked at him. In the background I could hear the café owner shouting for us to come and collect the pushchair from out front of his shop. I could hear the Main Street shoppers tutting in unison at Dick's forgetting his own children. But above all of that, I could hear the sound of little Tommy Peaker's laughter. It was echoing down to me from the creaking pub-sign for the Royal Oak. It was rustling through the shopping bags and creeping through the bins. It fair thunder-cracked across the Newton Mills promenade.

'I know what you're going to tell me,' I said softly, feeling tears pricking at my eyes. 'Lion's dead, isn't he?'

If it were possible, Dick's face grew even more pallid. A simple nod told me that I'd followed death halfway across the world and that I was too late.

Chapter Eight

*" Them good old boys were drinkin' whiskey
and rye "*

If some smarmy TV executive was looking for a decent location for a pub scene in some 1970s drama, they could have done worse than take a look at the Royal Oak (or the Royal Choke, as most Newton Millsians called it). It was a desperate place. Stuck in a time-warp; a living museum to the time when, most likely, women weren't even allowed to cross the threshold and men defined themselves as men by spitting into their own pints, as well as those of their friends.

My old grandfather, old drunk that he was, used to tell an amusing tale about the Choke. Apparently, there was this one guy used to go in on his own and prop up the bar all day every day. But he was renowned for being a tight-arse. Wouldn't stand even his next door neighbour a pint when the poor guy's wife had topped herself. And I don't know if the story's true, and it would be a typically Newton Mills story if it was, but eventually, the old bastard's tightness started to descend to new levels. Driven mad by the fact that someone *might* sup his ale when it was unguarded when he went to the toilet, he started to ask the landlord to stick the pint behind the bar, where nobody could get to it. But madness, and years and years of drink eventually made our guy even more paranoid. In the end, he started to suspect that the landlord himself was the one helping himself to the beer.

Eventually, he came up with a fool-proof plan. Or what he thought was a fool-proof plan. He wrote a brief, blunt note on a beer mat, with a pen he stole from the bookies for that very purpose. 'I have spitted in this drink,' he wrote, in his spidery, drunken hand. Oh the guy must have loved the fact that he could finally luxuriate in having a long horse-like beer-piss in peace, without that doubt constantly nagging at him. He could take the time to wash his hands and even try to use the broken old dryer in the corner.

But what he hadn't reckoned on was that Newton Mills spirit. The one which said *fuck 'em all*. The one which my grandfather and his pals held as their badge of honour. When our now totally-pleased-with-himself guy comes back from the toilet, he saw the beer mat still in place by the side of his pint glass. (And mind it was a pint glass one with no handles; my grandfather always used to add at this point: 'never trust a man that needs handles on his pint.') As our guy approached the bar, he saw, with a sinking heart, that his scrawl was not the only writing on the back of the beer mat. Underneath, in the confident block capitals of a younger man was written: 'SO HAVE I!'

Of course, our guy didn't know whether to drink or to look for any traces of spittle in the glass, or worse, hand the pint back. And as his internal monologue continued to play out in his head, he must have heard my grandfather and his mates from the toffee works spluttering with laughter; spilling their own pints in the desire to congratulate themselves on their own youthful ingenuity.

The sad conclusion to the story was the fact that the last time I saw my grandfather, it was he that propped up the bar of the Choke on his own. All of his mates were gone; dead, banged up, missing in action. And it was my grandfather that raged against the arrogance of youth, often reaching over to give me a clip round my ear for being too loud before he even realised that it was me he was chastising.

In a way, the Choke was the place that told the story of the misspent hopes and dreams of Newton Mills far more than the town library or the school or the graveyards. From the mottled brass table tops to the plates which were nailed to the walls, only slightly masking the yellowing stains from a hundred years of cigarette smoke; from the plastic carpet protector which surrounded the old bar and stuck to the soles of your shoes if you tried to walk away, to the constantly closed frilly blinds; nothing had changed. Every sad detail of the place seemed engineered to force the regulars to drink more. The place seemed to give off the same sense of hopeless decay as I'd felt clinging to me ever since Tommy's return.

I smiled gingerly at the barman – a young lad, surprisingly – and hoped that he'd finish pouring our drinks before realising just how bad a state Dick was in. I'd had to drag Dick in off the street, and he was now drumming his impatient fingers on the top of the bar, furtive eyes darting off here, there and everywhere. Behind the bar, where the barman couldn't see from his vantage point, Dick's feet were performing some impromptu jig. I'd already had to shush his constant questions.

'Wait until we sit down,' I said, giving him an icy warning stare. We were lucky that none of the crowd from outside had chosen to follow us in.

Dick moaned under his breath. Leaned down closer to the bar. Looked as though he was going to start smashing his head against the taps. As it was, he seemed to take all of his aggression out on a new piece of chewing gum; rolling his mouth around it as though pummelling it into submission.

'Is he all right?' asked the young barman, fingers itching to stop pouring the lager. Itching to be able to assert his one and only right; to be able to bar people that were too pissed-up to stand up.

'He's fine,' I breathed, taking care to smooth down the collars of my uniform. Making sure that he recognised me as a man of action, despite the leg.

'Hey; don't I recognise you from somewhere?' asked the barman. 'Are you from round here originally?'

I narrowed my eyes. It wouldn't do for too many people to know of my return. Not yet. Dick muttered something about people minding their own business and I faced the young barman down. It didn't take long for him to give up; they breed them that way at the Choke. Sighing, he passed over two over-full lagers, took my proffered note and returned to his crossword.

The pub was quiet again. So quiet that we could hear the whistling from an old man's nose as we passed him on our way to the back of the lounge. The man had smoked so many cigarettes that he'd practically turned cigarette now. And despite the fact that he could barely breathe, he was trying to light a new one off the dying embers of the last one in the ashtray. Involuntarily, I shuddered.

'How did you know?' whispered Dick as we took up our seats; under-sized stools which seemed as though designed for children. Perhaps they were; perhaps the Choke were so desperate for custom these days that they let primary school kids in to sup alcopops here, where they couldn't *quite* be seen if any passing policeman happened to pop their head round the door. 'How did you know about Lion?'

'Wait a minute,' I said, firmly. 'None of that crowd's going to come in here looking for you are they? Not that bloke from the café? We don't want some kind of scene…'

Dick took a long drink of his pint. Too long; bubbles must have gone up his nose and he choked some of the suspicious-smelling liquid straight back out over his tracksuit top. Now we both had matching booze-stains. Within an hour of getting back to Newton Mills, things were – on the face of them – right back to normal.

'Sorry Bully,' he gasped. 'This is all just…'

He made an extravagant gesture, taking in the whole of the pub and its dilapidated, condemned men. I knew exactly what he meant.

'We need to talk,' I repeated. 'But first: are we going to be followed in? What about your kids?'

Dick smiled bitterly: 'Let that Frank in the caff look after him for a while. He's the bastard that's been knocking-off my Laura. If he wants her, he can damn well take on the whole shebang.'

'Sure?'

'It's not the first time I've just left them up there with him,' said Dick. 'He'll be all right about it. He's actually an okay guy in a fucked-up kinda way.'

'Where's Laura?' I asked, not knowing who Laura was. Not really. Not knowing any of the story of Dick and Laura at all, come to think of it.

Dick waved my question away, pulled a half-smoked cigarette from his tracksuit pocket and tried to light it. Problem was, his hands were shaking too much, he couldn't get the lighter's little wheel to move. Quietly, I whipped out my Zippo and lit it for him, without the usual extravagant flourish I reserved for those kind of occasions.

He was in a bad way; in the harsher light towards the back of the pub – they needed a guiding light to ensure the more renowned drunks actually made the toilet – his complexion looked, if anything, worse than it had outside. Now his spots were spot-lit; his cracked and bleeding gums looked red raw and his eyes were framed by fear.

'Did the army tell you about Lion?' asked Dick, after taking a long drag from his cigarette. He bent low over the table, emitting the smoke. Looked like some kind of shady, underworld figure indulging in a spot of haggling.

'What do you mean?'

'I mean; I've seen the films. The army know all sorts. They can get information about anyone,' said Dick. He looked around him furtively, before lowering his voice: 'They probably know you're here.'

'Calm down mate,' I said in what I hoped to be a soothing voice. Obviously things with Dick were even worse than I'd first suspected. His paranoia, whether drug induced or Tommy induced, was even worse than I remembered, just before I left for what I believed was the final time. For the second time, I showed him my foot. 'The army's not looking for me, you or anybody, Dicko.'

Dick raised his eyebrows but said nothing.

'Tell me what happened to Lion,' I continued.

Dick's bruise-coloured bottom eyelid started to quiver. He started to scratch at his hairline. Seemed about to break down. I should have reached out to him; shown him my... my what?... My support? My compassion? My complicity in the whole damn thing? But I didn't. I couldn't. I just sat on my too-small stool and watched him try to wrestle with the tears that had clearly been building up inside him for some time now. I watched him try to keep playing the big man as we had when we were kids. I watched him try to maintain his grip on reality.

'He's... he fell... he was...' mumbled Dick.

'Tell me,' I said.

'The gorge,' breathed Dick. 'The river...'

'He fell off the bridge into the gorge?'

Dick nodded, mutely. Stared at the mottled brass of the table; the thin trail of beer which was flowing from his side of the table to mine.

'Accidentally?'

'It weren't suicide if that's what you're thinking,' said Dick, raising his eyes to meet mine. There was fire in those eyes now. Sheer, stubborn will.

'From the start then,' I said, in the style of some interrogator from the military police; the new Tommy Lee Jones or Chewing-Gum Breath perhaps.

Dick took a moment to compose himself and then began: 'Lion wasn't right in the head. Hadn't been for a while. Not since... You know?'

I nodded. He looked back, almost accusing.

'I suppose all of us apart from you got a bit fucked up by what happened. You got out. We had to live here with what happened. Every day. Worried that we'd get found out. Worried that the next knock on the door would be the filth with their handcuffs and their fucking moustaches.'

'Go on,' I said.

'After a while, we couldn't bear to be around each other, the three of us. I think we all found it out after you upped and left. Twinnie got bad first; you know what he was like. Always *this* close to the edge. He's been inside a few times. They let him out a couple of weeks ago, and I haven't seen him, but I've heard rumours. Stuff about what he's up to and that. It ain't good, mate.'

'What about Lion?'

'The big bastard thought Twinnie blamed him that first time he got sent down. Got scared, you know? First time Twinnie got let out, Lion admitted himself to the Looney Bin down at Stockport. After that, every time I saw him, Lion was a bleedin' mess. Kept saying all this stuff about needing to change his identity. And then there was the drinking.

Anyway, this went on for a few years. I'd hear stuff on the grapevine about the two of them. I worried something terrible was going to happen.'

'Something terrible did happen.'

'Yeah, but it wasn't like what the police said it were.'

I took a Dick-sized gulp from my beer. Prepared for the galling confirmation of what I already knew.

'They said that Lion tried to walk along the railing on the bridge. Two hundred feet up. All them rocks and shit at the bottom. Jagged like teeth. They said he was probably doing it to impress a bird. But Lion's not had no birds. Not since school, Bully. And he had no friends. No nothing. Thing is, and I only know this from a lad I know that happened to over-hear something at the police station when it all went off... Thing is, they found this... thing... on his chest. And even though the filth are playing it down as a suicide, it ain't.'

'What thing? Who's this lad?'

Dick winced at the thought of having to repeat what he'd heard out loud. I knew sort of what he was going through. Saying that kind of thing makes it real. When it's just in your head, you can kinda believe that it's just your fucked-up imagination playing tricks with you.

'There was this mark, above his heart. Like a scratch you get from claws, apparently. One of the police blokes said it looked a lot like a number one.'

I felt the colour drain from my face. And I felt that stabbing sensation in my chest, right where the spear had been.

'Lad at the cop shop that overheard all this was my dealer,' continued Dick. 'Said he heard the names of Twinnie and Lion mentioned in that same conversation. Oh, Bully, you don't think it was Twinnie that did Lion in do you?'

'Tommy?'

'Twinnie,' said Dick, looking a little confused. 'I said Twinnie... What you talking about Tommy for?'

'That's what I needed to tell you,' I said, slowly. 'Tommy's back...'

'Shut up,' shouted Dick. 'Shut the fuck up. What are you; mad?'

Dick's outburst stilled the steady lull of conversation in the Choke. The barman craned his neck to look round a pillar to see what all the fuss was about. The old, wheezing, chain-smoking bloke creaked on his stool and gave us a dirty look. Dick immediately flopped back down onto his stool. For a moment, nobody spoke. We could hear the unsteady ticking of the Choke's clock, once set ten minutes slow so extra last orders drinks could be bought, but now probably set ten years too slow.

'All right you two,' said the barman. 'You've had your fun. Now simmer down or you'll be out.'

'Sorry,' I called over to him. 'Won't happen again.'

Dick continued to stare at me with those same confused eyes.

Finally, he spoke. Actually, it was more like a snarl: 'Don't ever say anything like that again, Bully. I mean it. Don't mess with my head like that. I've got enough to worry about with Twinnie and Lion without you bringing up what happened all them years ago.'

'But we can't get away from it... Everything stems from that point.'

'You're starting to sound like Lion,' sighed Dick. 'Just as fucking-well mad as that big bastard.'

'He said it too... about Tommy?' I breathed, leaning forward on the stool, almost displacing my pint.

Dick shook his head. Sighed again.

'Do you remember that time we all went up to Grange Heights that time? When we took them tents and sleeping bags we robbed from the Outdoor Store?

I hardly knew what Dick was talking about now, but couldn't risk upsetting him again. One more scene from us would see us out on our ear, back on the main street of Newton Mills and visible again... Visible to Tommy.

'Yeah,' I said. 'Isn't that the time Twinnie and me set fire to the bottom of Lion's purple sleeping bag when he was passed out?'

'It was *my* sleeping bag,' said Dick, wearily. 'My sleeping bag you set fire to... Ruined my trainers and everything.'

'Shit, sorry mate,' I said, wondering where all this was leading.

Dick waved away my apology.

'That isn't what I wanted to talk about. Do you not remember what else happened up there?'

'Uh...'

'If you remember, that was the time all those people claimed that they saw that Black Panther roaming around. There was that

94

rumour that it had bitten a child and eaten some goats and stuff. Nobody could get a photo, like, but everyone said it was massive…'

I remembered the stories now. How, for a while, the Black Panther had been blamed for every accident or injury that took place in Newton Mills. How even the stuff that happened to Tommy had been pinned on the beast, which was probably just some over-sized neighbourhood cat.

'Anyway, we all sneaked out that night, remember? Even though the school had tried to get all us kids to be on a curfew? And up at Grange Heights, you started talking about the Black Panther, Bully. You told us all about how it had this real scary type of breathing. How you'd know even before it got hold of your neck that the Black Panther was about to kill you, and there was nothing anyone could do about it. I got shit-scared by your story. Believed every word. And do you know what? You even had me convinced that it was the Panther that did for… for, you know?'

Finally, Dick's tears were starting to come now, but he soldiered on with his story.

'In the middle of the night, after all that with the sleeping bag, I woke up again. I heard all this raggedy breathing. I heard what I thought was the padding of gigantic paws on the rocks. And it was sort of half-light but there were still shadows. The rocks and that sort of thing. And I became convinced that it was me that the Panther was after. I *knew* it was going to kill me…'

'Sorry,' I breathed.

'Do you not understand what I'm saying? You had us all convinced, Gaz. We believed every word that came out of your mouth. You were always more intelligent than any of us no-marks. And what you said went. Even for Twinnie. When we had to go down to the graveyard that day, it was all because of you. When I smashed my head running down from Grange Heights that morning, that was all because of you. And now you're saying something like this? The things you make up follow you around, Bully. And it's bad shit. You *create* bad shit.'

Dick stood up from his stool again. He didn't shout this time though. He simply walked out of the Choke with his tail between his legs. And I stared at my pint and wondered if what he'd said was true. Over the years I'd managed to convince myself that I'd been the one being led – the one under the bad influence of people like Twinnie and Dick – but had I somehow managed to block out what really happened? Was the only way I'd been able to build a life for myself because I'd built it on foundations which were actually a lie?

And now Lion was dead, and Tommy was back and I had absolutely no idea what I was supposed to do about it all. Well, that wasn't strictly true; I did have one idea, but to do that would require Dutch courage. Seeing Twinnie was not something that anyone should undertake on a beer-empty stomach.

Chapter Nine

"Moss grows fat on a rollin' stone"

I propped up the bar like my grandfather had done before me, mangled leg well hidden by my pack. Occasionally, some regular or other would try to engage me in conversation, but soon took my grunted responses as a sure-fire sign that I didn't want to talk. I had more pressing matters to take care of. Like pouring enough lager and whisky down my gullet that I could numb the pain.

Only the wheezing, chain-smoking old man managed to even get me to stop staring at my reflection in the dirty mirror behind the Choke's bar.

'Guilt does funny things to a feller,' he wheezed to me while waiting for his next half of bitter.

'What?' I asked, swinging round on my bar stool to meet his eyes, bristling with indignation. His face was as stained as the wallpaper and his eyes were rheumy and weak. I could hear the death's rattle of his lungs when he breathed, but his chin jutted out with something resembling pride.

'Whoah there, feller. Just saying: guilt does funny things to folk,' he more or less repeated, before undertaking some emergency repair work on his dentures with his tongue. In an instant, I knew without doubt who the old man was. It was Burt, the man that used to run the old sweet shop where we used to buy our single cigarettes. Where we'd have to brush off the dog hairs before smoking them. God, the man must have been in his eighties now, surely. How had he managed to survive so long in this rotten town?

'I can see you been in the forces, son. Been away from here for a while, no doubt,' he continued. 'And those that are left behind may feel slighted by your going away. Like your pal that left a while back. But don't let them get to you, son…'

Burt had been in the forces himself, I recalled, but now his face resembled more of a retired shop-keeper's face than that of a soldier. It was round and jowly, and kinda loose-fitted. But deep down, underneath the wrinkles and the jaundice, it was definitely the same man that had often shouted at us boys in his shop.

'Do you remember me?' I gasped.

Burt tried to smile. Old gravestone teeth collapsed in his mouth.

'I'm sorry, son. Got no recollection of nobody these days,' he said. But something about the new light in his eyes told me that he knew more than he was letting on.

'I had to come back,' I told him, without quite knowing why.

'I know, son,' he said. 'Everybody does. There's a pull about this place that you can't quite put your finger on, isn't there?'

I nodded. Spun my tot of whisky around the bottom of my glass. Watched how the liquid seemed to cling to the sides. Like it was hoping to escape.

'I was in the forces myself,' continued Burt. 'Way back when. But after the war, when my wife got ill, we just found ourselves stuck here. Couldn't go nowhere. Can't remember I left the town boundary last nowadays. But you can make something of a life for yourself.'

I must have grunted my disbelief then for Burt leaned in closer. I could smell the drink off him and also the stink of death. Time wasn't long for him now. And from somewhere deep inside me, I got the funny feeling that the only reason Burt was alive at all was so he could impart this advice to me in the Choke.

'Just don't listen to the voices,' he breathed. 'Keep your head down and your nose out of trouble and you'll be okay.'

But I knew I wasn't going to be okay. I knew that I was about as far from okay as I could get without passing go and collecting two hundred pounds. I lowered my head onto the bar and felt the weight of the world and of Tommy Peaker on my shoulders. Thing was; the voices Burt was referring to… Well, they were *my* voices, weren't they, if what Dick had said were true. I'd brought it on myself, this guilt, and there was nothing anybody could do about it.

'I'm sorry,' I whispered, to nobody in particular.

And then I heard everything as a mumble of indistinguishable voices. Someone, probably the young barman shouted something angry. Burt tried to pick me up off the stool and I heard his pained whistling burning a hole in my ears. Someone else was laughing. It could have been Old Tommy Peaker. Somewhere else, a stool collapsed. The sound of rushing feet. A scream as rough hands grabbed me under the arms just like in the C.U.M building way back when. And then it was all darkness as the black hole enveloped me again. Head loss.

Within the black hole, we were young again. I felt strength in my arms and even in my leg. I felt a kinda craziness in my head, like everything was being fast-forwarded. We were sat at the back of the dinner hall at school. On tables which had the chairs affixed to them so they couldn't be thrown, like in prison. Us slouching and posturing. A handful of girls looking-on with lusty eyes. Dinner ladies trying *not* to look.

Tommy Peaker was pinned into a corner, unable to go anywhere. To one side there was the big dinner hall window, to the other, Twinnie. Behind him was the wall, and facing him down was yours truly. Lion and Dick were kinda leaning across the tables, using their school bags like pillows. Trying to block the view from the other side of the hall.

'Why's your mam such a slag, then Tommy?' someone sneered. Painfully, the realisation came to me that it was me; it was me conducting this interrogation.

Tommy didn't speak.

Twinnie jammed a pencil into the smaller lad's ribs.

Tommy still did not react.

'Are you fucking her now, twatty? Is that why you don't want to say anything? Are you trying to *protect* her?'

Me speaking again. The bile in my voice, the pure anger shocked me.

Tommy blinked back the tears. Made this gurgling sound at the back of his throat.

Twinnie twisted the pencil in harder, as though he was using Tommy's ribs as a sharpener.

'Little prick like you must have a little prick,' laughed Dick.

'That's right,' I agreed. 'Show the girls here your little prick.'

The gaggle of girls screeched in mock alarm. One of them turned her face away but the others had that same blood lust on them as we did. Unfortunately, their scream alerted a teacher, and Mr. Swann swans up to our table with a busybody policeman's *what's going on here then?*

How could he have missed the agony which was etched across little Peaker's face? How could he have missed the fact that the four of us lads had him, Tommy, trapped in a corner like a wounded animal? But miss it he did. With a tut, he span on his heels and made for the opposite end of the dining hall, where his presence would have more chance of controlling the raggedy, half-wild children that made up our school. He was probably counting down the seconds until he could quietly slip out and have a crafty cigarette in his car.

'Right. Pull your fucking kecks down,' I ordered.

Tommy snivelled.

Twinnie drove the pencil in still harder.

Tommy tried to back away, but there was nowhere for him to go.

'Kecks. Now,' said Twinnie.

'Leave it now lads, eh?' said Lion, sounding concerned.

We didn't listen to his moaning. He was last seen backing away, probably going to re-join the queue for Swiss Roll, which was always his favourite pudding.

Dick tutted.

Tommy started whimpering as he unzipped his too-small trousers. Twinnie pulled them down for him. The girls screeched with laughter. Dick clapped his hand on the table with excitement.

A little Pooh-stick of an erection poked out of Tommy Peaker's boxer shorts. A nice n' spicy Nik Nak of a nobbled little cock straining for the light.

'Disgusting!' cried one of the girls, without taking her eyes away.

'What the fuck?' demanded Twinnie.

'Dirty bastard,' I roared.

'I can't help it,' snivelled Tommy Peaker, grovelling on the floor to grab at his trousers again.

'You fucking can,' I shouted, wheeling my school bag like some medieval weapon around my head and then cracking it into one of his sticky-out ears. Swiftly, we all vacated the back table and made for the exit.

Within the black hole, there was the me from then and the me from now looking on as we strolled past the big dinner hall window, laughing and gesturing at the slumped figure of Tommy Peaker in the corner of the room, still with his pants around his ankles. The me from now wanted to run to him and tell him that we didn't mean it. We just had nothing better to do and we were sorry.

The me from back then decided to inform one of the dinner ladies of the state of Tommy. That he'd been flashing the girls in the dinner hall... He was last seen being marched to the headmaster's office in tears. His trousers were ruined. But we knew he wouldn't tell.

I tried to shout to him.

'I'm sorry!' I tried to yell. But all that came out of my pig-ignorant young mouth was further abuse.

I came to, feeling gnarled old hands touching my cheek.

'What are you sorry about, son?' asked a soothing voice.

I tried to open my eyes. Anything to dilute the poison that they'd just seen.

'You're in a bad way, lad,' continued the voice. 'But you'll be reet.'

Burt, I thought. Burt touching my cheek. Back in the day, the very idea would have caused the rest of the gang no end of amusement. But back in the day, we were amused by anything that caused misery for anybody else.

I opened my eyes. Saw his face almost too close to mine. Almost flinched backwards but managed to stop myself. For in his own eyes was written concern rather than malice. He looked as though he wanted to help.

'Where am I?' I managed to gasp.

Really, I should have already known the answer. Really, the relentless smell of off-meat which permeated the place should have told me that I was in one of the upstairs rooms above where Burt's shop used to be... and where the butcher's shop of my dad's history books once was.

Burt creaked himself up to a half-standing position and shuffled away to a moth-bitten armchair by the curtained window. My eyes followed him and took in the room. Like the Royal Choke, it was stuck in a time-warp. Old prints of horses in the fields on the walls; the floral print on the three piece suite; the bare patches on the carpet. As well as the lingering smell of meat, there was also the sharp smell of a million cigarettes smoked over the years in this room. Burt lit up a cigarette now, struggling through a rack of coughing to get the damn thing lit.

'I'm above the shop,' I said eventually, answering my own question when it appeared likely that Burt's coughing fit wasn't going to cease in the near future.

He managed to nod his assent, before clicking on a radio – more a wireless actually such was its age – in order to muffle the sound. Finally, he managed to regain control of himself.

'These things,' he winced, holding up the Dorchester and Grey and regarding it as though he'd never seen the like of it before. 'These things put me in such a state that the only way I get to feel any better is just by lighting up once more.'

I nodded.

'And there hasn't been a shop down there in years,' he continued. 'Trouble with the school, and the parents of the kids from the school. They *advised* me that it would be better to close down than face whatever penalties they had in store for me. How's your leg doing now, lad?'

In truth it itched, just as Do-Nowt had said it would back in the British hospital. It itched to kick a football or to run or to dance. Not that I'd ever danced in my life, but you know what I mean. Or maybe you don't. Maybe you've no sympathy for me whatsoever, after what I'd done. Even Burt, the old sly trickster, might have a few things to say if he knew. And I'm not sure if the word 'rehabilitation' would enter into any of it.

'Wrecks,' I said finally. I tried to shift it on Burt's sofa, using both of my arms to lift it up like the whole thing was dead and never coming back, and not just my foot.

'Know the feeling, lad,' smiled Burt. 'There's some wounds you can't hide, aren't there?'

And there it was again; that mysterious gleam in his eyes which told me that everything was not exactly as it seemed.

'Do you honestly not remember me?' I asked.

'Nope,' said Burt.

I fished around in my wallet for a while before producing my old army ID card which I slid across the coffee table towards him, avoiding unknowable spillages and stains along the way. Burt strained and grunted as he reached over. For a moment, I thought he wasn't going to make it, but a sharp draw on his cigarette – like Popeye with his spinach – gave him the strength for that final push, and red-faced, he clawed the ID badge.

'Lance Corporal Gary Bull; Third Infantry,' he read. 'Gary Bull… the name sounds familiar…'

'I've heard it all before,' I replied. '*Terry-bull.*'

Burt shook his head.

'No… I've heard the name recently. Since all that happened with the shop and everything. Just give me a minute and it'll come to me…'

Burt stared wistfully through the curling smoke from his cigarette. I saw him counting through the years and faces and names that he'd long since forgotten. Saw him trying to wire up the old connections up there again. Then, suddenly, he ground out his cigarette and slapped his hand on his thigh.

'Gary Bull, the Duke of Lancaster's Regiment' he read. 'Now I remember. I have something I need to give to you.'

He made no move to get out of his seat. For a moment, I thought he was going to start ordering me around to find whatever it was in his own flat.

'Now where did I put it?' he mused.

'What is it? Who gave you whatever it is? *Why* did they give it to you?' I asked, trying to jog the old boy's memory.

Burt shook his head wearily, tossed the ID badge back onto the coffee table in front of me. I picked it up and looked at it, mainly so I wouldn't have to watch any more of the desperate guessing game which was going on in Burt's head. I looked at the photo but it didn't look anything like me, or at least the me that I saw when I looked in the mirror now. I had to check the name twice just to reassure myself that I'd not picked up the wrong badge by accident. What the hell was going on?

It's the guilt, said a voice which was not Burt's or mine.

I tried not to look panicked.

Guilt does funny things to a person, continued the voice. *Think of all of the guilty secrets possessed by this town. Think of all the skeletons which are liable to come crawling out of the closet at any moment.*

My eyes shot across to Burt. He was staring intently at the back of his packet of Dorchester and Grey. It was definitely not him that had spoken.

Ask him about the purpling, continued the voice. *He knows all about it and you need to know. Ask him about the purpling...*

I screwed up my eyes and tried to forget my burning desire to take a drink. Or to repeatedly bang my head against the hard wooden armrest of Burt's sofa. Why the hell had I come back here, to hell, after everything I'd done to rid myself of the memories?

Chapter Ten

"Do you recall what was revealed the day the music died?"

A sound; for a moment I couldn't work out exactly what it might have been, but it had certainly shaken me out of my reverie. Then I heard it again; a heavy thud coming from downstairs; the old shop. I glanced over at the armchair, where Burt was fast asleep, still gripping his packet of cigarettes as though they were the only thing ensuring that he'd wake up. Behind him, the thick curtains were still drawn. I couldn't tell if it was light or dark, night or day. To be honest, I couldn't even tell whether either of us was alive until Burt gave out a loud snore and my heart nearly did a runner up and out of my chest.

I tried to calm down. Tried to talk myself down from the precipice; at the bottom I could only see madness. Perhaps this was how it had happened for Lion. Perhaps the constant pressure had finally got to him and that was why he'd leaped from the bridge. And then been marked with the number one on his chest.

And how could I stop Tommy Peaker – the new Tommy Peaker – if it was him come a-knocking downstairs? How could I, a semi-cripple now, armed only with my cigarette lighter; protected only by an eighty-year old somnambulist, stop the new big Tommy from straddling my chest, pulling down my trousers and laughing at my shrivelled penis? How could I stop him from carving the great big number two on my hairy chest, above where my heart should have been?

When I heard the sound again, my only reaction was to whimper. Something heavy was being launched against the locked front door. Of that I was sure. I tried to gauge the weight of whatever that heavy object was; tried to decide how much it is that dead people weigh. Was the heaviness all wrapped up in the revenge thing?

My ears pricked up as I heard footsteps walking away from the front door. Heavy tread; purposeful. Strong, I thought.

Go away, go away, go away, I whispered to myself, or to God, or to Tommy Peaker himself. And for a moment, I almost believed that someone, somewhere had answered my prayer. But then I heard a sound which chilled my blood. Everyone knows what a smashed window sounds like, but at that moment, it sounded to me as loud and overweening as the peal of bells on a Sunday morning, calling the worshippers to one of Newton Mills's two competing churches. It was loud enough to wake the dead, and was probably intended to do just that.

Oh fuck, oh fuck, oh fuck, I moaned. Louder and louder I moaned, and yet old Burt still did not rise from his chair. I longed for the strength to pull myself up from the sofa, but now both legs felt numb. I was at the mercy of whatever was coming through that door.

One of the worst nightmares I could imagine was being buried alive, but only just behind that was being completely paralysed, like the man in the old Metallica video, where he was screaming to be put out of his misery and yet nobody could hear him. In that moment, I felt like that man. Trapped – buried alive – within my own body. And for the second time in recent memory, I involuntarily lost control of my bladder. I was becoming just like Tommy Peaker in our school days.

And Tommy Peaker was evidently becoming like me. Relishing the minor details which would build up and finally, make my life the living hell that his had been. I could clearly hear him tramping through the shop downstairs. It had been left, almost exactly as it was on the day Burt was *advised* he could not trade any more, or so he'd told me. Rather like the bedroom of a dead or missing child, I suppose. I imagined the chocolate bars and crisps on the shelves gradually rotting away. The cakes going hard like stones and the biscuits becoming soft and pliable; mossy almost. And through this vision of childhood hell he stepped, knocking over the display rack of birthday cards which were sun-bleached and out of date even when we were boys. Crashing past the arcade machines and their life support machine echo bleeps which probably still sounded once in a while.

Then the footsteps abruptly stopped. I couldn't help myself from imagining the monstrous Tommy Peaker helping himself to some monstrous snack to build up his strength before his strike. Perhaps a ten-year-mould covered pasty; one of the ones we used to claim contained dog-meat back in the day. Or perhaps he was helping himself to a packet of cigarettes from behind the counter. I listened out for the tell-tale cough as he inhaled. Tommy could never properly *take* cigarettes. Always duck-arsed them; I imagined what he left behind on the filter tip now. What with his half-face and decaying tongue, he'd probably extinguish the thing…

Soon he was moving again. And he reached the bottom of the stairs which led up to Burt's living quarters and our hideaway. He *told* me that he reached the bottom of the stairs by tapping his misshapen stick or cane – the spear that he had ripped out of me back at the C.U.M building against the door jamb.

Tap, tap, tap. Little pig, little pig, let me in.

I closed my eyes. Like a child does, hoping that the world will simply go away. Hoping that once they were open again, I'd be in a new, brighter reality.

Tap, tap, tap. Little pig, little pig, I'm going to come up there and find you whether you like it or no-ot…

I heard old Burt's breathing becoming more and more ragged. He was going to wake up and be subjected to whatever fresh hell awaited me. And I felt guilt again. Guilt for having dragged the poor old man into this mess.

Tap, tap…

Tap, tap, nothing. That third tap never came. I waited some interminable amount of time and then gingerly opened my eyes, half expecting Tommy to be rearing up over me, ready to spear me in the heart, but there was nothing there. Just the bare room and Burt, drooling in his chair, still clutching on to his packet of Dorchester and Grey.

I reached under the sofa, for where I hoped my crutch would be. I touched things that were unclean; items which had lain dormant for years. Tried not to think of what they might be. Tried not to imagine them starting to scurry and then bite into my flesh like the rats back at the British military hospital. I forced my fingers to search out the familiar cold, clean metal of the crutch. But it wasn't there.

Where the hell was it? Had I left it back at the Choke? Had Burt propped it up somewhere else? Or had he hidden it? Was he a part of this grand revenge plan? Was that why he'd lured me back here in my drunken state? Was that why he'd *kept* me here with promises that he'd something to pass on to me? Was Burt undead too? He certainly looked it. But then half of the people in Newton Mills did. Dick included. Me included…

And then I heard a voice on the stairs again.

'Bully!' it called. 'Bully! Come out, come out wherever you are!'

It was pitched higher than the booming voice that Tommy had used on me previously, but still seemed terrifying. The voice was so… inhuman. So unreal; so taunting.

'Bully!' it called. 'Bully! Are you up there? What the hell you doing to that poor old fucker up there?'

I'd heard the voice before. Recently. Very recently. But before I could properly put two and two together, Dick Featherstone ambled into Burt's front room. He was wearing the same tracksuit that he'd had on when I'd seen him last – looking even more dishevelled, if anything – but he also had on a massive, goonish grin and a kind of sheen of something. Like he was floating almost.

'What the fuck are you doing?' I demanded.

Dick flopped down onto the sofa next to me, barely even bothering to move my half-leg out of the way before he sank into the sofa's welcoming folds and ruffles.

'I asked: what the fuck are you doing?'

Dick spun his head around to face me. It took him about twenty seconds to achieve this feat, but once I saw the lolling tongue, the rolling eyeballs and the trickles of sweat which were rolling down his forehead, I knew exactly what was wrong with him.

'I asked at the Choke where you been, man,' said Dick, slowly. 'They told me old Burt looked after you… They told me you came here. So I found where 'here' was and then I came round here. Mate. Mate? Are you not pleased… ?'

'You smashed the old boy's window,' I snapped, trying to keep my voice down.

'Never did that,' said Dick. 'No, never smashed no windows or nothing. It was like that when I got here. And I thought you'd done it.'

Dick seemed to find the confusion over the smashed window fairly amusing. But not as amusing as the picture of the horse in the field which was stationed above the fireplace.

'Nice horse,' he said. 'I used to like horses.'

'Shut up, Dick,' I snapped. Louder this time. 'Are you sure it wasn't you that smashed the window?'

'I told you... Look I'm sorry about what I said in there. In the Choke. I was in a bad way mate. Strung out. I didn't know what I was saying. Or who I was saying it to. Lion going like that has fucked me up. I just needed a little taster again tonight, just to set my mind at ease again. I'm okay now. We can talk all you want. I'm glad you're back.'

Dick beamed over at me. I had the overwhelming urge to punch him in his stupid gurning mouth. But at least he wasn't Tommy Peaker...

'I'm sorry, man,' he repeated. Kinda wailing now.

And that must have been what finally roused Burt from his slumber. Not the thudding of the undead at his door; not the smashing of his front window as they slipped inside; not their *tap, tap, tapping* on the stairs; but a stupid junkie talking nonsense in his front room. He must have had a sixth sense for that kind of thing.

'Sorry Burt,' I said, meeting his fiery, yet confused eyes.

'What's this one doing here?' he growled. 'This one's no good. No good at all. Look at him...'

Then Burt launched into another machine-gun quick rapid-fire burst of coughing and spluttering. His round face turned blood red. To someone in Dick's condition, it must have looked as though his whole head was going to explode.

'Go on over to Burt's chair and light up a cigarette for him,' I whispered to Dick, gesturing to the packet of Dorchester and Grey which Burt had finally dropped on the floor.

Amazingly, Dick did as he was told; popped up from the sofa again, skirted the coffee table and reached down for the cigs. Still coughing, Burt tried to lash out, fearing that his prize was being stolen from him. His weak arm-swings only met thin air, but still Dick shuffled away a little before extricating a lone soldier from the pack and lighting it up. He took a long drag before passing it on to Burt's grateful fingers. Burt finally understood it for the act of kindness it was and calmed down. Or maybe it was only the nicotine that stopped him from being a raging bull.

'Thank you, lad,' he breathed, through a thick mouthful of smoke. 'But what was that you were saying about a smashed window? I heard you talking just as I was waking up… Smackheads are always round this way breaking windows. Is that what you've done, lad?'

Dick shook his head and again strenuously denied the accusation: 'Smackheads go on the rob when they *don't* have gear. Not when they do.'

I had to admit, Dick actually had a pretty good point. So did Burt, nodding away to himself and examining the perfect smoke ring that he'd just blown from his mouth. Thing was: neither of us believed him. Smackheads are great storytellers, or so I'm told. It *had* to have been him that smashed the window. Probably he just couldn't remember it, that was all.

'Well, what are we going to do now that you're here?' asked Burt, after a moment's silence.

Dick and I looked at each other, a little mystified.

'How's about I get us all a nice taster of whisky and we have a good old, honest-to-goodness chat about old times?' continued the suddenly back-to-normal Burt.

'That sounds nice,' I said, like a polite young Kingsman doing his duty in the community. *Not* like some fucked-up child killer that was being haunted by the very boy that he killed.

'That's a nice horse, Mr. Burt,' said Dick, by way of thanks. He was pointing at the picture above the electric fire again. Burt raised his eyes to the ceiling as he stumbled past on his way to the kitchenette to grab some glasses. As he rummaged through the cupboards, we heard him cursing and panting, but neither of us made a move to help him. This was his place, his refuge, and we knew better than to demean him like that.

He returned with three tumblers, two which looked as though they'd seen better days. There was a large crack running down the side of one of them, and another looked as though it hadn't been washed or dusted for about a hundred years. The other – his glass – looked pristine clean however. Burt was clearly not used to company of any kind. My heart, such as it was, went out to the old battler.

The whisky, it turned out, was stuffed down the side of Burt's chair, and was already half drunk. I wondered if he'd been drinking after he carried me home. I wondered *how* he'd carried me home in the state he'd been.

'Glenmorangie,' he said. 'The best.'

'You're spoiling us,' said Dick.

Burt poured lovingly. Even twisting the bottle at the end of his free pour as though he were a barman in some swanky airport lounge and we were travelling businessmen, ready with cash-dollar tips. He handed one over to me first, then placed one on the table in front of Dick. His own, he drained in one fluid gulp, before pouring another, larger measure. Then he took his seat.

'Well; what is it you lads want to know?' asked Burt.

'I...I don't know what you mean,' I stuttered.

'What brought you here, to my door? What questions do you need me to answer?'

'You brought me here,' I tried.

Burt waved away my comment: 'You were brought here by the wings of destiny. You were brought here because you need answers. Now fire away. We don't have much time...'

Dick nudged me in the ribs and made a rather too obvious gesture with his hand, indicating the fact that he clearly believed Burt to be drunk, or insane. I tried to ignore my smacked-up friend.

'I need to know where my crutch is,' I chanced. 'I can't see it anywhere.'

Burt smiled.

'Such an obvious question, young man,' he said. 'It's in the kitchenette. I couldn't have you running out on me before I had chance to tell you what I needed to tell you... or remember what it was that I was supposed to give you...'

'Why do you say that about us not having much time,' interrupted Dick, sounding remarkably compos mentis for about the first time since he'd arrived.

Burt smiled again. This time it was a cruel, knowing smile. Not a shopkeeper's smile at all, but the smile of a man who's seen it all and who knows what's coming.

'If it wasn't you that broke the window, lad, someone did,' he said.

'Who?' shouted Dick.

'You know very well...'

'We need to get out of here,' I said. 'Get me the crutch, Dick.'

'You've not asked what you need to ask yet,' said Burt, slowly, calmly lighting up another cigarette from the butt of his last one. The ashtray was overflowing now. Surely a fire risk.

'What is he on about?' asked Dick, not making any move to get the crutch.

'I'm *on* about guilt, boys. Guilt,' said Burt. And suddenly we saw the light in his eyes once again. 'I'm *on* about what you need to know about guilt and what it does to people in this town. We're killing ourselves, aren't we? Be it the smack or the booze or the fags or the jumping off bridges.'

'He didn't jump,' muttered Dick.

'That may well be,' continued Burt, 'but have you ever considered *why* so many people seem to be on a one-way ticket to hellsville in this town?'

'Do you mean all the graveyards?' I asked, remembering what my father had said in school that day. 'The processing of the people...'

'In the old days, it was the mills. Now it's the drug dependency,' said Burt. 'But what drives people into this mess in the first place? Tell me, have you heard of a thing called the purpling?'

I felt my face blanch. I had heard of the purpling. Why, in this flat, I'd heard of the purpling... But I couldn't answer Burt's question.

'It used to be that the purpling only came to certain people. A madness, it was. A death-wish so to speak. Where good folk feel that they have no other choice than to persecute themselves into living the lives that they don't want to live.'

I nodded my head, tried not to look at Dick, whose mouth was wide-open, catching flies. We were under his spell, and despite the fact that we should have just run away, got as far away as we possibly could, we just kept listening.

'But the more people came into Newton Mills – the more people that were poisoned by the town – the more it became like an epidemic. First at the mills, then in the schools where they taught you lack of ambition, and then when they let you drink and take drugs. Without ever caring what it did to you... I was younger than most when I began my purpling... At first I felt it as a... I don't know... a desire to inflict pain on others. And then I started to turn that hatred in on myself. The purpling is a desire to bruise and cripple what is innermost about yourself until there is nothing left.'

'How did you get away?' I breathed. My good leg was drumming up and down, wanting away from the place, but somehow, I stayed rooted to the spot. And helpless.

'I didn't get away, son,' said Burt, slowly. 'I just left for a bit and came back. And the purpling had already taken Sheila – that's my wife – in my place. I tried to take it back from her, but it took us both in the end.'

'But you're still alive,' I said.

'Am I?' asked Burt, looking me straight in the heart. 'Am I really?'

'You sold us bastard cigarettes when we were twelve,' said Dick, holding one finger up as though he were a case lawyer proving an incontrovertible point.

'Lads,' he said calmly. 'Do you not realise? You were already taken! I could see it in you that you were gone. Lost. The purpling had started in you boys even earlier than it had with me... And the purpling had a very specific job that it needed you to do, didn't it?'

We both drained our whiskies at the same time, Dick and I, unsure of the exact nature of the information that was being imparted to us, but both recognising, in our own fucked-up little ways that it was bad. Oh it was bad, and there was no escaping it.

'You've had a shock, lads,' said Burt. 'I'd better get us another bottle of the good stuff so we can talk some more about this. There's other things you need to know before you face what it is you need to face.'

He wrenched himself up from his armchair. I wanted to call him back; the whisky bottle on the table still had enough in it for at least three more shots. But the old man was determined, and we had to let him have his time. I turned round to speak to Dick, and all I saw written on his face was raw fear.

'It'll be okay,' I lied. 'It'll all get sorted.'

Dick wouldn't reply. Couldn't reply.

We sat in silence and listened to Burt rummaging around in the cupboards again. Heard him cursing and panting and moaning. Suddenly, the old man called through to us. 'I remember what it was I was supposed to give you now,' he shouted.

And then he gave this little half-laugh, half whoop of joy, as though he'd discovered buried treasure. And in a way, he had; his own memories. We listened some more as he rattled around behind the fridge, this time with far more speed and purpose. And then we heard a terrible, massive thud. And then we heard nothing.

Dick and I both lurched into the kitchenette as quickly as we could. But our uncoordinated three-leg race had only one winner, and it wasn't us. When we finally reached the sad little ante-room, we found Burt's body twisted on the floor. A look of complete and utter terror was burned into his face. His eyes were bulging out of their sockets and there was a strong smell of shit. Worse; worse than any of this was the sight of his right hand which was battered and bruised, but still clutching the spear that had been sticking out of my chest in the C. U. M building. The spear that Tommy Peaker had pulled out.

So that was what Burt was going to give me; the spear. The warning.

'Oh my God,' breathed Dick. 'He's dead.'

'We need to call the police,' I whispered, trying to bend down, frantically trying to find a pulse. Guilt was already quickening on me.

'We need to get out of here,' said Dick, coldly. 'Don't you see what this will look like? The two of us – me one of Burt's renowned smackheads – in his front room; him dead in the kitchen and a smashed window out front. Who are the filth going to believe? *What* are the filth going to believe?'

I crouched over the broken body of Burt. The man whose surname we'd never bothered to ask. The man who'd been trying to reach out to us. The man whose coffin nails helped the rot to set in. And I shed a single tear for him. I heard Dick moving away from me, back to the cupboards, where he started fumbling around, just as Burt had, only minutes before. I shot him a murderous look.

'What?' he pleaded. 'We're going to need money, aren't we? Where we're going?'

'Where are we going?' I asked.

Dick ignored me. Continued pulling out rusted tin cans and moth-eaten cereal packets. Finally closed his hands around the prize; an old money jar which contained a few old pound coins. He smashed the jar on the kitchen surface with a practiced ease and deposited the coins into the pocket of his tracksuit. And I swear in that one moment, Dick positively *glowed* purple. Like an aura or a fucked-up halo all around him.

Once a junkie, always a junkie, was all I could think.

We stepped along Dye Lane, keeping away from the glare of the streetlights. It seemed a pointless thing to do; Tommy could find us whenever he wanted, light or no light. But somehow it gave us comfort. Somehow, being on the move gave us comfort too. And we found a companiable stride in the half moon's light; me struggling along on crutches and Dick staggering through drink and drugs.

We passed the old graveyard where we'd go to smoke the single cigarettes from Burt's and I gave the place a two-fingered salute, just for good measure. In the moonlight, my fingers seemed to glow purple, just as Dick was back in the kitchenette. Quickly I pulled them down.

'What do we do now?' asked Dick.

'I thought you had a plan... You said we'd need money where we were going?'

'We'll always need money,' said Dick.

'We should find Twinnie' I said. 'Tell him what we know. Find out what he knows...'

'Twinnie's gone bad... And anyway, how'd you reckon we find him? He's off the radar...

'Do you not have a mobile number for him or anything?' I asked.

Dick started frantically tapping the side of his head. 'Don't have no mobile for anyone, mate. They're just tracking devices so they know what we're doing all the time. No. I don't have no numbers for anyone. I just use my instincts.'

I tried not to sigh with impatience. Stepping back into Newton Mills really was like stepping back in time. The town boundary sign should have read:

Welcome to Newton Mills, twinned with Level Six, Hell. Please leave all accoutrements from the twentieth century in the basket provided. You will find no need – or reception – for mobile phones, satellite navigation systems, Channel Five on the TV and anything else you might pull out of your candy ass. You are welcome to hang on to your weapons, however.

'Well what are your instincts telling you now?' I asked.

'That we're in deep, deep shit,' said Dick, stopping abruptly on the pavement. 'I saw shadows in there, moving. Before we found him. Didn't want to say anything 'cos I thought you'd think I was mad... and I never smashed that window... Bully? What if it really is Tommy Peaker, like you said? Out to kill us all...'

'Then we make ourselves ready for him,' I said, pulling Dick along with me, despite the searing pain from my leg.

Chapter Eleven

" The levee was dry "

How do you find someone that doesn't want to be found? In Newton Mills, the general plan would be to check some of the ropier pubs; the Choke actually being one of the better ones. For there are places in Newton Mills in which any sane person should fear to tread. Places where, in the golden days, and perhaps even now, bare-knuckle boxing is live and immediately *in your face*; far more diverting than the bore-draw in the football, being beamed by satellite - or more likely from some crackly Norwegian channel - onto the massive screen in the corner.

Or you could try some of the drug dens. Rented flats above the shops in the high street whose naked light-bulbs burn brightly through the night; places where everyone's welcome, providing there's a few crisp notes – no questions asked – in your back burner.

If the person that you were searching for was young, you could check some of the old, crumbling mill buildings down in the gorge, where me and Dick and Lion and sometimes good old Tommy – rock on Tommy – would skive school and smoke someone's mum's fags, pilfered that day from their handbag on the kitchen table. If the person was old, you could, of course, try the old warehouses, up by the toffeeworks; places where you'd share your breakfast with a veritable army of rodents and otherwise empurpled townspeople.

Where you'd never look is outside the town boundaries. Newton Mills has a pull about it. It draws you back in; wraps its icy claws around your heart and won't let go, no matter how much you kick and scream. Richard Featherstone told me that, and more on our lonely tramp along the early morning streets. He told me of how difficult he'd found it to make a life for himself and his children and for Laura. He told me about how he'd always *meant* to give up on the smack, but there was always a face in the pub that grinned and winked at you until you followed it, like a rat behind the pied-piper and found yourself in some squalid dive, squandering your kid's inheritance on a few hours of escape from the mundanity of life in a small town.

'It's hopeless; we could try every place in this damned town and we still might miss him. There's too many places to hide. Too many old buildings and *off the radar* places... Hell, the whole town's set up to be *off the radar,*' said Dick.

I simply nodded in assent. I already knew what needed to be done. I knew that the one man that might be able to tell me what I needed to know was my poor old dad. He would know, more than anyone else, where Twinnie would be. And although I'd not spoken to him for years – I'd cut all ties with everyone as soon as I left – I knew he'd hold no grudges. He, as much as anyone, knew what the town could drive a person to do.

I knew dad would still be living in the old house up on Hangman's Row. I knew that inside, he'd still keep the memories of my mum, my brother and me burning. But it was only when we crossed Meat Street that Dick seemed to divine where we were headed.

'Th- that's the first place anyone would look for us – for you,' he stammered, suddenly scared again. 'As soon as I hear the sirens, I'm outta there, Bully. No matter how much you wanna see your old dad.'

I grimaced.

'There won't be any sirens, Dick. Nobody will know or care that the old bastard is dead on his floor. There won't be any sirens.'

'But Tommy... Tommy Peaker doesn't come with any sirens on, does he?'

'No. No he doesn't, but he can find us anywhere. It doesn't matter where we are. When he wants to find us, he'll find us.'

'Like he has a tracking device?' asked Dick.

'Yes; a bit like that,' I confirmed, feeling like I was speaking to a child. And in a very real way, Dick was very much a child. He yearned for the company of others, despite his problem. He yearned for approval and for a nice pat on the head. He yearned for an encouraging wink and that sheen of unreality which had, up to this point, governed his hopscotch path of a life. Sometimes, he was just like Private Selly.

We cut through the allotments to gain some time. Most of them were weeded over, but I noted that my old dad's one was still looking relatively healthy. There was a broken window in his shed though, and graffiti on the far wall. Part of me longed to scrub it off for him; to make just that one part of dad's life easier to take. The allotment was his only escape, I knew that, but even there, the Newton Mills curse had started to encroach.

After the allotments, there was a steep slope which took us down to the old railway tracks. Not trusting myself on crutches, I slid down on my arse. Not a very dignified – or army-like – way of doing things, but it was the only way. Even the railway tracks were overgrown; thick grass crept up and onto the wooden slats. A rail crash here was surely only a few weeks away. That's if they even bothered to send trains out Newton Mills way any more. I didn't bother to ask Dick about that; I couldn't ever imagine a time where I'd have to do something as normal as catch a train again. Couldn't imagine stowing my crutch away in the luggage rack and then trying to seek out some kindly young scout that would help me get it down and escort me off the carriage. Couldn't imagine *what* I'd need to catch a train for; I was already on the runaway train to hell, and that stopped for no man or beast.

And then we were crawling up the opposite slope. Feeling the cut of broken bottles tearing at our knees; feeling the mud slipping through our fingers; feeling the fallen leaves slippy underneath us; everything trying to drag us back down from whence we came. I looked over at Dick, and his face was now blacked-up like a commando's. My own must have looked very similar. I wondered what the hell my dad was going to think when we turned up at the front door like that.

Oh, who am I kidding? The states I've turned up at that front door in my time; covered in cuts and bruises; drugged-up to the nines; soaked in chip fat after the time we stole a barrel from out the back of the pub, only to find it wasn't beer inside... Dad wouldn't be shocked at all. Turning up as we would do would be run of the mill in Newton Mills. It would be hardly worth a passing comment.

We gained Hangman's Row finally. I once asked dad about the name, and of course he knew. Turned out that the little row of terraced houses wasn't named after some town hangman that used to live there at all – something that really disappointed my blood-hungry teenage self – but because the row were built on an overhang above the gorge. He thought that the row used to be called 'Hanging Row', but it was changed because the townsfolk of Newton Mills *craved* bloodthirsty stories, just like I did.

The road was fully cobbled, as it had been for about two hundred years. There weren't many cars parked up, probably due to the fact that it was so difficult to get up the slope and onto the road proper. And the whole place looked like some model village representation of where I used to live. Everything seemed about a third smaller than it had once been. Even the old tree in the garden of the corner house – one that I'd been forbidden to climb, but had done so anyway – seemed less formidable than it once was.

I could already see our old house, tucked away unobtrusively between the stone-clad frontage of Mrs. Watkins' house and the new conservatory at the front of the Higginbotham family home. Memories came flooding back. Dad teaching me to ride my bike on this street; how it made my teeth chatter as I rode over every cobble; how funny it sounded when I shouted *wheeeeeeee* over all those bumps and heard my voice bouncing around like the wheels were. I remembered falling off that bike too, and smashing up my arm. Having to be taken to hospital. Staying in for three days and dad never going home once, so far as I knew. I also recalled breaking into another neighbour's house – although I couldn't for the life of me remember their name – and stealing four cans of Special Brew from their fridge and pissing on their carpet. Had that really been me?

There was one thing on the street that surprised me. There was a plaque on the wall of a house about four doors down from ours. I'd never in my life seen it before. I stopped to read it:

The Drunkard's Reform: Here lived Thomas Mellor, who washed his hands of that purple demon drink in the year of our lord

1876. He joined the family of the Church and lived for the rest of his life as a good Christian and a valued member of the community.

'Have you ever seen that before?' I asked Dick.

'What: the plaque? We used to laugh about it. Said you an' your dad should've lived there. You never could take your booze, Bully.'

Dick moved away, but I stayed and read the plaque again. My eyes kept returning to that one word: 'purple.' And I couldn't help but notice, out of the corner of my eye, that Dick, his silhouette ringed by the rising sun, glowed purple once more.

Madness, I thought, shaking my head. *This whole town is riddled with madness.*

Our front door was so dark blue that it was almost purple. Another sign, I thought. But as my hand clenched around the old rusted knocker – the one with the angel's face on it – I could barely bring myself to use it. Seeing my hesitation, and already jumpy from the drug withdrawal, Dick reached past me and rattled the letter box a little.

It took a while, but eventually, through the frosted glass of the small window, we saw a small, stooped figure shuffling towards the door. I reeled back in shock. But the figure, who I so wanted *not* to be dad, didn't click open the latch. Instead, he shouted through the letter box.

'I told you last time; no doorstep preachers. I'm not interested in going to damn church. And I'm certainly not interested if you're trying to sell me something this early in the bloody morning. So, kindly, go away.'

His voice was strong; stronger than his body looked. Even through the frosted glass it had been a shock. I wanted to run away, but already Dick was readying himself to perform his part of this unique letter-box communication ritual.

'Mr. Bull, it's me, Dick... uh... Richard Featherstone... Oh and I've got your...'

Before Dick could finish his sentence, dad had wrenched the door open. And had wrenched me into him, clasping me into his once great chest with all the strength he could muster.

It took all the strength I could muster to ask: 'What *happened* to you, dad?'

I pushed myself away from him and took in the whole of him; the worn slippers with holes at each big-toe; the faded blue pyjama bottoms; the creased shirt. And he was unshaven. I'd never seen him unshaven before and somehow it made him look ill. His eyes were ringed with dark lines – the eyeliner of worry, I thought – and his hair was receding badly.

But then he smiled: 'I could ask you the same thing myself. Look at the state of you. Covered in crap the pair of you. Come in; get washed up. I'll stick the kettle on.'

It was only as he ushered us over the threshold that he held me back a moment, looked into my eyes and I saw pleading.

'I got the call from your CO. He told me you'd been honourably discharged. That's the truth, isn't it, son?'

I nodded my head down towards my foot. Or what was left of my foot. I watched as he lowered his head; at once wanting to see, but not wanting to see. Then, he simply shook his head and wandered back off down the hall, following Dick into the kitchen. I swear that I heard him mutter something like: 'fucking idiot. I told him not to join the army.'

I followed them; there was no other choice. And I tried not to make the comparison between dad's single man lifestyle and that of old Burt. But it was hard not to, given the smell of the place. Although dad had tried to cover the lingering smell of defeat with that of Pledge air-freshener, there was no disguising the loneliness of the place now that mum, my bro and me had abandoned ship. Deserted. Gone AWOL. Everything looked spick and span but tired and worn, too. As though it was all about surfaces, and underneath, the decay was just fighting to get out.

The kitchen was so much like Burt's that I wanted to cry. The same fake-wood cupboards and 1970s white goods, the same lino even. It was as though whoever sold kitchens sold in a job lot to Newton Mills, flat-packed, flat-lined and flat-fucked. There were bits of paint peeling off in the corners, by the ceiling, where once dad would have borrowed a ladder to reach, but now couldn't really be bothered. One cup and one plate and a single knife and fork lay draining by the sink. I felt purple with rage.

'What do you both want to drink?' asked dad, clicking on the kettle. It looked scaly, like it was a half-alive reptile or something. 'Can't offer you any alcohol, but I can do a nice pot of tea.'

'Tea's great,' said Dick.

'Can I have a coffee, dad?' I asked.

Dad raised his eyes to the ceiling and creaked open a cupboard door. Started rooting around for the offending jar.

'I didn't know you'd be coming back,' he said, to the cupboard. 'Otherwise I'd have been down the shops. Got some stuff in special.'

'We're not staying,' said Dick.

'No? Well what you doing then?' dad asked the cupboard, perhaps hoping that it would come up with some better answers than his wayward son.

'Just wanted to see you, that's all,' I said, pulling at a frayed edge of the table cloth. Hearing it start to rip.

'But what are you going to do with yourself?'

'We're looking for Twinnie, Mr. Bull,' interrupted Dick. 'Paul Morton. Gaz here thought you might know where he was.'

Dad spun round, coffee jar in hand. Evidently, he was having trouble unscrewing the top.

'And why on earth would you think I knew where he was?'

'Just a feeling I had, that's all,' I muttered. I'd been wrong to come back, I knew that now. Wrong to think that all the unspoken wrongs between the two of us could just be forgotten about over a nice pot of tea. And yet dad still couldn't find it in himself to yell and bawl at me, despite the fact that he'd been the one left to tell my Jane that I'd *done one* and fucked off into the army.

Dad shook his head, took the kettle off its base even though it hadn't boiled yet. Started to pour out drinks into three faded old mugs. One of them, I thought, had our own school crest on it. It was a branch – supposedly an olive branch, I thought – but it always struck me as though it was the bony hand of someone giving the rest of us a two-fingered salute.

'Cheers,' said Dick, moving over to the sink where he ran a little cold in to the mug in order that he could drink it straight away. Then, as an afterthought, he turned on the hot tap and stuck his head under it. Dirty water splashed everywhere. I could tell dad longed to pull him away from the sink, kick him up the arse and send him away from the house with a flea in his ear. Instead he just stood there, leaning against the fridge, cradling his brew like it was a life-support system. Like Burt's cigs.

The brew didn't need a splash of cold. It was already drinkable anyway. I drank in the sour coffee and felt the energy already beginning to course through my veins.

'What did the army tell you about the accident? My leg?' I asked.

Dad sighed: 'Just that everyone else died in there, but you got out. You're lucky, Gary. You know that don't you? Don't go ruining the rest of your life just because you were injured. You're lucky. Make something of...'

'I can't listen to stuff like that, dad. Not now. Not now. Just don't worry about me, that's all,' I groaned. Already, he was starting to remind me of Montaffian... Or had Montaffian reminded me of dad? Was that why I'd taken to the old doc so easily?

Dad looked away. Looked out of the window over the gorge.

'Your mate Lion died. Did they tell you that?'

'Yeah,' I admitted.

'Well don't go the same way as him,' he said, softly. 'And I *do* worry about you, Gary. That's my job.'

I took a long gulp of my tea; watched as the half-clean Dick poured most of his down the sink. These sort of conversations took me right back to the old days. The awkwardness of the meetings between my friends and my dad. The fact that they forced us to go out, looking for trouble. Anything but face the questions and the demands on our time that he always seemed to make. Always there was some scheme he tried to interest us in. Like building a goddamn pigeon coop in the back garden. That was one of his worst ones. He never had the slightest interest in pigeons.

'Right: we're off now, Gaz,' announced Dick from over by the sink. He tried to wink at me, and dad caught the implied meaning.

'Better had, I suppose,' I said, making a great effort to sound as though leaving would be a great effort.

'So soon?' asked dad, and I was sure that for a second, I heard something in his voice crack. 'You not going to even attempt to clean yourself up, Gary?'

'We ain't going birding, Mr. Bull,' said Dick. 'Not at this fucking time in the morning.'

He roared with laughter at his own joke. Dad and I stared at each other across the frayed-edge table top and I found myself shaking my head. What I was saying no to, I had absolutely no idea, but eventually dad nodded. Dick made as though to help me to my feet, but dad ushered him away. Grasped me under the arms just like Tommy Peaker had, and then Burt after him. All three of them had a strength which far outweighed mine. Perhaps it was because they had righteousness behind them, or some such crap. I didn't care. All I knew was that I had to be out of the house, and if that meant dad carrying me out the door, then so be it.

Dick was already outside kicking his heels on the cobbles when dad let me loose from his iron grasp.

'Paul Morton's trouble. More trouble than that idiot that you're with already. Don't get messed up in what he's messed up in,' he said.

'I already am,' I sighed.

Dad clapped a hand on my shoulder.

'There's always ways out. Whatever the mess may be.'

I shook my head. *Not this time.*

'He's camped out up at Summit Farm,' said dad, quietly. 'Been living off rabbits and suchlike but he caught one of old Maurice Dailly's sheep the other day... There's going to be a mob going up there later on this week. Probably tomorrow. Whatever you do; don't be there tomorrow. They're taking pitchforks and things. You know, sometimes this place reminds me of some medieval village. It's the same mentality.'

I grinned. For once, my father and I agreed on something.

Chapter Twelve

"Jack flash sat on a candlestick"

Summit Farm was situated, or so an estate agent would tell you, on the brow of yet another hill overlooking the town of Newton Hills. 'Stunning views,' they'd tell you. 'Marvellous panorama of the hills which form the gateway to the Peak District. You simply have to see this property to believe it. Ancient, rustic farmhouse; acres of land where dogs and horses can roam free; kitchen comes complete with an Aga, dontchaknow.'

In fact, it was yet another building that had been left to decay. Its greatness was now a thing of the past. Now, all that remained of the house was an empty shell. The land was overgrown and riddled with rabbits and moles and ragwort. The view, such as it was now, was of the billowing smoke from the toffeeworks, and if you could see through that, you'd see the teeming council houses and graveyards that made up the rest of the town.

Story was, an old man – *another* old man – had gone completely mad stuck on his own up there. Turns out, he'd killed his wife and daughter and buried them in a woodpile in the barn. After a few weeks, he dug them out and started dressing them up like they were members of the family again. Police found them spread out on the lawn on a rug, taking tea and cakes on a sunny afternoon. But the old feller didn't go down without a fight. Took two coppers down with him and badly wounded another before they dragged him kicking and screaming into the barn, where they fired round after round of shots into his bearded face.

Of course, most of the story was all hearsay, but, like the rumours about the Black Panther, they'd seemed to stick. The town's will was that things like that could still happen, even in the twentieth century. Wild West lawlessness was what the townsfolk voted for, and nobody would touch the place with a barge-pole for years after.

Of course, Dick told me that there were rumours and stories that started to mix the Black Panther and Mad Farmer myths into one unholy crap-fest. According to him, people had started saying that the Black Panther had been bred – rather like the Hound of the Baskervilles – in that very barn by our mad as a coot farmer and that the reason he offed his wife and daughter in the first place was so as to give the poor old cat a taste for human meat.

I wondered what they'd all say about us, once this whole thing with Tommy Peaker came to a head one way or another. Maybe they'd say we got what we deserved. Maybe they'd say that we got what was coming to us. But I just knew that in some of the drug dens and the alehouses, on the factory production lines and the too-long shop queues, there'd be whisperings.

Boys will be boys, they'd say.

They were only rough-housing, another would agree.

And the whole damn thing would slip into the annals of history and myth. Problem was, if I tried to excuse our actions like that, all it would bring was more guilt. Because no matter how I tried to look at things, we'd still done what we'd done and this lunatic from beyond the grave was still looking to put us where we'd once put him.

We walked up past Grange Heights on the way to Summit Farm. Up there, I got the funny feeling that Dick was sticking rather close to me than usual. Perhaps he still believed in the Black Panther, despite all the things we knew. So I trailed cigarettes in front of him for him to follow; leading him like he was a donkey and I held the carrot. And he quivered and quaked his way onto the top of the hill as though he was going to collapse at any moment.

Once we were at the top, the wind picked up, buffeting into our clothes like it didn't want us to get where we were going. Dick pulled up the hood of his tracksuit top and drew the cords tight, so all anyone could see of his face was his nose, which was becoming like a dripping tap. I just pulled my army jacket tight around me and narrowed my eyes. I had to keep seeing things as a mission. Had to keep my eyes on the target, otherwise we were lost.

'This is a nightmare, I'm sure it is,' muttered Dick. 'At some point I'm going to wake up, passed out on someone's bloody kitchen floor with my works by my side having had one helluva ride. You're probably not even here, Bully, are you?'

'Nope,' I said. 'Not here at all. I'm sunning myself on a lovely beach in Spain, with a nice cold cerveza in hand and a nice old view of the birds on the beach.'

'Are they topless, Gaz?'

'They certainly are, mate. And I'm wearing these dock-off aviator shades so they can't tell I'm staring straight at them.'

'How's the beer going down?'

'A beauty, mate. A bit cold, like, but the bubbles are dead refreshing. Hold on; some bird's coming up to see if I want her to light my ciggie.'

I looked over at Dick. He was watching me with rapt attention, so wanting to believe that everything I was saying was true; that we weren't up here on some godforsaken hill being chased by the Frankenstein's monster we'd created in our own stupid carelessness; that we weren't walking towards our doom.

I sparked up another cigarette. I was running low now, but couldn't let Dick know. That was the kind of news that was liable to push him over the edge. He reminded me more and more of that dog-gone mummy's boy Selly. And Selly had always been a little *distracted* out there, like Dick was now, but one day when the toilet paper ran out, he just exploded. Started firing off round after round into the toilet bowl. Blowing it to smithereens. Of course, out there, boys being boys, we all had a right laugh about his reaction. But I think deep down, we all shared that fear of his; we were so close to the dividing line that all it took was one push and we'd fall headlong into that other world where Tommy Peaker can exist and spears from some lonely desert rebel hideaway can suddenly appear in a flat in fucking Newton Mills.

As soon as we reached the dry stone wall which marked the far boundary of Summit Farm lands, we saw the signs of Twinnie's presence. It was clear now why it had been so obvious to the neighbouring farmer that something was amiss. Because the whole top field was littered with dead livestock. Some had had their throats ripped out; others burned where they were killed; still more were speared to the ground with what looked like makeshift arrows. It looked like a scene out of *American Werewolf in London* or else some awful scene of ritual sacrifice.

'Fuck,' whistled Dick. 'He's not exactly hiding himself away up here is he?'

'That's if it's him killing all these animals, and not Tommy,' I said.

Dick shot me a baleful glance. A wounded glance. He didn't want me to mention Tommy's name any more. And in a way, I couldn't blame him. But at some point soon, he'd have to face the reality of the situation. There were no more drugs…

I vaulted over a low part of the wall, where it looked like something heavy had crossed and dislodged a number of the stones. Even I didn't want to think what that heavy thing might be. Dick followed, somewhat less successfully than me, despite my half-foot, and ended up collapsed on his arse on the Summit Farm side of the wall, just missing a cow pat. For a moment, I felt like cracking up laughing, but decided against it.

Perhaps the main reason I decided against laughing was because I felt the whistle of a bullet rocketing past my ear. So close, I thought, that it may have even clipped me. Just afterwards I heard the echo of the gunfire ricocheting back off the hills. I threw myself down on top of Dick and tried to cover him as best I could.

'What was that?' he whimpered.

'Bullet,' I said, starting to crawl down the slope, pulling him after me. I was aiming for the cover of a small mound of earth a few feet away.

Another gunshot. Louder than the ones out there in the desert. This one was using some older weapon. Something like a good old-fashioned blunderbuss. Absently, I wondered what the kick-back on those things was like; liable to take a feller's shoulder right out, I suspected. Unless they knew what they were doing.

Thankfully, this shooter didn't really know what he was doing. The second shot cleared the dry stone wall. And the third barely even made the top of the small mound. But sooner or later, everyone finds their range. Even halfwits like Twinnie, if that was really him shooting.

'Don't come any fucking closer,' someone shouted. 'I'm fucking armed and fucking dangerous.'

It *was* Twinnie. I'd have recognised the voice anywhere. The fact that his speech was peppered with swearwords was a dead-giveaway even if the strong Newton Mills accent was not.

'The only person you're a danger to is yourself!' I yelled back.

And I swear Twinnie let that fourth shot go even though he must have recognised *my* voice.

'Dickhead!' I shouted. 'Shot shooting.'

I hadn't even stopped to think where the fourth shot might have landed. Until I heard the groan from Dick underneath me. Somehow, he'd allowed his leg to slip into Twinnie's wayward sights, and somehow Twinnie had made a direct hit. Blood was now shooting from the fleshy part of Dick's thigh. Quickly, I tore off my fatigue jacket and wrapped it around the leg. A makeshift tourniquet to try and stop the bleeding.

'I'm hit,' cried Dick. 'I'm dying man, I'm dying.'

And then someone who vaguely resembled the Twinnie that I once knew was standing on top of the small mound, looking down at us, shotgun still cocked.

'You're not fucking dying you twat,' he growled.

It was only when we found Twinnie – or when Twinnie's shots found us - that I truly understood what Burt had meant by the purpling. Because even the man's *skin* was purple. He looked like he'd applied too much hair dye and it had started to run off his hair and onto his face, staining it in the process. And apparently, that first time we saw him, he'd even been wearing a thin layer of flour over his face so as to disguise the colour somewhat.

He had long, lank hair now and a thick beard; all purple-tinged. And his eyes burned fiery bright with knowledge and pain. The only aspect of him that was recognisably Paul Morton were those sharp features; the long, thin nose; the tiny mouth which we once joked – but never after that first time – looked like a cat's arse; the jagged edges of his cheek bones.

Without any compassion whatsoever, he dragged Dick off the top field as though he were one of the animals that he'd shot; I crawled behind this terrible twosome, too much in shock to even attempt to walk. When I got to the front door, Twinnie pulled me to my feet by the collar of my t-shirt and sneered into my face.

'You look after the fucker,' he said. 'He'll only end up dragging me down.'

I tried to stare him down. Tried to see if there was anything human left inside him, but couldn't see even the remotest of signs.

'Dragging you down?' I tried. 'Why? What are you doing here? Who are you hiding from?'

'I think you know that as well as I do,' he said and crashed through the door into his hideaway. Inside the farmhouse at Summit Farm, he'd set up a cranky looking camp bed and a small gas-powered cooking stove. He'd surrounded this by a series of traps that he must have found in the barn. I couldn't think where else he would have picked them up from. On the whitewashed walls, either he or the demented farmer from myth had scrawled the words:

You'll never take me alive.

'Well; what you looking at?' he shouted at me. 'Drag him in here and either cut his leg off or kill the fucker.'

I still couldn't move. A million questions raced through my mind. At what age do you become fully responsible for your actions? When does the irrepressible desire to be boys being boys suddenly change, and you become negligible for your actions? When does *blame* start to be bandied about?

Twinnie picked up a spade from underneath his camp bed and walked towards me, swishing it this way and that. Eyes ablaze. I still couldn't move. Perhaps this was how it should end.

After all; how do you live with yourself for the rest of your three score years (or whatever it is) knowing that you've done something so terrible that anyone who knew would shun you and treat you like the leper you are? Sure, you can change your identity. You can become *Lance Corporal* Gary Bull, but deep down, you'll know who you are right down to the rotten core of yourself. That black hole which is there in place of your heart, just like Twinnie's. Your identity is *killer*. Your stock in trade is killing. Your name hardly matters any more.

My eyes appealed to him: Do you walk down the streets of your home town knowing that everyone that passes can somehow look right through you and see the emptiness within? Are you like me; broken and maimed, so the only thing you can do right is keep on punishing yourself and punishing yourself until there's nothing left on that photo on your ID badge that remotely reminds you of yourself as you once were?

The spade connected with the side of my face. The same side that I'd thought had been skimmed by the bullet. And all I could think was: Once there was family and a fiancé and living a lie, but that could only last so long. The purpling had begun. The bruising of yourself until you were black and blue and bloodied and not a man at all, but an amalgam of half-finished apologies and guilt that grows until it can remain buried no more and erupts.

Blows rained down on me. I saw my own blood waterfalling into the air. And I saw the madness in Twinnie's eyes. I saw how he was pinning the blame on me for how his life had panned out, just as I was pinning the blame on him.

And then, just as suddenly as it had started, Twinnie's attack stopped.

'I'm sorry, Bully,' he said, half-smiling. Wiping away my blood from the side of his face with the sleeve of his big black Barbour coat. 'I had to be sure that it was you, mate. And now I am. Nice to see you, me old mucker.'

I flinched away from him as he knelt over me, but he didn't touch me. Just stared into me with those fiery, beady eyes.

'You'll be reet,' he said, in a voice devoid of any emotion. 'Just rest your head a minute and then go out and see to Dick, will you? He's making a racket that'd wake the fucking dead.'

With that he sloped back off to his camp bed and flopped down, picking a porn magazine up from the floor. He didn't bother looking back over at me. Evidently there were some engaging articles in *Twat Weekly* these days. The only issues I'd seen out there in the desert had been at least two years old and well 'thumbed.' I lay on the cold stone of the farmhouse kitchen, gradually becoming aware that Dick was indeed screaming the place down. Occasionally, I tried to get up, but the pain in my head, and in my foot was unbearable. Some hidden, Twinnie-like part of me kept telling me that we should just leave Dick outside, to attract the thing that was once Tommy Peaker or perhaps the slavering mob of men from Newton Mills. But I argued myself down. At some point in this whole damn mess, surely my brain would kick into gear and some sort of feasible plan would present itself. And besides, if there was anyone I wanted left for dead, it was Twinnie.

Dick was in a bad way when I finally got out into the courtyard to see him. He'd lost a lot of blood despite my tourniquet and was sweating profusely, although some of that may have been down to his lack of drugs. As soon as he realised that it was me crouched by his side and not Twinnie, he grasped my hand.

'I told you; he's off his head, Twinnie is,' he gasped. 'We should never have come up here.'

In the distance, the wind began to howl. Or at least I hoped it was the wind. It reached the farmhouse, trickled along the corrugated iron of the barn and whipped into the plastic sheeting which covered some farm truck or other. It was as though Tommy was reminding us that he was still watching; still laughing.

'Twinnie saw Tommy as well. He must have, judging by what's written on that wall… That means we all have, Dick,' I said, trying to cover up my wounded friend as best I could. 'This thing's going to come to a head sooner rather than later, I reckon. He has us where he wants us, and now it's up to us to decide how we play this. But don't worry, I'll try and sort your leg out for now at least.'

'We'll be legless together, just like the old days,' said Dick, but there was absolutely no trace of mirth in his eyes. I gave him a wink, and that probably just looked as though I was trying to blink back the tears.

I climbed to my one and a half feet again. Felt myself almost buckle and fall, but righted myself by holding on to a drainpipe. From inside the farmhouse, I caught the faint smell of cooking. Whatever Twinnie was cooking did not smell good. I tried to ignore the sick feeling that it inspired in my gut and looked around for some way of getting Dick under cover. It was going to rain soon – in fact, a full on storm seemed likely judging by the thick black clouds overhead – and I didn't think I had the strength for any more dragging. Neither, for that matter, did Dick.

I made up a makeshift stretcher for him out of a decorative wheelbarrow in the garden and somehow managed to wheel him across the courtyard and into the barn. Without any natural light in there, it was difficult to see what was lurking in the corners, but I consoled myself with the fact that at least it wouldn't be Twinnie.

I slipped back out of the barn and into the courtyard. Already spatters of rain were pebbledashing the concrete. Already, the clouds overhead were starting to breach and the first signs of the storm were beginning. I lurched over, back to the farmhouse, guiding myself along the walls. Propping myself up. When I reached the door, I took a deep breath and entered the stench.

'You chopped his leg off?' barked Twinnie, from his camp bed. 'Otherwise that was fucking fast work, soldier boy.'

He gave me a mock salute and nearly spilled whatever crap was in his plastic bowl all over his purple legs. I simply smiled back at him.

'Well?' he asked.

'I've managed to get him in the barn. Thought I'd come back in here. I'm looking for a knife to cut his tracksuit bottoms off him. So I can get a proper look at the wound *you* gave him.'

'Or is the knife to slit his moaning, drug-addicted throat? Huh?'

'Do you have a knife?' I asked, rapidly growing tired of this game.

'I'm using it,' said Twinnie, spearing a huge piece of what looked like barely cooked flesh with a hunting knife and plunging it down his cat's arse of a mouth. I heard the point of the knife scrape against his jagged little teeth as he pulled it back out.

'I like what you've done with the place by the way,' I said, while I was waiting for Twinnie to finish his extravagant chewing of the meat. I pointed at the blood-red graffiti on the wall. Smirking as I did so.

Twinnie barked something back to me that was almost totally incomprehensible. A trickle of blood slipped down his purple chin.

'Knife?' I said, holding out my hand, half expecting Twinnie to twist it into my naked palm. Almost expecting the jarring pain as it cut through sinew and bone. It looked damn sharp that knife. Probably Twinnie had it singing off a butcher's steel hymn sheet every morning these days.

He continued his exaggerated chewing, sounding like some predatory animal. And I knew from watching my nature documentaries that an animal like that doesn't really want to be disturbed while they are eating.

Finally, he stopped; spitting out some gristle onto the floor right by the side of his camp bed. For some reason, all I could think of was how *unhygienic* that was.

'Think you can come back in here ordering me around like you're the fucking alpha male of the pack?' he growled, still accentuating every word with a baton-twirl of the knife. 'Think being in the army gives you some divine right to be the big boss man?'

I shook my head. 'Nah Twinnie, I don't think that at all. I just wanna at least *try* to patch him up...'

'It's every man for himself nowadays,' spat Twinnie. 'You made that very fucking clear when you went off to the army. You can't turn back time, mate. You can't have everything just like it was before you went off on your own like goddamn Rambo.'

'I just wanna...'

The knife whistled past my ear and twanged into the wooden door, sticking into the flesh of it by at least an inch and a half.

'I'm only messing with you, Bully!' laughed Twinnie. 'For Christ's sake, chill the fuck out.'

I didn't laugh. I didn't chill the fuck out. Dick was right; Twinnie was way out west now. He was so far gone that he probably didn't even know where he'd come from in the first place. He was as much monster as Tommy Peaker now. Somehow, I preferred him as snarling animal rather than his other schizophrenic incarnation; this laughing, faux-friendly madman that would stick you in the back as soon as look at you.

I clenched my fist around the hunting knife and twisted and turned it until it finally came out of the wooden door. Had half a mind to launch it straight back at Twinnie, but when I turned round to face him again, he had the shotgun cocked on his lap. It was pointed directly at me.

'Just making sure you don't wanna use that knife for something else,' he sneered.

'I'm not like you, Twinnie,' I said. And then I repeated the same phrase in my head for about the next half hour. What the hell had happened round here while I'd been away?

I managed to put together a rudimentary dressing for Dick's leg using some of the stuff in my pack, and also some woefully out of date medicines I found under the smashed-up sink in the outhouse next to the barn. I copied the treatment techniques I remembered from the military hospitals back in that desert place; remembering Nurse Thomas tending to Do-Nowt's stump. I remembered Dr. Montaffian, and started whistling 'Purple Rain' as I worked. Part of me wondered whether even that old doctor's choice of song had been a sign that I hadn't heeded. Had he been trying to tell me something of this purpling business?

Even after I cleaned and dressed it as best I could, the wound couldn't stay like that for any more than a few hours, tops, I thought. When I cut Dick's tracksuit bottoms away and seen the mangled mess that the scattered shotgun pellets had made, I'd been inextricably reminded of my own foot. When I'd not been able to tell what was skin or flesh and what was boot or sock. Dick's tracksuit bottoms had become so saturated with blood that bits of material clung to the wound and refused to be budged. Dick screamed when I pulled the material away.

He also screamed when I applied the ointment from the outhouse and a bandage from my pack. He screamed whenever shadows moved in the barn and begged me to either stay with him or let him come back into the farmhouse.

'Please,' he said, tugging at the sleeve of my t-shirt like a kid would. His breathing was raggedy. Dangerous breathing; like how he'd described the Black Panther breathing. Or how we'd all imagined the Black Panther breathing at any rate.

'Let me back inside. I'm so c-c-cold…'

'Too dangerous,' I said, trying to sound stern, not-to-be-messed-with. 'I'll keep checking up on you though, Dick. You'll be fine.'

I managed to find a few tatty old blankets in that same outhouse and wrapped Dick's body inside them so tightly that he started to resemble a cocoon. On top of all the blankets, I placed the yellow tarpaulin which I'd wrenched off the broken body of the farm vehicle out in the courtyard. I didn't know which I felt more sorry for; the rusted, abandoned body of the machine, now left open to the elements after all those years of protection, or Dick; so warped by drugs that he hardly knew where he was any more and hence probably didn't even know that one of the main reasons I was wrapping him up so tightly was in order that he didn't try to crawl away in the night, looking for treatment of a different kind to that which I could provide. Treatment which could only be found in the flats above the shops in the main street, with their naked bulbs buzzing with energy that they'd sapped from the drugged-up townsfolk.

And I started thinking about what Twinnie had said about every man for himself. I started to ask myself whether I wouldn't be better off facing Tommy Peaker alone, without these two crazies holding me back. But that wasn't the way Tommy wanted it, was it? He wanted us all together, driving each other mad just like we used to. He wanted us to experience that same head loss which had driven us to kill in the first place. And right then, I knew that he had us exactly where he wanted us. He'd be coming, and soon.

Chapter Thirteen

"No angel born in hell"

Twinnie and I sat around the flickering light from the small blue flame of the camping stove. It wasn't providing much heat, but as the only torch we'd thought to bring was rapidly running out of batteries – refusing to play ball like every other goddamn piece of equipment we had up here apart from the gun, of course – it was at least providing us with some light. And both of us wanted light. We wanted to be able to see what the other one was doing.

I was sat, cross-legged like in school assembly when we were good little boys, or at least not so bad little boys. God, I couldn't remember the last time I'd sat like that. Nor could I really remember being a not-so-bad little boy. Every memory I had seemed soured by the knowledge of what was to come later, like when I remembered that last day we were all at school together. How we'd all scrawled our names across our school shirts. How we'd got the girls to plant big lipstick kisses on the collars. But then we'd got drunk and someone had attempted to burn the school down. Not us, you understand, but we'd been the ringmasters. The ones who'd whipped everyone up into such a frenzy that it all got *waaaaaaay* out of hand, and far too quickly.

Or the time Tommy Peaker got that certificate in assembly for managing to make it in to school every day for two consecutive weeks. The way some of the spods had complained. You know the type: 'I've not had a day off in two *years,* let alone two weeks. Why can't I have a certificate? Oh sir, please present your penis to me so I can suck it. Please, pretty please...' How we'd all rolled about laughing when Tommy collected his certificate and started trying to make a speech,

139

holding the crappy piece of scrap paper aloft like it was the FA Cup or something and not just sweet FA. Tommy pointed out to us who the main complainers were, and in the spirit of the day, we set about them all; robbing lunch money here, burning school bags there, pretending to pierce their fucking smarmy faces with their pristine compasses for maths class. How in the end, as always, we took it one step too far and ended up going for the easiest target of the lot; Tommy himself. Twinnie wiped his arse on the certificate and blu-tacked it to the wall of the lad's bogs using his own shit. Unbelievably it took a whole two weeks for the certificate to be removed by the cleaners. And a whole two weeks for us to see Tommy at school again.

As I thought about the old days, I'd been rubbing at the stump which was formerly known as my foot. When I looked down, I saw that my over-long fingernails were tearing into the plasticy-flesh; trying to scratch the itch that was not really there. Like Hannibal Lecter quizzing that senator in *Silence of the Lambs,* I wondered where it itched on Twinnie. Maybe it itched on his fucking dead twin.

Jesus, I have to lighten the mood, I thought.

And for some reason, I thought that the best way to re-establish some kind of bond between Twinnie and I was by bringing up some other incident from our past.

'Does this remind you of the time we went camping up at Grange Heights?' I asked, trying to massage some life into my stump.

Twinnie flashed me another of his unreadable smiles.

'Yeah mate,' he said. 'It might well remind me of that night, but I can guaran-fuckin'-tee it won't remind you of that night. I bet the only reason is you mention it is after something fucking Dick let slip.'

'What you on about?' I asked, calling his bluff. 'I remember everything about that night... I remember the Black Panther stories... All of it.'

Twinnie started laughing. He laughed for so long that it soon became obvious that he was mainly doing it to prolong my discomfort.

'Bully,' he said, finally, 'you were so drunk that night that there's no chance you'd remember anything. Staggering about all over the place. Never could take your booze, could you?'

His comment may or may not have been intended as a slight on my manhood. I certainly *felt* it that way. In a town like Newton Mills, drinking all day is respected; making a show of yourself is not. Beating your wife behind closed doors is expected; striking her in the pub is a big no-no. She shouldn't be in the pub in the first place, some wag might say.

'Piss off, Twinnie,' I snarled.

He laughed again.

'Pack it in.'

'What's up, Bulls-eye? Don't you like a bit of ribbing? A bit of dissent in the ranks? Can't you take it?'

Can't you take it? It was what Twinnie always asked of his victims. As though the fault was somehow with them. And do you know what? When he asked the question of me, I sort of felt like it *was* my fault that I couldn't take him bullying me as he was attempting to do. I sort of felt like I deserved it.

'It's not that... I just...'

'Just what? Just what? What are you stammering like that for? You sound just like Tommy fucking Peaker.'

Suddenly there was silence in the room. We listened to the wind whip round the farmhouse and the far-off cries of Dick in the barn. I'm sure we both felt that by saying Tommy's name, we were simply drawing him closer. For the first time, I saw a quiver of fear in Twinnie's face.

'When did you first see him?' I asked. 'Second time around, I mean?'

This time it was Twinnie's turn to go on the defensive. He shrugged his shoulders, muttered something typically incomprehensible and picked up his porno mag, feigning nonchalance.

'He came to the hospital... After what happened to my foot. Why haven't you even asked about my foot, Twinster?' I continued, pressing home my advantage.

'Don't fucking care about your foot,' sniffed Twinnie, sounding like Dick, like a child. 'Doesn't bother me what happens to you. Not after you left.'

Were you lonely, Twinnie? Was that what fucked you up? Lonely for your dead twin? Did you kill him too? Did your purpling begin before you could even walk and talk properly?

I longed to be able to ask him those questions, but knew that I had to save them up. Save them for a time when we were gripping on to the edge of the precipice with just our fingernails, and he'd be trying to scramble all over me, just to save himself. Besides, Twinnie was stroking the shaft of the shotgun in a way that suggested that any mention of his twin brother, and I'd be chucked in the woodpile, just like that mad old farmer's family.

Suddenly, he spoke again: 'I presumed *he* did it to you. I thought that I didn't need to ask. Not after Lion. Not after Lion.'

'Not *him* actually,' I admitted. 'Rats did it.'

'Rats?' barked Twinnie, suddenly sitting upright on the camp-bed. 'What you on about?'

'Rats tried to eat me alive.'

'Fuuuuucccccckk,' groaned Twinnie. Then: 'Still; look on the bright side, you're still walking. Sort of…'

Twinnie's words reminded me so much of my dad's that I was taken aback. Still, the conversation was the first sign that Twinnie wasn't completely turned to the dark side. There was still something of the old him left, wasn't there? Or was that the problem all along? Should he have been trying to *get rid* of the old him?

Later, after a silence which could hardly be described as companiable – I'd had to listen to some suspicious sounds from Twinnie underneath his sleeping bag – I started to feel the pangs of hunger eating away at my stomach like… well, like the rats that had gnawed away at the top-side of my foot.

'Is there anything to eat?' I asked.

'Should've brought your own,' Twinnie snapped. 'You not pass any shops on your way up here. Like Burt's or something?'

'Why'd you say Burt's?'

Twinnie bolted upright again; sensed the tension in my voice.

'Just said it, that's all. Blast from the past, like. You were the one bringing up all sorts like that camping trip at Grange Heights. Chill out mate, for fuck's sake. Thought that by mentioning that old gormless fuckwit, I'd be able to make you laugh.'

'Burt's dead,' I said.

'Figured as much; not seen his shop open in donkey's years; maybe the environmental health finally got hold of what shit he was trying to sell in them dog-meat pasties...'

'No man; I don't think you get what I mean. I mean he died *yesterday...*'

Twinnie whistled through his teeth, clearly still not understanding.

'I mean he died from the same thing as us!' I cried. I longed to take his head and smash it against that whitewashed wall or on the blank space on the concrete where the Aga must have used to reside, before some hardy, and strong thieves managed to disconnect it and make off with it.

The fire returned to Twinnie's eyes. 'We're not dead yet, man,' he said. 'Look at us. Alive and kicking... Well; some won't be kicking as well as others...'

He twisted round on the camp-bed, gestured to the blood-red graffiti on the walls: *You'll never take me alive.*

'That's what I mean! He doesn't want to take us alive; he wants to...'

Twinnie climbed up from the camp-bed. Towered over me. I couldn't remember him being so tall.

'Well, what do you suggest we *do* then, soldier boy?'

I didn't say anything.

'Huh?'

I still didn't say anything. Twinnie returned to his seat, but picked up the spade from under the camp-bed again. I could see glints of blood on the blade. My blood.

'You were talking about that night up at Grange Heights earlier, Bully,' said Twinnie, in a soft voice which didn't quite tie-up with the violence he'd so nearly inflicted just a few seconds earlier. 'Well let me tell you about that night.'

'Member it was around that time that everyone was afraid of the Black Panther. Some fucking busybody or other claimed she see'd a big black cat stalking through her garden messing with her washing or some such. Called the old filth in to report it. An' of course they laughed their piggy-little heads off at the story. A big cat in Newton Mills? Where'd that come from? The travelling circus?

Anyway, turns out that because the woman's garden backed on to the school playin' fields, the filth *had* to go check it out. Just in case, like. Look for dock-off paw-prints and the like in her rose beds. And of course, they found nothing out of the ordinary. Whatsoever. But you know what it's like in Newton Mills. People like to talk. There isn't much else to do round here save killing yourself on drink or drugs or by joining the army. So this busybody starts talking. She starts talking in the shop queue and at the bus stop. She tells her neighbours. And before you know it, it's like Chinese Whispers and *everybody's* talking about this big old cat with sabre-tooth fangs that's strutting round the town like he owns it. Men in the pubs start talking about the cat making off with a baby from a pram like that woman down under who had her baby snatched by dingoes. Women in the... wherever women go... start talking about pulling the kids outta school. Just in case.

'Member the special assemblies they had round that time? How they told us we had to go straight home from school. Do not pass Burt's. Do not collect two hundred 1p sweets. How they told us not to go out at night until that beast was caught? Do you not remember even *why* we went up Grange Heights in the first place?

It was after... after what happened with you know who. And nobody knew where he was still. So we decided – *all* of us – to go up the Heights and say we saw the Panther and that he had a piece of you know who's clothing on him. In his fangs or something. Or that we saw the Panther carrying you know who's school trousers – remember them shit ones that he always wanked in. I dunno, we just kinda decided that the best way of putting everyone off our scent was to set the bloodhounds on the trail of that imaginary cat.

But of course, once we got up there, we had nothin' to do but drink and smoke, like usual. And it turned into a good party for a while. Dick was being a dick, but funny with it. Lion was trying to wrestle all of us, but playful-like; you know how he was. Me and you sat around sharing this dock-off bottle of cider that we'd pinched from the offie down on main street. You know the one; the one where they had that bird from a couple of years above us – well, a few years above us – and she always just gave us booze so we'd stop pestering her.

You got drunker and drunker. And more and more… maudlin. Yeah, that's the word. Maudlin; like my old mum used to get when she got stuck into the gin. You were snivellin' and cryin' and everything. Just like you know who. Then you passed out for a bit. And that's when Dick and me set fire to your bloody sleeping bag with you in it. You woke up like a man possessed. Wouldn't see what we'd done as the joke it really was. But you stayed when we bribed you with more drink.

Anyway, after a while, we all had too much to drink and went to sleep – you in your half sleeping-bag, shivering away like a girl – everyone else wrapped up toasty warm. But after an hour or so, I got woke up. You, white as a sheet, like you'd seen a ghost, shaking and shaking at my shoulders. Claimed you'd seen the Black Panther. I mean *really* seen it. Not just as part of the story we were going to make up. Kept talking and talking about how it breathed. Even how it smelled. You said it smelled like fish. I'll always remember that.

We all tried to calm you down. All of us. Lion sat on you for a bit, Dick tried telling dickish jokes. I just told you that we needed to stick to the plan. But then you said it: you said that you were going to go to the police. About you know who. Said you were going there straight-off. Gonna run all the way down to that piggy station like a good little pig. And you just scarpered, leaving us clutching on to your burned-out purple sleeping bag. Dick tried to run after you and you just increased the pace. But as you did so, you started slipping down the slope. Came a-tumbling all the way down, didn't you? Bashed your arm up big-style. And your head.

Of course, we went knocking on the door of Maurice Dailly's farmhouse like good little boys. And Maurice called your dad and the ambulance. You were in for two weeks. Your dad stayed the whole time. But when you came out, it was like you'd forgotten the whole thing. It was mad, like. But we thought it might interrupt your recovery or something, so we… get off… get off my throat…

I had my hands clasped around Twinnie's neck. I could feel the grease and *purple* sliming its way off his skin and onto mine. I felt the old power in my hands and the righteousness of what I was about to do. Outside, the wind howled louder, like it was laughing away, ever so merrily about some fart joke in assembly.

I loosened my grip. Twinnie seized upon my moment of weakness and kicked out at my half-foot. Knocked me over. I crashed to the floor, still gripping him, but weaker now… weaker.

I ran my fingers across the ridges on the stone floor, tried to map my way back into a reality I could cope with. But suddenly, Twinnie's story about what really happened at Grange Heights that night started to ring true. But it couldn't be, surely?

'You're lying,' I breathed.

Twinnie, who was still lying next to me, fingering his purple neck, started laughing.

'I swear on Dick's life that I'm not,' he said, finally. 'It was you that broke down up there… You that wanted to confess…'

'But it was Dick's sleeping bag,' I pleaded.

'It was *your* sleeping bag… Come on, you remember really, don't you, soldier boy?'

I screwed up my eyes; tried *not* to remember.

Twinnie grabbed onto my shoulder and squeezed. I felt his fingernails slipping into those old scars left by Tommy Peaker back at the military hospital. Felt the searing pain of memory sting through me.

'It was you that was in hospital. You that has that scar on your arm where the bone poked through…'

'That scar on my arm is from when I fell off my bike… on the cobbles… on Hangman's Row.'

'Is that really what you think?' demanded Twinnie, digging his fingers deeper into my flesh. Twisting them now too. Twisting so's I'd finally understand what he was trying to tell me.

'But why did Dick tell me all that stuff he did… back at the Choke? Why did Dick say it was him?'

Twinnie laughed.

'He'll say whatever he feels like depending on what the drugs tell him. Come on; you know that.'

I gasped, stared down at the familiar circular scar on my wrist, just down from the elbow. It glared purple.

'Or he'll say whatever I fucking well tell him to say,' said Twinnie.

Chapter Fourteen

"It landed foul on the grass"

I must have passed out. When I came to, I had the strange feeling that a lot of time had passed, but I couldn't pinpoint exactly how much. Through the cracks in the farmhouse walls, I could see that it was still mostly dark, but it was the kind of dark in which there's light at the end of the tunnel. Or at least I hoped there was.

My fingers ached. They remembered what I'd tried to do to Twinnie. I must have had the heavy weight of memory, of truth and of righteousness behind me in that moment. I rolled over on the stone floor and saw Twinnie. He was sitting, back propped up against the camp-bed, just staring at me. There wasn't malice, or love, or compassion, or regret or *anything* in those beady eyes of his. Just blankness. Just inhumanity.

'It's you know who that's driving us crazy like this,' I whispered, trying to make some kind of connection with my childhood friend. 'His poison is infecting this whole farmhouse.'

Twinnie snarled. His upper lip quivered and his jaw clenched.

'You tell yourself that, soldier boy. You tell yourself that,' he said.

'You looked in on Dick?' I asked, trying to be as normal as possible.

Twinnie simply resumed his staring match. I felt the hairs on the back of my neck starting to stand on end.

I tried to climb to my feet, using a broken old workbench to help me up.

'Watch out for those old animal traps,' said Twinnie, not making any effort to come and help. But I didn't want him to. I didn't want his cold fingers touching me again. I could still feel their impact on my shoulders; digging into my very soul just as Tommy Peaker had.

It was only when I'd finally got to my feet that Twinnie lit the cigarette. I heard him click open the lighter and light the cigarette in one move; something that could only be achieved with a Zippo. With my Zippo. I turned to look at him, extravagantly puffing away on that extra-long Dorchester and Grey – the cigarette brand he'd always taken the piss out of me for smoking because, apparently, old ladies did – and stroking his beard like he was performing some kind of meditation. Again, his eyes were fixed right on me.

'Where'd you get that cigarette from?' I asked.

Twinnie blew a smoke ring – not as impressive as the one Burt had blown a day or so ago – and picked up my Zippo from the floor in front of him. Started spinning it around with his fingers, occasionally snapping it open and sparking the flame.

'Where'd you get that *lighter* from?'

'In your pack, man,' he said. 'Chill. I went looking for some... uh... medicine I could bring you round with. I only helped myself to a couple of your ciggies... honest.'

I picked up the pack from the floor. Checked the small front pocket. Saw that the last *two* packs were missing.

'Where's the rest of them, then?'

'In safe keeping,' smiled Twinnie. 'Don't you worry about that. I'll keep 'em safe from this bogeyman that you're so scared shitless of.'

I felt my fingers twitching for his neck again. I felt the cold burn in the marks on my shoulders.

'Toss me one over. Now,' I ordered.

'Now wait a minute, soldier boy. I ain't just one of your cadets or something that you can just boss around whenever you've had a bad day. Now be a good little soldier and fuck off out of here, or else you can go find somewhere else to hide away until your bogeyman comes after you.'

'He's your bogeyman too,' I breathed as I unbolted the farmhouse door and stepped into the freezing mist which had descended on the courtyard.

Fucking hell it was cold. And eerie too. Like the mist was trying to tell me something. I felt it brushing up thick against my face. Felt it creeping under my t-shirt and caressing the nail-marks on my shoulder. Felt it buffeting against me, trying to make me lose my footing. I reached for the now familiar uneven stonework of the farmhouse wall. Traced my way along that same path I'd already walked a dozen times since I'd been here. Followed it like it was a thread and the courtyard was a labyrinth.

It was only when I heard my grunts and pants echoing back to me that I realised that I'd entered the barn. It took a while for my eyes to get accustomed to the dark, but soon I managed to pick out a row of pitchforks lined up against the wall; I picked out old bails of hay which were rammed into the corner; I picked out the now dilapidated woodpile. And finally, I picked out Dick's cocoon; he'd evidently kicked off the yellow tarpaulin in the night and it now lay sad and battered and useless half out the back door.

I crouched down over the pile of blankets. Felt the dampness of them; dew perhaps. Ran my hands along the once-soft material, trying to feel Dick's body underneath. Started to panic when I couldn't feel anything. Crawled to the other end of the cocoon. Thought I saw Dick's face, shining white despite the gloom, but slowly realised that it was my eyes playing tricks with me.

And then I kinda threw myself into the cold blankets, hoping to touch any part of him. Just wanting to feel body-warmth. Wanting to make him say something like; 'Get off me Bully. What are you; a puff?' But there was nothing alive inside the blankets.

Oh God, what has he done? Oh God what has been done to him?

My mind raced through the possibilities; first, and least terrifying of them was the chance that Dick had simply wanted the drugs so much that he'd managed to extricate himself from the cocoon and tried to crawl back into town to the welcoming numbness of the main street flats and their naked bulbs. Second, and only marginally worse, was the possibility that Twinnie was fucking about with me. That he'd used the time when I was passed out to do more than just steal my cigarettes; perhaps he'd simply moved Dick. Perhaps he was in the outhouse or something. And then there was the option that I wanted to think about less than any of them; the fact that Tommy Peaker might well have come for him in the night, while Twinnie and I lay in the relative comfort of the farmhouse.

Hell, we'd offered Dick up like some goddamn sacrifice or something, hadn't we? Although I'd tried to convince myself otherwise, through years of trying to make myself a better person, there was still a hidden part of me that only cared about number one. And now Dick was number two. He'd have that number carved into his chest, above the heart, just like Lion had the number one carved into him.

I let out this massive bellow of torment and pain and I don't know what, gripping the blankets to me, trying to inhale the scent of Dick. But all I could smell were the horses that the blankets used to cover. All I could smell was the past, coming back to haunt me. Cantering back to haunt me, with a fucking lunatic highwayman in the saddle wielding a bloody spear that was destined straight for my cold, cold heart.

Somehow, I managed to wrench myself upright and using the crutch, I staggered back out and into the courtyard. Despite the fact I knew it was hopeless, I tried the door for the outhouse. But there was no Dick in there; no stupid, childish junkie shouting 'surprise' as soon as my worried face poked through the gap.

I staggered on. Past the farmhouse and round to the front, to the lawn where I'd picked out the ornamental wheelbarrow. Where was the famed view of Newton Mills now? Where was the belching factory and the school? Where were the garish council houses and the decrepit old mills? They'd all turned their eyes away, hadn't they, and pretended that they didn't see. They pretended that it was too misty, or that their minds had been too clogged up with drink. Or that they had better things to do than look in on other people's business.

Oh, but they'd be whispering about it, wouldn't they? They'd be creaking into each other; *nudge nudge, wink wink; did you hear the one about the soldier boy up at Summit Farm? The one that fell asleep on his watch and allowed his injured comrade to just be carried off into the night. And he didn't even stir. Just lay there feeling sorry for himself. That's what happens when you take the boy out of Newton Mills; Newton Mills is taken out of the boy.*

I picked a careful path through the middle of the garden and back to the fields. This, surely, if Dick had effected his own escape, would have been the way he had crawled. But the mist was still too thick to check whether there were any tell-tale crawl-marks on the grass. The mist was still too thick to see more than a few yards in front of me.

My throat burned for a cigarette, and for the comfort of my pack on my back. I tried to play 'mission' again, but all I could think of was the time we were up at Grange Heights yesterday, Dick and me. How he'd appealed to me to look after him. How my story about being on a beach in Spain was like an unwritten contract between us which said that I'd never let reality encroach upon his sheen of fantasy. Well: I'd broken my promise. But then, I couldn't remember a single promise that I'd actually kept in all my life. And even if I did - if I could remember - would I even be able to trust my own memory any more? After what Twinnie had said? The memory of falling off my bike on the Hangman's Row cobbles: a fiction. Setting fire to Dick's or Lion's sleeping bag? Made-up. And what about all those things I remembered about my brother and about Jane? The things that made me who I was? Were they fabrications too? I supposed that the only thing I could really trust now was the fact that the four of us had done what we'd done to Tommy. *That* was who I was.

Eyes stinging from the mist, I pressed on; stared into the middle distance and into nothingness. I could have been walking on the moon or in the desert or across a beach in Spain for all I knew. But all I knew was that I had to walk.

And so, I can't actually pinpoint the moment that the mist began to clear; that Newton Mill's self-imposed blindfold was lifted. All I remember is that suddenly, I could make out the bumpy, grassy terrain of the fields. Amazed that I'd not fallen over, I looked back at the house and saw that I'd not actually walked that far. When I looked back, I could see about half of Newton Mills town, as though it was emerging from the deep like some long forgotten sea monster.

'Blind bastards!' I yelled at the town. 'Your heads are up your arses!'

I staggered on, still yelling.

More and more of the town became clear. I could see the toffeeworks now; for some reason it was not spouting candy-coated smog into the air this morning. I could see the half-basketball dome of the library at school. It was winking at me in the early morning sun.

'You should all be punished!' I yelled again. But knew now I was clutching at straws. Blaming society for the way I'd turned out in a way that I hated psychiatrists doing.

And then I saw him. A figure in the distance, stealing over the low part of the dry stone wall just as Dick and I had done yesterday. I crouched low to the ground and watched. The figure had a loping gait, but walked with a purpose which belied his stooping frame. Perhaps he was the first of the Newton Mills mob, come to descend on Summit Farm; come to burn Twinnie like the mad witch that he was. But I could see no pitchfork. In fact the figure carried no weapon of any description. Not so far as I could see. Or else it was Tommy Peaker, and decomposition was already increasing at a breakneck pace, half-crippling him; giving him a kinda hunchback.

Either way, he was rapidly gaining on my hidey-hole amongst the long grass. That limpy-gimpy stride swallowing up great swathes of turf and molehills and dead rabbits.

I decided there was only one thing for it. I lifted myself on my crutch, bit back the pain and ran towards the man on my one and a half feet; the crutch held high above my head like some primitive weapon.

'Gary!' shouted a voice. 'Stop!'

But I couldn't stop myself from barrelling into, through, over the figure. Couldn't stop my half-foot trampling down onto something soft and unprotected. I fell headlong into a gigantic molehill, and face full of dirt, tried to catch my breath for whatever would come next.

But when I felt the figure's hand on my shoulder, I did not feel the ice-cold certainty that death was just around the corner, *tap, tap, tapping* with impatience. I felt warmth flowing through his fingers. I felt peace. I craned my neck around to see my old dad. He had a big smear of blood coming out of his ear-hole, but was standing strong and proud, holding out a thick hand to me, offering to help me to my feet.

'Dad?' I gasped. And then I could say nothing more. The tears just wouldn't stop coming. The single tear I'd shed for old Burt had now become a torrent and threatened to overwhelm me. Dad simply held me up and pressed my face into his once great chest.

'It's all over son; all over,' he whispered, over and over again.

And I so wanted to believe him. I wanted to be able to let him carry me down off that fucking hill, back to the house where I'd get washed up and then get started on building a bloody pigeon coop or pretty much whatever he fancied turning his hand at.

'All over,' he whispered. 'I came up here as soon as I knew. I'm sorry son.'

'About Burt? Have they found Burt?' I sobbed into his chest.

Dad took my face between his two meaty hands like he used to when I was a child. He lifted my head off his chest and looked into my red raw eyes.

'Not Burt, Gary. What are you talking about Burt for? Which Burt?'

'Burt from the shop. On Dye Lane,' I blubbered. 'He helped me out the other day. That's where I slept the night I came back. But he had some kind of heart attack and... I'm sorry dad... We left him there...'

'Son?' said dad in a strong voice, like he was talking to someone stuck down the bottom of a well. 'Son? You know that old Burt from that shop in Dye Lane... Well, he died years ago. Right at the counter of his shop, just like everyone said he would. He just loved the place so much that he...'

'Someone else has moved in there. Some other old guy,' I said.

Dad brought my head back against his chest. I could hear the haphazard beating of his heart that was once so true. I used to sit on his knee and listen to its metronomic progression every evening when I was little, when he thought I was sat watching cartoons. I always had my eyes closed... Or did I? Was I remembering something else? Was it someone else's memory I was clinging to? Was it some film I'd seen at the barracks or rented from M & S Video Supplies?

'You're in shock son. Everything must have been building up,' whispered dad. 'What with your leg and everything. And coming back here to find out about Lion, and now *this*... Well, it's hardly surprising... We can get you help, lad.'

'I can't take it any more,' I sobbed. 'Help me, dad.'

'I'll always help you, son,' he said, stroking my hair. 'That – along with worrying – well, they're kind of my only profession nowadays. But listen; first I need you to come with me to the police station. You need to tell them about the state he was in. Rule yourself out of the enquiries, so to speak.'

'But... but... you said that it wasn't Burt that was in the shop on Dye Lane. You said there was...'

'Not Burt, Gary; Dick. You need to tell them about Dick.'

Chapter Fifteen

" The sacrificial rite "

Now I'm not sure what real or fictitious memories are any more, I don't know if this is true or not, but I do seem to have this nagging recollection of dad always saying to me: 'If I've told you once, Gary, I've told you a thousand times.' That morning, up on the top field of Summit Farm, dad must have had to explain about Dick's death about a thousand times, and still I had questions. Still I couldn't get it through my 'thick skull' that two of us were down now. Fifty percent. Old Tommy Peaker was half-way through his revenge mission, and I'd barely even had time to formulate a plan.

So, it's probably best that I just let dad explain what happened to Dick, or at least, what the police figured happened. Because it's all still mucked up in my head.

It was one of the early shift that found him. They start at six am. In fact, the only time the toffeeworks has *not* got workers in it is between the hours of five and six, so that's when they thought he must have done it. They try to keep the machines running for twenty-three out of every twenty-four hours, only closing down because of new noise and environmental regulations. Honestly, it's a surprise they haven't got round that by employing quieter machines. They're still processing the workers here, Gary; they still are.

Anyway, I'd better get off my high-horse hadn't I? A young lad found him; lad by the name of Mark Birch. Nice boy. The quiet type; I used to know his dad. Now Mark was a dedicated worker. Would never complain because he just thought himself lucky to have a job. Just the type that the toffeeworks like. Now Mark was always charged with getting in there early; going round and switching on the machines and getting them warmed up. Done it for the past ten years now, so it's second nature to him. I suppose they made him into a kind of machine himself.

Anyway, yes; I'll get on with it. So Mark gets to work at a quarter to six in the morning. Has to walk there every day as there aren't any buses running at that time in the morning. How convenient for him, eh? And when he gets to the gate, he can tell that something isn't right. You know that feeling you get that you can't quite put your finger on. Like you've suddenly had an eighth of a premonition and you just know something bad is going to happen.

Don't give me that look, son, you know that if I'm telling the story I'll tell it like this. I suppose I'm trying to soften the blow for you in a way...

He checks all the locks and they're all fine. So he tries to forget that feeling that he's just had and he opens up just as he always has for ten years. And he goes into the kitchenette and makes himself a brew, and then ever so slowly ambles into the main hall where the machines are; the mixing vats and the like. And I don't know about you, but once you know a place like the back of your hand, you just don't really look up. Ever. You tend to stare at your feet or at the cup of steaming coffee that you've got in your hands. You don't really feel the need to look right up there in the rafters.

Now this is all second hand – third hand maybe – but this is what I heard. For some reason – perhaps it was the funny feeling that he got outside the gates – Mark Birch looks up into the rafters this morning. And he sees your friend Richard Featherstone hanging from a noose which has been tied around one of the rafters. How he's managed to get himself up there nobody can really tell. How he's managed to get in there without breaking through the chains on the gate, nobody rightly knows. All they know is that he'd hung himself.

Of course, could be that he managed to slip in during the night shift. Most of the people that do the night shift take in hip-flasks and the like just to get them through it. And you can't really blame them.

Or I suppose you can if they fail to spot someone slipping into the building that'll then go on to kill themselves.

Anyway, police think open and shut case despite the fact that it would have been so difficult for him to get up there. I suppose they reckon that it would be just as hard for *someone else* to get up there and do it to him, and suicide's the easiest explanation. Less questions asked. Less leg-work. Less misery for all concerned. Apart from poor Dick's kids and that girlfriend of his that he treated so badly.

What did Newton Mills do to those boys, Gary? What did it do?

Oh, and before I forget, there was one other thing. One other thing that was pretty weird to tell you the truth. And I only know this because I spoke to Mark's dad. When they cut Dick down from the rafters, they found this strange sticky substance on his chest. At first they thought it was blood, but when one brave soul actually sniffed the stuff, they realised that it was from the mix that goes into make those Strawberry Skulls sweets. You know the ones?

Anyway, yes; he'd daubed red candy on his own chest. Now why on earth would anyone want to do that?

I screwed up my eyes and tore at the grass we were sitting on. I had to feel something tangible. Had to hold on. It felt like the grass was the only thing keeping me from falling off the precipice.

'What had he daubed on his own chest, dad?' I asked.

Dad shook his head; he thought he'd already gone too far. Probably thought he shouldn't have broken the news to me while I was still so fucked up. But *he thought I knew*. And that's why he thought I was fucked up in the first place. Only too late did he realise that instead of actually discussing Dick's death like rational human beings, he was breaking the news to me…

'Was it a number?' I continued.

'How do you know that?' sighed dad. 'Or should I not ask. Was this some stupid prank gone-wrong, Gary? Did Twinnie have something to do with this? Did you?'

'No prank,' I managed to say. 'Not a prank at all.'

'Well you clearly seem to know more than you're letting on,' said dad. 'Would you mind telling me what the fuck is going on?'

I thought of all the times I hadn't been able to explain myself to my dad in the past. I thought of all the opportunities he'd given me, but it just hadn't been the right time, or I hadn't been in the right mood, or I just *couldn't* tell him any more because it had got that bad. And suddenly I wanted to tell him everything.

'It's bad shit,' I said. 'Rotten to the core.'

'And this *bad shit* started before you got back? You just happened to get mixed in with it, like you used to?'

'No,' I breathed, attempting to bite the bullet. Finding it cold and steely and not at all easy to grip between the teeth. 'This bad shit started a long, long time ago. Back when we were kids. We did something that was unforgivable...'

'Everything's forgivable,' said dad, reaching out and draping an arm over my shoulder. 'You just have to know the right people to ask for forgiveness.'

'But... if you knew... You'd walk away from me now and you'd never want to see me again.'

'I never see you anyway, Gary. Where would be the difference?'

He was staring out over the town and in that moment, I knew he hated it just as much as I did. But he loved it too. I could see the way his eyes followed the path of the river in the gorge or the shape of the hills across the way... Or maybe it was the geography of the town that he loved, and the buildings and the people that he hated. Maybe he, like everyone else, was seduced by the beauty of the place on a summer's day, and never saw until too late what it was like on a damp winter evening, when all of the insects came out from under their rocks looking to feed on the hope and blood of those that weren't taken yet.

'Just trust me on this, dad. You wouldn't want to know me...'

'I should have moved away from here after your mum... after your mum died. I should have taken you and your brother away. But I was too worried about how we'd cope with all the upheaval. I put too many obstacles in our way...'

'Dad; me and Steve would never have stood for it if you made us move away from here. It's in our blood. You can't help it. Nobody can help it. It's just the way things were meant to be.'

Dad nodded, wiped away one of his own tears.

I shuddered at the thought of what I now had to do. What I was now going to force myself to do. I was going to come clean; they have it just right that term. Because that was what it was starting to feel like, the more I was starting to open up to this stranger; my dad. It felt as though years and years of grime were about to be washed away. And I didn't care what would happen to me.

I shivered again.

'You all right, Gary?' asked dad. 'You don't have to tell me if you don't want to.'

'I'm all right,' I breathed. 'I *need* to tell you...'

'But you're not right, Gary. Look at the state of you. You're turning blue with cold. You're nearly *purple* with cold,' said dad. 'Let's get you back home and in front of the fire. We don't have to go up to the police station today. Not if you're not up to it. You've had a shock son.'

I raised my eyes to the sky, suddenly remembering why it was I could never tell dad anything. He just didn't want to listen. His heart was already pummelled and battered to a pulp by what had happened to mum and to Steve. He knew he couldn't take any more and so he just talked and talked and talked but never really *said* anything. And here was me thinking old daddy would be here to save the day. More fool me.

Dad climbed to his feet and dusted down his jeans. I don't know why he bothered; they were covered in mud anyway from when I'd knocked him to the ground. Dried blood coated one side of his face too. He wouldn't exactly pass muster walking down the main street like that.

'You coming?' he said, offering me his hand. Again, he said it like he was shouting down a well; like his hand was a bucket being lowered. A bucket containing my life preserver.

'I can't dad,' I said, coldly. 'Deep down, you know that. This whole thing has to finish and it'll finish up here, at Summit Farm.'

Dad jogged from one foot to the other, trying to get the feeling back. I had the feeling that he'd been doing similar ever since mum died.

160

'It doesn't have to be like this,' he said, finally, without looking at me.

'Yes it does, dad. Yes it does.'

And he walked away from me then. Walked away although I knew it was the final spear in his heart to do so. Walked away and back into the town that he so loved and so hated and which had ruined his whole family's life. I hoped that he wouldn't do anything stupid. Certainly not anything as stupid as I was now planning to do.

Chapter Sixteen

"Fists of rage"

After we killed Tommy Peaker, everything went on as per usual. It was mad – 'fucking mad' as Twinnie put it – but nobody seemed to give a shit at all about the disappearance of that poor little boy from Newton Mills School. We sat in soulless classrooms and barely listened as the register was read out and Tommy once again didn't answer his call. Of course, there were the whisperings in the dark corridors or in the toilets, probably in the staff room too. Rumours were spread about the Black Panther. One rumour in particular involved a group of boys that had gone on an ill-advised camping trip up at Grange Heights. Apparently one of them had seen the beast carrying a piece of young Tommy's clothing between his teeth.

But the police scoffed at the tales. They had enough trouble dealing with Tommy's mum who made herself an ever-present in the police waiting room, bringing along her hip-flask and occasionally a male associate for company. The police could always tell when it was time for her to go home because she'd start trying to climb on the counter like some demented chimpanzee, mascara lines streaked down her face. She'd attempt to beat whichever officer was manning the reception desk with the spike of a stiletto shoe until whatever male companion was with her beat a hasty retreat, realising there'd be no nookie tonight, and the policeman in question would simply knock her off the desk. She'd usually then just lie there and wait for someone to come off duty and drive her home like a regular taxi service.

They ran a couple of stories in the local rag for the first few weeks after Tommy didn't come home. But the tragic fact remained that he didn't have the proper angelic features in order to spur the public into action. In the photo which the family provided – the one that they used for all the media stuff – Tommy looked rather like the younger incarnation of a sex pest; even the teachers said it, in the quiet of the staff room. Even the neighbours said it. And they said more. They told all about how he was such a strange little boy. 'Always running about with his penis in his hand,' they said. 'Once wanked off a stray dog,' they said. Used to try and stare through their curtains and steal their milk bottles. Couldn't be bothered with school and hadn't achieved anything noteworthy even when he had.

Nobody knew who said it first, but someone did and soon everyone was saying it: 'I wouldn't have blamed the kid if he'd run away. He was always trouble, and the state of his mum... well... he's probably on the streets in London or Manchester now. He'll cope. There's nothing we can do any more.'

And in the school, girls that had never known Tommy, but who'd skriked their eyes out and won sympathy off all and sundry for weeks on end, stopped mentioning his name. Stopped trying to get petitions signed, although there was never any purpose to the petitions in the first place. They ran out of excuses not to do their homework and started looking for the next victim to claim as their own.

Mrs. Peaker still turned up at the police station, but now she was pretty much turfed out as soon as she made it through the doors. And no lift home was offered now either. Instead she lurked like a ghost in the dark pockets of pubs ready to shriek at anyone that would listen about her darling son Tommy and did they know what had happened to him? And wouldn't they kindly buy her a drink?

The Peaker family home, if anything, got into a worse state of disrepair. One day a window simply fell out of its frame, nearly decapitating a poor paper boy that was simply minding his own business, trying to skirt around the pack of baying dogs that had gathered in the front yard. Apparently, the damp inside the house had got so bad that everything was simply rotting away or breaking or fusing or collapsing into dust and mould.

Some on the estate, the more house proud amongst them, started to feel like the Peaker home was an eyesore. A slight on all the

163

hard work they'd put into their herbaceous borders and scissor-trimmed metre-square lawns. Committee meetings were held in local pubs – the ones that Mrs. Peaker was already barred from – and it was decided that a letter should be drafted to the council. They wanted her removed, they claimed, or else rent would not be paid. *We may only be tenants, but we have rights too, you know.*

At school, Tommy's name passed from being mentioned in whispers to being used as the butt of sick jokes within weeks. His legendary wanking and his fishy smell and his too-short school-kecks were all valid subjects for a dig. But then, eventually, the teachers stopped bothering to read his name out at all in registration. They blanked him out, just as we had.

And us boys got on with doing what we did best; making everyone else's lives a misery. We found other hangers-on to coerce into doing our dirty work for us; other willing boys that would steal from the tuck-shop and then pass on their ill-gotten gains hand-over-fist; other boys that would steal Mr. Sharp's hubcaps; other boys that would daub blood-red graffiti all over the headmaster's office door, informing him that he was a 'right cunt.'

Of course, they didn't ask Twinnie or Dick or Lion to bother coming back for the exams. They advised them to go out looking for jobs. They were always looking out for fresh blood up at the toffee works, dontchaknow? But none of them listened; Twinnie carried on the small-scale drug-dealing business he'd started at school. And his best customer kept coming a-knocking on a daily basis. Yeah, even at that stage, Dick was too fucked-up all the time to get himself a job. Lion did a bit of manual labouring at a local building site, but his poor time-keeping – he never was any good at getting out of bed before midday – soon caught up with him. As did the site foreman once he found out that the four of us were using the little portacabin on site as our temporary – and I was tempted to say 'clubhouse' here, but that wasn't what it was at all – fallout shelter.

We'd go in there and play cards and have a couple of trips or a wrap of speed or a bottle or two of Ice Dragon. But already things were starting to change between us all. I could sense it; *I* had changed. I'd stayed on at school for some reason. Probably because I couldn't be arsed arguing with dad about it. And anyway, I took my medicine. I numbly slipped into my seat in that exam hall – the dining hall, actually, just made over a little bit – and blankly filled out their forms. Got reasonable grades too, believe it or not. Then slipped numbly into college and more exams and met Jane.

Me Tarzan; you Jane.

At first, it really did feel as though I had been raised in a jungle and she in her posh suburban home where they had crockery and condiments and everything. Maybe she saw me as a bit of rough – although she said later that it was something crap like the 'wistful look that came into my eyes when I thought nobody was looking' that first attracted her to me. And of course, I never introduced her to Twinnie, Dick or Lion, because I knew that the first thing that attracted me to her would be the very thing they comment on. Loudly and to her face.

She had an excellent rack on her, did Jane. And for a while I was the envy of the college. All of the spods in the classes kept looking over and you could see them thinking: *Is she really going out with him?*

Fuck 'em all, I thought. And in the end, so did she. When her family found out we'd got engaged at eighteen, they went ballistic as only good middle class parents can; all smashing inanimate objects and screaming at the light fixtures and hugging cushions. Promises that she should never 'darken their door again', were hastily followed up, within a day or two, by hourly calls which my dad had to field from a gin-soaked mother and a father that just didn't understand how his daughter's tits had caused them so many bloody problems when all he wanted to do was weed the acre garden in peace.

Jane lived at our house on Hangman's Row, off and on, for about eighteen months, I think. I say off and on, because I often had head loss periods. Weeks or months in which I'd spiral off on this whirlwind path of self-destruction. Anyone that got in the way was likely to be carried away with me and plunged off whatever precipice I'd reached. In the end, she stayed on longer than I did.

But I'm getting ahead of myself. She aced the exams in college and was offered a place at a fair to middling university. I didn't see myself moving off to some fucking suburb of some big city somewhere, fading away into nothingness like her dad and mine, and so I forbade it. I stopped her from going. I used every trick in the book, most of which were emotional blackmail-related. I told her that the job at the metalworks that I'd somehow wisecracked my way into, had always been my mum's dream for me, or somesuch crap, and she took it. She took it hook, line and sinker.

And sinker I did. Although not yet. First there was the world of work.

I don't know what I'd been expecting. Certainly I hadn't been expecting it to be just an extension of school as it was. In fact, in that metalworks, there was actually *more* childishness, more pettiness, more bullying and more gossip than I'd ever seen at school. We dished it out for breakfast, lunch and supper, along with the slop they served us from the godawful work's canteen. And it was easy to fall in with lads similar to Twinnie and Dick, too. I seemed to have some sixth sense for wrong-'uns. And they seemed to have a sixth sense for me. We were the alpha males and we ruled the roost.

Until I first thought I saw Tommy again. Sitting on his own in the smoking room looking as pathetic and piss-stained as he always used to. I saw him a few times after that; always hunched over his roll-up, which he'd be making over a pristine copy of *The Sun*. Only after a while did I pluck up the courage to go in there. But as it turned out, the person I thought was Tommy was actually his brother; Danny Peaker. A 'right little scrote' according to the other metalworkers I spoke to. Apparently, he wasn't 'all there upstairs', but he was handy with a sweeping brush when he needed to be, and so they kept him on, half in the capacity of general dogsbody, half as court jester.

I tried to speak to Danny Peaker once. Got nothing in return apart from some incomprehensible mumble and a shower of rolling tobacco on my trainers after I'd made him jump. And right then, I knew that we'd got away with it forever. The whole of Tommy's family were so pathetic that nobody even cared about them. They'd been chewed up and spat out by a resurrection of that same system which cleansed Newton Mills of the millworkers in the last century. Only now, instead of actual machines, there were little walking time bombs like our lot doing the work for them. What a fucking laugh, eh?

That night, the dreams started again. And the only way I could get them to stop was to run and run as fast as I could. Away from Jane. Away from dad. Away from Twinnie and Lion and Dick. Away from Tommy Peaker. Straight into the army. Straight on that massive boat across the many seas and oceans we crossed, until eventually, I became just like everyone else for a time. We were all killers.

So I suppose, as I hold the hunting knife over my wrist, you could say that I got what I deserved. Nasty all my life; deserves a nasty end. But do you remember something I told you a long time ago, about bullies being insecure deep-down? Well at that moment, I knew it to be true. Because I was scared to see my own blood. Sounds stupid after everything that had happened, but I was. Just like when the military policeman that so looked like Tommy Lee Jones was fiddling with my tubes at the American hospital…

And I just sat and I sat in the barn at Summit Farm, listening to the faraway sounds of Twinnie singing – yes singing; he knew what I was planning to do – and I teased the blade along my wrist. But I was never really serious about it. I was still waiting for something – anything – to happen that would make everything okay in the end.

And then I heard another sound. Coming from right behind me. Snuffly breathing. Kinda whistly, through nostrils that weren't properly all there. Through a face that had been ravaged by time…

I sat up, erect. Felt the hairs on the back of my neck become erect too. And I almost felt like ghostly fingers were being run through them. *Tickling, tickling, tickling.* But not in a nice way. More like in the way that just tells you that you can't do anything about it, even if you want it to.

I knew straight away that I wasn't in the presence of a fox, or even Black Panther, that had just strayed into the barn by accident, say. Without even turning my head, I could sense the size of the thing that loomed behind me. It cast no shadow; it was all shadow anyway. But it somehow implied that it could snap my head off like it was the top of a dandelion.

'Who-who's there,' I stammered. Already knowing the answer. My fucking nose could have told me the answer immediately. That same salty, fishy smell that I remembered from the military hospital.

My mind began to slip over the precipice:

Doctor, doctor, my ghostly stalker has no nose.

Oh really? How does he smell?

Well, he is a supernatural force, see, so he doesn't really use the sense of smell to be honest. He can rely on things like the fabled sixth sense... Oh hold on, this is a joke, right? Let me start again. He smells awful. Smells like the fucking grave, doc. He smells like someone that's been buried in his own shit and piss, half eaten alive by animals, then died, then rotted, then somehow come back to life, but still without any proper control over his bodily functions. That okay doc? That answer your goddamn question?

I tried to allow myself to fall this time. Tried not to rely on memory as a crutch to keep me limping along. The thing was stroking my back now, like particularly sex-starved teenage boys do to girls that have drunk too much at parties. Girls who have been sick, but the boy *still* thinks there is a chance of a bit of how's your father.

How is your father?

He's as fucking purple as the rest of us. He's so purple that he won't even listen when his son tries to confess murder to him.

The thing continued to stroke my back. Wax-on, wax-off, like Mr. Miyagi. And I felt myself being dragged back from the precipice again. The wind was no longer rushing through my hair. The ground was not rushing up to meet me: splat. I was already *on* solid ground.

Not yet, said the voice of Tommy Peaker. *Not yet. It's not ready yet. There's still something that needs to happen.*

'What? What needs to happen? You want me to get eaten alive by rats again? You want to hang me from the rafters like Dick or push me into the gorge like Lion?' I gasped.

Tut, tut, tut, said Tommy Peaker. *They did that to themselves, Bully; you must know that by now. After all that bloody idiot Burt told you...*

'Gonna carve a bloody number three on my chest, are you?' I wailed. I tried to move the hunting knife up closer to my chest, but felt heavy weights attached to my arms. I looked down and Tommy wasn't touching me; what was it that stayed my arm? Hope, perhaps? *Gimme one more chance, please gimme one more, I'll be a good boy now* hope?

There, there, Bulls-eye, said Tommy, who'd resumed stroking my back now. *You know you're not number three, don't you? Just like you know that I never had a brother called Danny. I had three sisters, Bully. Three sisters; you used to say that it was one each for you, Lion and Twinnie. Always left Dick out. Quite ironic that, given his name. Your memory's shot to shit though mate, isn't it?*

When I finally dared myself to turn round, there was nobody there, but I knew there had been. And I knew he'd been there for a long, long time. Since the metalworks. Since before then, even.

Chapter Seventeen

" I saw satan laughing with delight "

Twinnie looked particularly pleased with himself when I limped back into the farmhouse. He had one of my Dorchester and Grey's sticking out of the far corner of his mouth and one eye half closed as a stream of smoke billowed upwards and settled just below the mouldy ceiling.

'Couldn't do it then, soldier boy?' he asked, through the other side of his mouth, like a cowboy. Like Clint Eastwood. 'Better give me that knife back then, just in case.'

I tossed it back to him, handle-first. It bounced a little way in front of him and then landed blade-first on the stone floor. The blade sang out in complaint.

'Careful, soldier boy; wouldn't want anyone else getting hurt,' said Twinnie. 'It's a bloody epidemic around here at the moment.'

Seeing that I wasn't going to pose any threat to him, he tucked his legs inside the sleeping bag and made himself into a nice, snug cocoon. He was settling in for the evening, like there was a good solid detective drama on the telly and the female lead was one of those actresses that always got her tits out, no matter what role she was playing; grieving mother, nun, detective, victim.

'Can I have one of my safe-keeping cigarettes now please?' I asked.

Twinnie made this face as though he was umming and ahhing over some great universal subject like life or death. He sucked his thin jaw one way and then the other, pursing his cat's arse lips.

'Well,' he said, finally. 'I'm not really sure what I can say to that, Gary. After all, the whole rationing situation was re-assessed when you proposed that you were going to do yourself in. You can't very well expect me to go through the whole paperwork, the whole red-tape of beaurocracy, just so's you now fancy a cigarette rather than killing yourself. What's it going to be next, eh? You gonna ask me if you can have a go on my camp-bed and then claim it as your own? Is that your game?

'No game,' I said wearily. 'Just thought we could have a nice talk that's all. And it's better to talk when you have a ciggie on the go.'

Twinnie chucked over the remaining third of the Dorchester and Grey which had been hanging out of his mouth ever since I'd made my return to the farmhouse. It landed on my arm, fiercely burning the hairs on the wrist.

'There you go, soldier boy,' he smiled. 'Don't say I never give you nothing.'

'Okay Twinnie,' I said, through a cloud of smoke. 'I wondered what your plan is. If you even have a plan. Because I've just seen – well, felt – you know who right behind me in the barn and he told me that there's something we need to do.'

Twinnie started evil-laughing again: 'You telling me that you know who has come and saved you *again?* That you've miraculously survived death twice because of the fair hand of the very thing that is trying to kill us?'

'How do you know he's trying to kill us?'

'You told me he was…'

'No; how do you *know* that he's trying to kill us. You seemed to know that before Dick and me got up here. Lion seemed to know it too. Now I'd like to know exactly what happened when you saw him?'

Twinnie sighed, sparked up another of my cigarettes and rolled over on the camp-bed. For a while I thought he wasn't going to say anything, but slowly, and in this pathetic-sounding voice that I thought I remembered from a long, long time ago, he started to recount the tale.

I'm not saying that I'm sure or anything, but it was Lion that first said something. And you know how mad he can get. Could get. Fuck; I keep forgetting. Anyway, I tried to meet him a couple of times, in the pub, like. Tried to get things back to the ay they used to be. I missed the big bastard, I really did. And I'm not saying I don't like my own company, but sometimes I just need someone to bounce off. You know what I mean?

Like I can get these great ideas in my head when I'm on the bus going nowhere in particular and I'll suddenly think of some great joke about the bird that's sat in front or the spak that's had to be wedged in by the luggage rack. And I'll turn around, you know, like I expect someone to be there. And then they ain't there and I have to stop smirking at what's going on in my suede or people will start thinking I'm a loon.

It was all right inside. It really was. Whenever I thought of something to say, I could just kick the bottom of old Shuffty's bunk – that was who I was sharing with – and he'd grunt and then I could just go on and on about whatever it was that I fancied going on about. Could be something important, could be something about why the chips from the canteen always stunk so bad when you shat them out in the can.

So when I got out that second time, I wanted someone around that I could bounce off. Not because I was lonely, just because… Well, I thought people might benefit from hearing what I had to say. And I tried meeting up with Dick for a while, but the daft fucker was so unreliable. Sometimes he'd never show up. Sometimes he'd show up and he was *itching,* literally itching for some more of that shite that he enjoys pumping in his veins. Other times, he *had* that shite in his blood and you just couldn't get on a level with him; know what I mean? Sometimes, I'd try and drink, like, a whole bottle of whisky or something, but it was like one of them platform computer games and our levels never seemed to match exactly. Like he'd be Sonic on some rising platform and I'd be Tails and I'd be sinking down, man. Do you know what I mean?

Then Dick told me that he'd started seeing Lion round and about the town again. Apparently he'd been inside too, but a looney bin for him, not the slammer. Anyway, so I kept going out round the pubs looking for him. Tried the Choke, the Three Legs, the Shire, the Bucket of Frogs. *Loads* of them, I tried, but the people in there always told me that Lion had just moved on. Funny thing was, there were a couple of times when I swore I saw him legging it out to the bogs just as I walked in, but then, if that was the way he wanted to play it, then fucking let him. I wouldn't go chasing the big bastard.

First time I saw him when there was no way he was getting away was up at that offie on main street. 'Member the one? The one where they had that bird from a couple of years above us – well, a few years above us – and she always just gave us booze so we'd stop pestering her.

So I was walking down the aisle and there was nowhere he could hide unless he dived into one of the fridges, and you know what he says to me:

'All right Twinnie, I been looking for you.'

Well, I couldn't believe that. The fat fucker was clearly lying, and I could see that he was scared of me by that shifty look that he got in his eyes. So I tried to calm him down by jabbing him a few rabbit punches right on his flabby arm. But he didn't like that one bit. In the end, I calmed him down by shouting him a couple of cans of the old Spesh Brew and sitting on a bench on the prom on main street with him. I did ask him if he wanted to come to the pub, but he kept muttering something about 'enclosed spaces' or shit like that.

So we sat on the prom and talked like old times. Well, I did. And we drank a couple of Spesh Brews together and we even had a bit of a laugh. After an hour or so of that I told him I had somewhere better to be, but I told him where I'd be that next day, and of course he never showed up.

So it went on like that for a while; the near-misses, the oh-so-closes, the 'he's just popped-outs.' And then I bumped into him again. Pure chance. Right outside his gaff, or where some fucker or other told me his gaff was. At first, like last time, he looked like he was shitting bricks. Tried to blend in with the wheelie bins or whatever. But I soon coaxed him out with booze.

'Why you scared of me?' I asked him.

And he went all sheepish white and that. Could hardly speak for a while.

And then he said something which, well, it fucked me over for a bit, to be honest with you. Daft fat bastard said that every time he'd seen me, and I mean *every* time, I'd not been alone. He said that there was another 'presence' – that's what he said presence – at my shoulder. Said it was a big dock-off feller, but that he smelled a lot, you know. And he also said that the smell was unmistakable. Told me that I'd had fucking you know who sat on my goddamn shoulder for the best part of six weeks.

Course I didn't know whether to laugh or cry.

I asked him: 'Is he there now?'

And Lion just nodded, all sheepish again and then said that he had to go back inside as he was expecting his social worker round at any time.

When Twinnie finished his story he was quiet for a long time. For a while, I wasn't sure whether he'd fallen asleep he was that quiet. There was no lighting up my cigarettes, no cruel laughter, no knives thrown. And I worried that I'd pushed him too far by making him tell me the story. I worried that the memories might mess with his head too much and stop me from achieving the next part of the plan.

I needn't have worried. Twinnie turned back over on the camp-bed eventually, looking, if anything more purple than ever and let out a revolting burp.

'I fancy some scran, Bulls-eye,' he said. 'Fancy cooking up some scran for us?'

And I knew beyond a doubt that he was all right, or as right as he'd ever be. The story he'd told could have been about anyone, I supposed. To him, it was just a story. He could always seem to put barriers in the way of him and whatever was worrying or threatening him. This was the essence of him. It was what made him what he was, for better or worse. When I was younger, I'd have termed the whole psychological mess of him as 'loose cannon'; now, I suppose, with the benefit of age, I suppose I pretty much accepted that it was in his nature to be so changeable, so divided. So hungry to make up for the part of him that he felt was missing since his twin brother died. And it was this that I hoped to play on if my plan was to pay off.

'What have we got in?' I asked.

Twinnie gestured over towards a couple of discarded rabbit carcasses in the corner; the remains of something bigger which was pretty much unidentifiable; dozens of empty crisp packets. I was struck, suddenly, by how much that corner of the room, behind his camp-bed, resembled the lair of some carnivorous beast. It was starting to smell like one. I wondered if Twinnie performed the cardinal sin of shitting where he ate.

'Told you rations were running low,' he said, by way of explanation, as though I was responsible for gnawing at the bones of the carcasses. I'd not eaten anything since... since... Well, I couldn't remember. But I supposed that nothing was better than eating the uncooked, unhygienic crap that Twinnie had shovelled down his cat's arse of a mouth. No wonder he never seemed to leave the confines of the farmhouse kitchen; he was probably too ill to do so.

I was reminded of watching a documentary once, about a bunch of eight or nine year old lads who'd been left to their own devices in a house for a week. It had taken them little over a day to turn feral; scavenging for food in bins and scrapping for scraps with their best friends of the day before. There was plenty of food in the cupboards, but the lads simply did not know what to do with it unless it was pre-packaged between two buns and came in burger form. They'd eschewed the vegetables in the tray in the fridge; chucking most of them out in fact so they could fit in more cans of fizzy pop.

Most had been unable to understand what a tin-opener was. And even if they had, they wouldn't have known what to do with the tins of chopped tomatoes, red kidney beans, sweet corn and the like. In the end, the documentary-makers had to suspend filming after four days, when one of the boys had attempted to stab another with a fork after being accused of stealing the last cheese straw. And the families had complained; said there would be a lasting impact on their sons. Probably, I reflected, the little fuckers would have forgotten the whole thing as soon as they walked through the door to their bedrooms and booted up the games console.

'We could order a takeaway,' I giggled.

'Fuck yeah,' said Twinnie.

'And if this is to be our last meal - our last supper – we should push the boat out. Go for something proper extravagant. I fancy a couple of nice juicy steaks. Some chips perhaps. Maybe a little bit of garnish, but no bloody peas.'

'Not just one steak, eh, soldier boy?' asked Twinnie, but not unkindly. He was playing along for once.

'Nah mate, I could eat a horse now,' I said.

Yeah, a horse in the national. The one with the number three on it; just like you, Twinnie. Just like you.

'Know what I'd have,' grinned Twinnie. 'Pizza. Pizza every time.'

We both laughed. Whenever we discussed food when we were younger, we'd always start talking about pizza. Generally this was in order to make Dick feel as bad as possible about his world-renowned pizza-face.

Laughing with Twinnie again, and I mean really laughing, with no... well, little hidden agenda felt good. It felt like coming home.

If that home was like the home for the nine year old boys...

'What would you really have? Honest to goodness if it *was* your last meal?' I asked.

'We did talk about it in the slammer once, me and Shuffty. I think it must have been around the time they fried this English boy on death row in some state in America. 'Member that, Gaz? Round that time everyone was talking like *what would you do if it was your last day,* or *who would you do – or do in- if you got one last chance.* Think I might've said good old Shepherd's Pie first time, but now, when we might... you know... one of us actually might... I'd go for Christmas Dinner. All the trimmings. Like we had when we were kids and we just ate and ate and ate.'

'Not sure about the trimmings, but there's gotta be some chickens or turkeys round here somewhere,' I said, trying to keep the tone light and chatty, 'up in one of the neighbouring farms or something. How's about you give me the shotgun for a while and I'll go on the hunt?'

Almost imperceptibly, the mood in the farmhouse kitchen changed. Twinnie edged along the camp-bed so his feet were blocking my view of the gun. But he still carried on like we were laughing and joking, like a minute ago.

'Some huntsman you gonna be on that gammy leg of yours, Bull,' he said.

'There's life in the old dog yet,' I answered.

Twinnie cocked his head to one side and regarded me carefully.

'Tells you what,' he said, 'I know I'm not feeling the best at the moment, but I reckon I'd still be better than you. Why don't you let me go out on the hunt and you go see if there's any vegetables out front in that garden of theirs?'

I waited for him to add *like a good little woman* but he didn't. This game was being played for high stakes now and both of us knew it. Thing is, Twinnie had absolutely no idea that he'd just stepped right into the trap that I'd laid for him. Hell, he couldn't have been more caught had he stepped on one of those old rusted metal things that he'd scattered around the kitchen.

I watched his stand to his feet. He did it gingerly, as though he was worried that his legs would give way beneath him. I caught the wince on his face before he hid it behind his customary sneer. He was in a bad way; we were all in a bad way now. Weak beyond all recognition, just waiting to be picked off by Tommy. But at least I wasn't number three, and that gave me some room for manoeuvre.

He walked to the door, trying to make it look like an easy stroll, but I could see that it was not. I also caught a faint whiff of something *off* about him as he walked past. He'd eaten things he shouldn't have been eating, had probably got food poisoning by now. Probably it was the best he could do not to shit himself right in front of me. Maybe that was why he always insisted on that purple sleeping back being nearby.

'Oh, Twinnie,' I said, as though it was an afterthought. 'Can I have my Zippo back? I'll get the gas cooker warmed up for when you get back...'

Twinnie wasn't sure, he wasn't sure at all, but he probably felt a more pressing need from his bowels and so he dug the lighter out from his pocket. He also tossed me a single Dorchester and Grey, for old time's sake.

'Don't say I never give you nothing,' he said, and walked out the door. I heard him whistling his way across the courtyard, but it wasn't an easy whistle. Half-howl, if truth be told.

I lit the fire off the dying embers of the Dorchester and Grey. I was almost sorry to see it go. It had been a good companion for the past few minutes. Thing with Dorchester and Greys is that they're Superking cigarettes, which means they are about a third longer than normal tabs. Some people call them 'lamppost cigarettes', or 'Dot Cotton snouts' because of their extra length and because they are primarily smoked by older women. Older women that have been smoking all their lives and who need that little bit extra from their ciggies.

Most people who smoke normal cigs, when confronted with a Dorchester and Grey will simply grind it out when they get as 'full' as they usually do on a normal length cig, leaving that extra third untouched. But I'm not most people; never have been. I always smoke them right down to the filter. Those last few drags never fail to burn the back of your throat.

And so with that satisfying sour taste on my tongue, I watched the small flames start to lick at my honorary discharge papers, and then some wood from the pile out in the barn. The old army ID card took a while to go up, but when it did, it kinda shrunk in on itself like when you throw an empty bag of crisps on the fire. When it finally disappeared, it went with a slight 'pop' which was a delight to my ears.

Soon, I had a decent fire going. The Zippo lighter fluid in my pack had helped of course, but I'd also thrown all kinds of stuff on there, some of which *must* have been flammable. Like the remainder of my small first aid kit and Twinnie's porno mag; a half-full tank of liquid which I found by the old farm truck which certainly *smelled* like red diesel but may have simply been home brew made by the mad farmer; some of the old blankets that had cocooned Dick in his final hours; the ornamental wheelbarrow. It was like a bonfire of the past; a kind of cleansing before Tommy got the chance to perform the real thing. It was the wiping out of our histories so that it seemed, we'd died at the same time as him. The saddest thing was that there was so little to burn. We'd done so little with the extra time we'd been had.

And in those flames I saw the faces of those that we would leave behind. Dick's children, content in their pushchair behind the counter of the main street café, being fed the occasional – don't tell mum – spoon of ice cream; Twinnie's dead twin who would finally be left in peace; Lion's grandmother who'd always struggled to contain the big brute and who could now shuffle off this mortal coil in her own time without having to think about what effect it would have on him. And then there was the face of Jane, which was framed by one of those daft mortar board things that they make you wear at university graduations; and dad, sipping on a pint of home brew down at the allotment, in front of a pristine clean wall. No graffiti no more; no wasted inheritance; no runaways in the army. One way or another, it was all going to come to a head, the flames agreed, and this would be the quickest, and most painless way of doing it for all concerned.

Staring into the fire kinda hypnotised me after a while. After a while, when I couldn't even see the outline of the toffeeworks in the gloom. Soon it seemed like Funnel's Fine Foods no longer existed at all, even. And all that was left were the massive shadows of the rolling hills and the faraway rush of the water as it passed down the falls in the gorge. Dad would have liked it up there with me now. I suppose just by being here, he might have understood a bit more about me.

The flames climbed higher. For a moment I feared that they'd started creeping too far over; that the barn would go up, and not the farmhouse, but no, everything stayed on course. The beacon had been lit.

'What the fuck is this?' screamed Twinnie as he rounded the corner. He had a sweat on him and had clearly been running. Must have seen the fire from a way off, which was pretty much the whole point of the thing.

He dropped two scrawny looking chickens onto the pathway and rushed at me, but I was ready for him and brought him down with the crutch. Which I then held tight against his purple chicken-neck.

'Now then Paul,' I roared. 'Why don't you chill out a little, eh?'

Twinnie struggled and kicked against me, trying to release himself from the choke-hold, but when they did for my leg in the army, it took nothing away from the strength in my arms. I'd felt it earlier, after he'd told me about what really happened at Grange Heights, and now I felt it again. I felt almost as though Tommy's strength was being added to mine and we were both grinding the gunmetal grey of the crutch into his sickening throat. He soon realised as much himself and raised both arms in the universal surrender gesture, barely able to speak.

Gradually, I released him from the grip of the crutch. He started coughing and spluttering. For a moment, I feared that I'd taken it too far, but eventually he rolled away and (I think) was sick in some of the garden's longer grass.

'What you do that for?' he gargled as he came crawling back. Purply slime and saliva covered his beard. I wanted to shield my eyes from him. Twinnie had to shield his own eyes from the fire, which was now starting to spit menacingly at us, having clearly swallowed something it shouldn't have, just as Twinnie had.

'The cooking stove was running out of gas,' I said, calmly. 'I thought we'd have a nice barbecue out here instead. What do you think?'

Twinnie spat out more of the saliva-vomit combo like some tramp that had drunk too much Mad Dog. There were tears in his eyes, but I didn't confuse them with the real thing. People often get teary-eyed when they are sick.

'I think you're crazy; why'd you build a bloody fire out here? It's like a sign to you know who saying *look where we are; yoo hoo, come and get us,*' he spat.

'You'd have preferred it out back or in the courtyard, Twinster?' I asked. 'Where he's already shown himself? Where he's already made off with Dick and he's come to pay me a visit?'

'But *round the front,* where the whole fucking town can see?' he cried.

'Let them see,' I said, tasting burning on my lips. I was too close to the flames but didn't want to move away. Didn't want to show any sign of sanity to him.

'I'm going back to the kitchen. I'll get some water. Put out these fucking flames,' he coughed. 'Before it's too late.'

But it was already too late. The fire was out of control now; already licking at the wooden beams on the roof of the farmhouse; already catching around the window frames and tickling at the barn at the side.

'Come on, Twinnie,' I said, still staring into the flames. 'Get the feathers off those chickens and we'll have fried chicken for dinner. Sorry it can't be Christmas Dinner, but I think the vegetable patch might have been underneath where I started the fire.'

Twinnie staggered away from me: 'You've finally gone off the fucking edge, Bully,' he spluttered. 'I think you've gone looney-tune. You're just like Dick and Lion were just before they were done in.'

Then Twinnie seemed to put two and two together. If Tommy had gone for the maddest of the bunch first – the bonafide nut-job Lion, who'd actually been housed in a looney bin more than once – and then the second craziest second, then, to him, it made sense that he'd go for the third craziest next. And that would be me. Suddenly, his mood seemed to brighten. He started to dance around me, prodding at me with his finger.

'Bu-lly; Number Three. Bu-lly; Number Three. Bu-lly; Number Three.'

And I let him do it. I let him prod his finger into my ribs and twist, like he'd once done with a pencil to Tommy, before we made him take his pants down in the dining hall; where we uncovered his embarrassing erection. And I grinned as he did it. I actively encouraged him, letting purple saliva of my own start to foam out of my mouth and down my chin; letting it drip down onto my t-shirt; letting it start to infect me. Because it didn't matter any more. None of it mattered any more. I'd made my choice between the two monsters and now the cavalry was coming. The cavalry was coming.

Chapter Eighteen

"Fire is the devil's only friend"

The cavalry did come. And they came bearing pitchforks and wielding baseball bats, although where they could have purchased these in a place like Newton Mills was beyond me. They came carrying burning torches, although the point of bringing more fire to a place that was already burning out of control was also beyond me. They came yelling and chanting songs of death. They'd come for Twinnie, who they believed was responsible for the bad spell of events that was erupting in town like a burst sewer pipe. And I'd just shown them exactly where he was.

They moved en masse up the slope at a constant pace. I heard once, probably in some army morale boosting exercise or other, that the wisdom of the crowd always beats the wisdom of the individual. They backed up their research with some half-baked statistics, and everyone knows that 109% of all statistics are completely and utterly made up, like most of my memories probably. But in watching that crowd moving so purposefully up that hill with the common goal of they weren't exactly sure what, and with the overall plan of... um, ask me another one, I can honestly say I believed in the blind stupidity of the crowd.

How many times have you joined a queue even though you didn't even know what you were queuing for? How many times have you seen people grouped in some identikit city centre somewhere and simply gone over to watch whatever mad religious freak was on show there just because everyone else was rubber-necking.

Approximately twenty percent of the crowd that stamped up to the burning of Summit Farm that day probably actually thought they were going to attend a barbecue, despite the fact that it was *actually very late for a barbecue, Maurice, and don't play that music too loud.* I reckoned about another twenty percent had joined in because their friends had.

Miss, miss I did it because she did it.

Would you jump off a cliff of she did?

Well yes actually, miss. Most people *are* like lemmings; you're a lemming yourself simply for coming out with such a cliché.

Okay, so we're up to forty percent of that crowd, that had now reached the dry stone wall by the way, having absolutely no clue what they were doing there. Let's start picking on individuals now; take that man in the luminous yellow fleece that was just then trying a novel approach to climbing the wall; by trying to shuffle up and over it on his balloon-like belly, like a sea-lion on land. What did he really think he was doing that evening? A nature walk? If not, why the binoculars?

But I digress. Perhaps the smoke was starting to get to me just as Twinnie suspected it had. But I didn't care. As the baying mob stamped and stomped closer they must have picked me out, madly half-limping, half-dancing around the fire singing one particular bit from Don McLean's *American Pie* over and over again.

"Oh, and there we were all in one place,

A generation lost in space

With no time left to start again.

So come on: jack be nimble, jack be quick!

Jack flash sat on a candlestick

'Cause fire is the devil's only friend."

They probably wouldn't have seen Twinnie; he was hunkered down under a collapsed piece of garden furniture; a tea-for-two I believed they were called. He'd been there ever since he'd first laid eyes on them. Perhaps he thought Tommy had opened up the gates of hell and these were all of the tormented souls come to claim him as one of their own, and in a way, he might have been right. He may have hit the coffin nail square on the head with that assertion.

Only when the slavering zombies reached the thin white fence which surrounded the farmhouse garden from the fields did they stop as though by unspoken command. Some planted their flaming torches in the ground and looked as though they were up for a siege; others tried to douse the flames of their own torches in the wet long grass. Perhaps these people finally realised the stupidity of bringing coals to Newcastle. It *did* stop me dancing though.

I stared them down; individually, by the light of the fire, the folk of Newton Mills seemed to glow with greens and yellows and reds, but blended together it simply became a mass of purple being poured forward, colouring everything in its wake. I waited for one of them to step forward. One of them to make a claim to be their leader. In the meantime, I listened to the fire crackling and roaring and otherwise having a whale of a time and I smiled to myself. It was getting closer and closer to the time. It was getting closer and closer to the realisation of the plan. I just hoped Tommy was reading from the same script as me. But then, he didn't need a script did he? Not when he could read my mind…

'Do you realise that you are trespassing?' bellowed a man from the middle of the crowd. He had safety in numbers there.

I laughed at his question.

'Do *you* realise that there is a farmhouse on fire?' I shouted back.

'Have you tried to put it out?' shouted a small woman at the front. 'It looks pretty dangerous, you should be…'

The rest of her politely concerned question was drowned out by dissent in the ranks. The people were getting braver; their old wise heads decided that it was time to be brave. Luckily, their combined wisdom hadn't seen fit to call the fire brigade yet, much like when the school burned down and everyone just stood and watched, open-mouthed as classroom after classroom was engulfed.

One man decided to speak for all of them. I didn't know him; no doubt my dad did though. He knew everyone; couldn't go to one shop in town for a bastard toilet roll without having at least three half-hour conversations with people he knew. By which time he'd probably have shat his kecks.

'We know who you are,' the man said. 'We know who both of you are… Where is the other one?'

I simply stared back at the fat, bearded man. I just had to keep them talking for long enough and Tommy would come.

'Look,' shouted the man. 'We know you've had a hard time of it, son, but you can't just go round setting fire to things. That's arson you know.'

'Sorry Pavarotti,' I yelled back. And I swear that a couple of the crowd had to stifle their sniggers.

'Is there a working tap in the kitchen that we can get water from?' he asked. 'Is there still a kitchen we can go in? This farmhouse was a listed building, you know, and we don't want to see it wiped off the map, son.'

The whole scene was rapidly descending into farce. Tommy probably hadn't shown his face yet because he was probably laughing too much. This was what he'd left behind. This is what he'd clawed and scrambled to try and get back into. What a fucking laugh.

But I wasn't laughing any more; Pavarotti started to move over the fence. A couple of the other men followed; handy-looking men, probably just been poured out of the pub. They were bringing weapons. I watched them moving forward, aping the army moves that they'd seen in countless movies no doubt. One of them was going to shout something stupid like 'cover me' in a minute.

'You're not gonna be any trouble are you, lad?' asked the meatiest of the men. I wasn't wrong about him being lured from the pub, only he'd probably been lured from the *outside* of the pub. He looked like a bouncer and he looked like he wanted nothing more than to have a bit of fisticuffs with me. He was probably one of those types that have been rejected from the army young and then spend the rest of their lives working out, cursing the forces under every breath, and trying to pick fights with squaddies on leave at the weekend. He'd seen my khaki t-shirt, the obvious army pants and boots and he wanted a piece of me.

I started to back away a little. Started to have my first quiver of doubt that Tommy would come. But I felt the fire at my back and knew I couldn't go any further. I was trapped. From under the garden furniture, Twinnie would have been loving this lunacy. The obvious number three that was probably burned into my flesh on my chest at that very moment. Maybe Tommy had been playing me all along?

The pub bouncer must have been five paces away from me at most when he abruptly stopped. Certainly he was close enough so I could smell his angry sweat and the cologne he'd tried to mask it with. Certainly I could hear his muscles crinkling and cracking back into place over and above the fire. Certainly I could see the way that his eyes suddenly became like flying saucers. How his mouth dropped open and a piece of chewing gum slipped out and dropped onto his black bomber jacket, where no doubt it would stick and be a nightmare to get out.

It was as though I was stuck in a freeze-frame. Pavarotti had one leg still up in the air, mid-stride; the other big man had his arms up, covering his face as though he feared he was going to be hit by something. It was only then that I decided that I should probably look round...

...to see Tommy Peaker. Undoubtedly Tommy Peaker, despite the black balaclava covering his half-face and the black gloves covering his rotten hands. And he was massive. At least eight foot tall; it was as though being so close to something which so closely resembled hell's burning fires gave him extra power. He was wearing a black leather jacket now which fair strained to keep his burgeoning biceps in check. It looked as though at any moment, his revolting body might break free, like the Incredible Hulk.

Somewhere, someone screamed. Somewhere else, someone yelled 'no'. But Tommy only laughed. He was being a showman for only the second time in his life. And just like that time he got the attendance certificate in assembly, he milked it for all it was worth. He lifted the huge barrel of petroleum above his head just like he had with that certificate; just like it was the FA Cup. Like it weighed nothing to him. And with those arms, you could see why.

He paused a moment and stared back right into the crowd. Hatred burned in his eyes, but something else too; vindication perhaps. And then he brought the barrel crashing down right into the middle of the fire. Flames leaped up all over him. For a moment we could hardly see him, but eventually the black figure emerged again, his leather jacket looking virtually untouched. All around him, flames crawled all over everywhere. The barn became a raging inferno; the farmhouse simply collapsed in on itself like a packet of crisps or my ID badge. When it finally gave up the ghost, it did so with a 'pop'.

Something exploded over in the courtyard. Probably the farm vehicle, whatever it was. And then the Newton Millsians were running. Full pelt down the field; trampling over the bodies of their neighbours and relatives; children and wives. There was no such thing as the crowd mentality any more; it was every man, woman and child for himself.

I felt myself being overwhelmed by the fire. And I welcomed it. It felt toasty and *right.* Tommy let me know that it was right. His laugh rang out over and above it all. At one point, I swear I could hear him singing, too, as if in answer to my previous verse when I was dancing round the fire:

"And as the flames climbed high into the night
To light the sacrificial rite,
I saw Satan laughing with delight
The   day   the   music   died."

Chapter Nineteen

"Helter skelter"

Apart from the past month or so, the only other period in my life in which I can remember passing out and waking up in various random places more would be in the height of my teenage years; in the height of the 'head loss period', as I'd come to know it. But perhaps the 'head loss period' never really went away. Perhaps it was just me that did, and now I was back, clutched to the corpse-like bosom of Newton Mills; I was forever a teenager. Certainly Tommy Peaker was, and part of me had ceased to be completely piss-myself afraid of him, despite his immense new size and despite that new voice of his.

The fact remained that the more time I spent with him, the more even this incarnation of Tommy reminded me of a fourteen year old, which he was, when you got down to the bare bones of it. As soon as he sensed me stirring, he was on me; rabbit punching me on the shoulders, shrieking into my ears, blowing smoke rings into my face.

To be fair to Tommy, I don't think he *meant* to blow the smoke rings. I don't think he was showing off or acting the alpha male like Twinnie had been. He couldn't help it really, what with the massive gouge in his neck which was painfully apparent now we were out in the open and it was morning. I couldn't take my eyes off the hole. Smoke was trailing out of it – he couldn't have been properly taking any of it in – and around it, dark, slippery mould was growing. At first I'd thought it the first spoutings of a typical teenage bum-fluff beard, but now I could see it for what it really was; just another part of him festering away.

'*Rise and shine, fuckwit,*' he said, finally climbing off me and allowing me to breathe. The more he used that voice, the more I was struck by the fact that it sounded like a fourteen year old boy, using one of those special voice disguiser things. I don't know how to explain it, but it was just the *way* that he said things... As though he was mimicking a bad-guy from an action film he'd seen once. Part of me believed that when he left hell, or wherever he'd been, he'd probably been given a choice how he could come back, and had picked that voice to match his new tree-trunk torso. An off-the-shelf *scare the living shit out of someone* costume, with all the accessories to match.

'Where are we?' I breathed, or tried not to breathe. The stench of him was overwhelming now, even in the outdoors. It smelled as though something had crawled inside him and died, which I suppose it had.

Tommy laughed. '*Have you not worked that out yet, Bully-boy?*'

And for the first time, I allowed myself to take my eyes off him. We were sitting – well, Tommy was; I was lying in a foetal position – on a grassy knoll which looked out over a graveyard that I knew very well. It was one of the places that we used to come and smoke and drink and eventually fuck girls, and generally raise hell. Like many of the graveyards in the town, there was no church attached – Newton Mills folk don't generally go in for that sort of thing – but it was unmistakably the graveyard from my memories because of the imposing gates. Big wrought iron things with what was supposed to be angels on the top, although they actually looked more like devils, or gargoyles.

The whole place was overgrown; nature was reclaiming it as its own. Long grass strained through the gates to grab for the legs of passers-by; small trees were erupting from some of the graves; in some places you couldn't even see the graves at all any more. But strangely, despite all of the trees which flanked the old bone-yard, and the fact that it was day-break, there was absolutely no sound of birds welcoming the dawn. In fact, there was no sound of anything at all, save Tommy's raspy breathing, and the staccato drumbeat of my own heart. It was as though the place was a vacuum, removed from everyday reality somehow.

'I know this place,' I whispered. 'It looks...'

Of course I remembered the place; it was the Cutter Street graveyard, not far from my house on Hangman's Row. And the fact that the graveyard had long been concreted over was not the most remarkable aspect of the place must have said something about the strangeness of the situation I now found myself in. Because those of the graves that still could be seen through all the undergrowth and bush were open, as though they'd just been dug by some council lackey keen to earn some overtime, and they were just waiting for the bodies to fill them. There were scores of them; long rectangular channels in the ground, and from the looks of things, they were empty. There was nothing as comforting as fresh flowers by any of the graves.

'What. The. Fuck?' I spluttered, or asked, or pleaded.

Tommy slapped me on the back.

'Good, isn't it?' he said. *'Very... Apt.'*

'Wonderful,' I said. Despite the fact that I'd been passed out for the past God knows how long, I suddenly felt immensely tired. I couldn't remember the last time I'd eaten and my foot felt as though it was being amputated all over again. And now I was at the decisive moment, that moment when I could plead for my life or change my life or at least try to make everything better, I just couldn't summon up the energy to argue with any of it. All I wanted was for it to be over with. I was like one of those mountaineers that spends their whole lives planning to conquer some unconquerable peak; spends their whole pension on flying out to whatever far flung place that peak may be in; spends all their available determination on actually reaching the top and then... And then when they reach the top they just have a look out over the rooftops of the world, maybe pose for a photo and plaster a fake smile on their face, and all they can think of is getting back down again. *Getting it over with.*

'I know what you mean,' said Tommy. *'You feel like you've had more than you can take. You feel like you just don't care any more. But that's how I felt every day of my miserable fucking existence. And that's why I wanted to make you go through all of this.'*

'But I get the point,' I moaned. 'I realise that we did something terrible. I realise that we had to be punished.'

'Sure, sure; you get the point,' sneered Tommy. I tried not to look at what he was doing with his neck while he spoke. He was always a-fidgeting - always chewing at his nails or at the skin around the nails - but now he was picking bits from around the gaping hole in his neck and popping them into his slavering maw like they were popcorn and we were sitting back and watching his favourite film of all time.

I sighed, tried to massage my half-foot back into life. It was numb from the way I'd slept; wrecked like a...

WHAM!

Tommy's fist caught me completely by surprise. Left me keeling over, coughing up whatever was left in my gut; my courage, perhaps. I tried to control my breathing. Tried to ignore the fact that it felt like the right hand side of my face was about to fall off.

'We're not on one of our school trips now,' said Tommy, standing over me. *'We're not on some joy-ride that you can just pick and choose when to get off. This is my world now.'*

He picked up the spear - the spear from the C.U.M building; the spear from Burt's flat; the spear from my heart – and started to trace the point against my chest. Traced a number four on me, but didn't commit. Didn't drive the spear *into* my flesh.

'You want to know why you're the last one, don't you?' he demanded.

At that particular moment, knowing why I was the last one was the furthest thing from my mind. Now the pain in my heart had come back. My heart felt like it was about to explode. It was as though it was reminding me that it was still there after all I'd said about it; all I'd inferred about there just being a black hole in there.

Tommy knelt by my side and started stroking my hair. In a way, it was far more disturbing than when he'd had the spear poking into my chest again, giving me that invisible tattoo of a number four.

'Some part of you wants to know what happened to your friend Twinnie, doesn't it?' he continued. *'Tell you what; why don't we go take a look at him now?'*

Somehow, I don't think I had a choice in the matter. And that was soon made abundantly clear when Tommy grasped me by the collar and started dragging me off the grassy knoll, down towards the open graves. I felt my half-foot bang and crack against every hidden broken bottle, brick, stone and bramble underneath that long grass.

Tommy barely decreased his pace when we reached the bottom of the slope, and for a second I thought he was going to drag me right on into one of the open graves. Instead, he left me dangling over the lip, on my back, screaming in agony.

'Bully; meet Twinnie,' he said, gesturing into the open grave.

And I looked. I knew that I shouldn't have looked but I did. I couldn't help myself. Some deep-down part of me *wanted* to see what had happened to the other monster in my life. Some deep-down part of me wanted to know that Twinnie had gone and would never be coming back.

I don't know if you've ever heard about what happened at Pompeii; chances are that you have. But it was only when we were doing our pre-op training in Southern Italy that I found out all about it. Mount Vesuvius; the volcano. The eruption. The fleeing Pompeii citizens trying to outrun time and fate and geological fact and then being caught by the lava and preserved in mid-stride, mid-prayer, mid-scream *forever.* Turned to stone, over time. The piss-artist previously known as Twinnie was just like one of them. In half-crouch, a look of sheer agony on his pinched face. His hands splayed out as though trying to stop the fire from overwhelming him. It looked strangely unreal, or as though a single gust of wind would dismantle all of the dusty particles which now made him up. But then, I figured, there probably wouldn't be any wind. Not here, not in Tommy's world.

And the most horrifying thing of all was the fact that Tommy had now leaped into the grave next to this human statue and was using the spear as a kind of rudimentary chisel with which he could carve the number three, like he was a professional sculptor or something.

'What happened to him?' I gasped.

Tommy looked up from his work, hand still hovering over Twinnie's chest, ready to make the final incision.

'I thought you didn't want to know? I thought you just wanted this over with?'

I clutched my head in my hands and started to rock back and forth.

'I don't know, I don't know,' I wailed, as though I was offering up some primitive prayer to some primitive deity; good or bad, I didn't know. Didn't care.

Twinnie was the easiest of the lot. So far. He'd always had a death-wish. He was broken-up inside. Always thought that there was something better going on somewhere else, somewhere where he was not; where his dead twin brother was. Twinnie lived like he wanted to make everyone else in the world feel the way he did; lonely, abandoned and lost.

It was his lifelong ambition to find somebody that he could be as close to as he remembered that he was with his brother in the first year of his life. But the ironic thing was that he never let anyone get close enough to him anyway. He always fought people off; either through fists or through verbal cruelty or through sheer ignorance. I don't know...

You probably don't know this, but during the last year I was alive, I used to go round and stay at Twinnie's house nearly every night. Sometimes he used to beg and plead me to go round. And when I did, I'd take the top bunk, he'd take the bottom and we'd talk all night. It was like he couldn't stop sometimes. And I'd sit, with my legs dangling over the edge of the bunk, and it felt like I was sitting on his shoulder.

Of course, he didn't want any of you lot knowing about the fact he always needed people around him, or how he'd cry out in the night, so he swore me to secrecy, the poor deluded fucker. And after a while, he came to rely on me being there. And he hated the fact that he relied upon someone like me. Sometimes when I got there, he'd punch me in the face, just so I knew where I stood.

He spent all his life with a heart of stone so I turned the whole of him into stone. Apt, don't you think? At the end, up at Summit Farm, he denied me again. He'd been denying me for years although I'd sat on his shoulder almost the whole time, even after I was killed. But eventually I realised I'd been wasting my time with him, when you should have been the one that I was speaking to. It was you that I had unfinished business with...

That fire turned him to stone because he'd purpled more than any other person that Newton Mills has ever known. That fire, Bully; have you not wondered why you have no discernible scar tissue from it? No burns? I'm not the monster that you think I am. Nobody else in that crowd got remotely hurt, you know. It was an illusion, just like so many things have been. Only, it was a chemical illusion – an illusion in space and time - and that just happened to react with Twinnie's particular chemical make-up. In essence, he self-destructed, just like the others...

Dick hung himself from those rafters at Funnels toffeeworks no matter what you might think. He was so determined for a fix that when I told him the Strawberry Skull mix was laced with the brown stuff, he couldn't help himself. And he was sooooo disappointed, so hopeless, that he couldn't stop himself. He just gave up. Just like the rest of you have. Some value you lot put on life, eh?

Lion? He was always fleeing the scene wasn't he? Always diving away from the chaos when it all got too much for him... And so he dived into the gorge. I had nothing to do with it. Not really...

Tommy put the finishing touches on the number three on his masterpiece statue and the finishing touches on his story. I'd examined pretty much every part of bare skin on my body while he'd been speaking and could find no burns. The only scar I found was the one on my arm. The one from my flight from Grange Heights, and not from falling off my bike on the cobbles, as I'd previously thought.

'I'm not lying to you, Bully,' said Tommy, wiping the sweat from his brow, as well as some flesh, I noticed. Evidently carving into a statue was not as easy as it looked.

'But Dick wouldn't have… couldn't have…'

'You'll discover reserves of strength that you never knew you had, Bully. When your time comes.'

'I tried to tell the police,' I breathed. 'Afterwards…'

'But you didn't, Bully. And you were the only one amongst them that had any decency at all. After you fell up at Grange Heights, you just became like someone else.'

'Grange Heights... you were there?'

'I've always been there. In a way. Or I suppose that you could say that looking back, I've always been there. I suppose I'm your guilt, Bully. That's who I am at the end of the day, and that's why I looked different when I appeared to each of the others. Lion saw me as I actually was. Under every bench, every streetlight, every bar, he saw the fourteen year old Tommy Peaker. Twinnie saw me – eventually – as a tiny little devil on his shoulder. Dick saw me as the endless thirst that he had to quench with drugs. You see me as a nine foot tall monster, don't you?

'Eight...' I stammered, but then Tommy hop-skip-an-a-jumped out of the grave and I saw that he was clearly nine foot now. And growing all the time.

Tommy winked at me when he saw that I'd put two and two together. Unfortunately, the effect of this was somewhat lessened when his bottom eyelid fell off and then his left eyeball started hanging by a veiny thread. As though embarrassed by his appearance he tried to pop it back in, but seemed to struggle a little. When he looked back at me he seemed a little sheepish for a moment, just like that time when we'd pulled his kecks down in the dining hall and revealed his erect penis.

'Oops,' he laughed. *'I'm falling apart a bit here, Bully. But not as much as you are eh? Your mind's all over the shop now, isn't it?'*

'Are you saying this is all in my imagination?' I gasped.

'Not at all, not at all,' said Tommy. *'But what used to be your imagination is now a graveyard of broken dreams and memories that don't compute. That make any sense to you, eh?'*

I shook my head.

'Think about it like this,' said Tommy. *'Let's say I've dragged you back and forth in time over the past few months. Made you a bit confused about what's happening and what's not... Well just think about how it's been for me for the past twelve years. That's how I've lived, Bully. Or died, you might say... I've been constantly*

remembering things but I've not had anyone around to confirm if it was true or not. Thought I was going mad, Bulls-eye...

Dreaming, waking, dying, it all became one to me, so it felt sometimes that I'd never lived at all.

Did you never wonder why all your memories seemed so mixed-together? How you couldn't pinpoint when one ran into another? Where you really were, all this time?'

'I don't understand,' I muttered.

'Here's an example for you: remember your friend Do-Nowt from the military hospital? Sure he was there. But he was never there at the same time as you... That's why you thought he just disappeared. But I had no beef with Do-Nowt; never touched a hair on his Yorkie head. It just so happened that you were there a long, long time after the place was deserted. Just you never really knew that...'

'Is... is... Do-Nowt really okay?' I stammered. The illusion that I'd spoken to him had felt so real... The pain when he'd been taken from me had been so real. Why was this happening to me?

'He's okay, right?' I cried, looking for further confirmation.

Tommy shot me a frosty look: *'Of course he is. But keep your voice down. Here's something else: that fire at Summit Farm that I've only just pulled you out of? That happened way back when you were seventeen, eighteen. I'm afraid I've been playing with your lives... all of your lives... ever since you stepped into that C.U.M building and I saw that I had to act. I couldn't have no desert-folk taking you for their revenge when I wanted you for mine!'*

I remembered something: 'My dad told me something about Burt having been dead for about ten years or something... but it really felt like I was with him the other night... In his flat.'

'Course it would. Because you were there. It's just that you weren't there when you thought you were there, if you know what I mean? Most likely, you and Dick broke in there on one of your 'head-loss phases' back in the day... Spoke to the old loon then... Memory has a funny way of playing tricks with you like that.'

'So what now?' I asked. It wasn't the uppermost question in my mind, but it would do. It would do.

'Now, Bully, I'd like to take you on a tour of a few of the other graves. Just to give you the heads-up on what I've got planned for my little memorial garden here... Hey, here's a thought; bent down like that, we could almost turn your mate Twinnie into a seat for the elderly when their poor feet get too tired of wandering round admiring the sights. What do you reckon?'

I kept my mouth clamped shut.

'Wanna see some more of my garden?'

'I don't think I really want to see any more...'

Tommy grabbed my t-shirt collar, started dragging me along the first row of graves.

'Now this one, of course, is for our old pal Dick. And I was sorely tempted to have my grave-digger dig it out in the sign of a massive dick, just like the ones he used to force me to draw on the blackboards before the teacher walked in, every lesson. I got chucked out every time, didn't I? No wonder I never learned anything. No wonder I never had the sense to stop hanging around with dead wood like you.'

Dick's grave was as yet unoccupied, but inside I could see that some of the traps from the Summit farmhouse were already being put to good use.

'Just in case something happens to him like it did to me,' winked Tommy.

And we moved on. I could already see the massive headstone hanging above the next grave, as though it was readying itself to jump in. Already knew it was being prepared for Lion.

'Just need to wait for the Newton Mills coppers to release their bodies and then I'll take custody of them both,' he said. *'And I'm sure you'll agree, they are very, very valuable additions to my collection. Sure they don't have the shock-value of a Twinnie, but they'll be worth a lot in their own right in a few years mark my words.'*

It struck me that Tommy was starting to sound like some rare art collector, and certainly the 'frames' that he'd made in which to hang his works were impressive. The graves looked... distinguished. Much better than the graves I remembered in the Cutter Street

Cemetery; graves which hadn't been tended, let alone visited for over a century.

'And now we move on to exhibit "d". I know what you're thinking, Bully, but this one really isn't for you. As I'm sure you'll eventually hear, through the graveyard telegraph or somesuch; this one's for Mr. Swann. Remember him? Nice feller, but had no idea, or no gumption how to tackle the very real problem of bullying at Newton Mills School. I'm sure you remember the time at the dinner hall? When you and your friend Twinnie sexually abused me? Well, I found him complicit in that crime and I decided that Gerald Swann, of 24 Turner Street, should also join us here.

Right about now, his friends will be waking up in his house. They had a heavy night last night, although they can't remember why – they only thought they had a couple of pints... Anyway, pretty soon, one of them will wake up busting for the toilet. They'll go in Gerald Swann's bathroom and they'll find him dead in the bathtub. Of course, it'll look as though he's drowned, but there'll always be that nagging doubt. You see they won't find any water in the bath, and when they check a little bit more, they'll discover that the water was turned off about two days ago. You see Gerald Swann was drowning in his own ignorance all of his life. He couldn't even see the misery that people like you were inflicting on people like me. Couldn't see the wood for the trees... And what a nice, apt way for him to go, eh?

When he plunged his head under that imaginary water it was one of the funniest things I've ever seen... Oh, I would have taken you to see it too, only you were passed out up there on that grassy knoll. You miss a lot being passed out, don't you Bully? It's almost like you're burying your head in the sand...'

I had the sudden feeling that Tommy was trying to tell me something, but to be honest, it was so hard to think when my head was banging off old, decrepit gravestones; the ones that had been moved out of the way to make room for Tommy's new 'garden' that in the end, my only concern was trying to make sure that I blocked out what was happening to me as best I could.

'*This next one's one of my particular favourites,*' continued Tommy, approaching the last grave on the first row. '*In fact, it's such a favourite that I'm going to save it til right at the end.*'

My grave. I was looking headlong into my own grave. And for some reason I couldn't take my eyes off a worm that was nonchalantly crawling across the bottom of it. All I could think was that the poor worm was going to be my company in there for whatever remained of my life… and what came after of course.

'*A very spacious grave, don't you think; for a terrace? And sure, the décor needs a bit of work, but with a healthy attitude, the occupant could give this place the real King's treatment. The Kingsman's treatment… The square-footage is also good for the sell-on value; out here, death-space sells by the foot, you know, Bully? Quite funny that, isn't it, after what happened to your foot?*'

I didn't laugh. Neither did Tommy for once.

'*Okay… bad joke. But back to more pressing matters; do you know who the ideal occupant of this particular death-space would be? A retiree. Someone that really doesn't care whether they have a room with a view any more. Someone that doesn't ever really have any visitors, and so doesn't need the extra space. Someone that takes pride in digging in the ground and in having dirt underneath their fingernails when they get home…*

Someone that just needs a bed in which to rest his head and a few friendly neighbours like Gerald Swann, Twinnie and Dick to look in on him every once in a while. Of course, he wouldn't really like it if any of these visitors asked him for a coffee or washed up in his sink. And he certainly wouldn't like it if that visitor started trying to talk about very serious things.

I tell you what, Bully; let's call it an old folk's home. And do you know who my very first resident will be?'

At first I couldn't bring myself to even say his name. At first I *didn't* want to say his name in front of Tommy. But it was already clear that Tommy knew everything it was possible to know about my old dad. And it was clear that this was going to be how the final game was played out. This was what Tommy had been keeping me alive for all this time. So I would know what real, raw pain felt like. And how that pain can somehow feel even worse when it is inflicted on someone other than yourself. Someone who you care about more than life itself.

My life, my world, had been collapsing in on itself like an empty packet of crisps in a fire. And now, finally, it imploded with an audible 'pop'. All of the seasons I'd ever experienced; all of the conversations I'd overheard; all of the spinning plates which made up my life suddenly spun into each other. Newton Mills as it was, is, and will be engulfed me. Things I'd done, secretly hoped for, and tried to deny swished around my face like branches from some overhanging pussy willow. The steady drip-drop of water torture memories became a full on torrent which spewed me out somewhere, I hardly knew when.

I was a-time-travellin' man, and the whole goddamn thing was giving me the worst kind of jetlag ever. I'd finally fallen off that precipice; madness raced up at me, ready to crack me on the jaw.

Chapter Twenty

"A long, long time ago...
I can still remember"

Autumn always made Newton Mills look a bit dishevelled. Maybe it was because when the leaves were on the trees, it went some way to hiding the run-down nature of the town. In autumn, it had nowhere left to hide. The school in particular looked like some kind of shanty town from a documentary about South America that we'd watched in Geography; none of the buildings seemed to match. There were the prefabricated buildings running down the hill which the teachers euphemistically called the terrapins; next to them was the brand spanking new metal and concrete leisure centre which had to be built after local goodfornothings burned down the old one (I remember cheering and dancing in the flames but didn't start it, all right?); then there was the main block of the school, the old posh grammar school bit with the domed roof on the library and the sweeping driveway out the front.

The four of us had bored of terrorising the new first year students and had retired onto the fields down below the terrapins where we could listen to some tunes on this little radio we'd found in one of the ruck-sacks that we'd ransacked outside the assembly hall. And we could maybe light a cheeky cig if none of the teachers happened down that way. In the main, hardly any of them did; they all got in their cars at the end of lessons and drove to the end of the road where they could have their own cigarettes in peace and not be pestered by the over-enthusiastic head-teacher for smoking on school property. Mr. Swann was a particularly bad one for that kind of thing; always sloping off when there was work to be done. Always ignoring what was going on around him as though he couldn't hear or couldn't see. It was like he was encased in some kind of fish bowl which he couldn't be bothered to look out of.

We were playing this new game we'd invented called 'raps'. Raps used to be used as a punishment in card games - you were supposed to gather the whole deck together and lightly rap the knuckle of the opposing player - but we'd soon grown bored of the actual games and moved on to pure torture instead. Just taking it in turns to hit each other and hurt each other for no other reason than that we were bored. Bored of school, bored of lunch-times, bored of Newton Mills. Twinnie in particular had the fine art of getting a whole deck of cards into a sharp point which would break the skin on first contact. He'd already drawn a fair amount of blood from Lion's hand and was now getting ready for his final shot. He narrowed his beady eyes and pursed his lips in anticipation. Although much the bigger lad, Lion looked very worried…

'I'm sure you've already had your three goes,' he pleaded. I noticed that his right eye was twitching a little bit as though he was close to crying. His big face was getting redder by the minute and his freckles seemed to be twinkling like shitty stars.

'*Two* goes,' said Twinnie, flicking through the cards, seemingly injecting them with some kind of static charge. 'This is the last one. Then you get to have a go at me.'

Twinnie wasn't worried about the reprise attack from Lion; Lion's hand was knackered now and would be no good for getting the cards nice and tightly packed and ready to hurt.

The artist formerly known as Paul Morton stuck his tongue out of his cat's-arse mouth in concentration as he made his own final preparations and then lifted his hand with the deck of cards in it into the air. This was where Twinnie's true skill for the game came into play. He made the opponent wait. He made the opponent imagine the pain in his head *waaaaaaay* before the actual hit, so in fact the hit was at least twice as bad as it ever would have been. My eyes darted to Lion, whose own eyes were pleading. His clenched fist trembled. He looked as though he was going to surrender. He was going to hand the game to...

'Wait!' shouted Dick. 'Not yet.'

Twinnie sighed deeply, dropped the cards onto the grass and turned to Dick. Lion took the opportunity to withdraw his battered hand and shove it into his armpit to alleviate the throbbing. We heard the tinny echoes of Don McLean's 'American Pie' from the stolen radio in his jacket pocket.

'That little shithouse Tommy Peaker's coming,' continued Dick, nodding his shaven head up the hill. We all turned to look. Tommy Peaker was indeed snowballing down the hill on legs which were whirring like tiny wheels in a cartoon.

'Look at the state of the little twat,' sneered Twinnie. He, more than any of the others, made no secret of his hatred for the hangers-on that we attracted. I suppose that it had maybe something to do with the loss of his twin but he never seemed to trust anyone but the three of us, and even that, I thought, was a kind of trust for convenience's sake while we wasted five years at upper school and before we could go and do our dad's jobs in the factories.

'Little bell-end,' said Dick. He was always one for following Twinnie was Dick. Maybe he wanted to be second in command or something. Not that Twinnie was the leader either, just that he liked to think of himself as such.

We all climbed to our feet and waited for Tommy to come to us. Poor bastard was almost slipping in the mud off the path now but none of us stood forward to lend him a helping hand. And even if he had have slipped, it couldn't have made his clothes look any worse. Our school didn't have a proper uniform but 'encouraged' students to wear white shirts and black trousers; Tommy's get-up was what looked like his mam's cast-off white blouse and black leggings of some description. There were whopping great tears at the knees, I already knew. On his feet, he wore black PE pumps like we used to wear at primary school. We, of course, were all decked out in the latest Nike trainers with the pump-up cushioned soles. We'd managed to stab compasses into the air bubbles on the trainers of nearly every other no-mark in the school that dared wear them.

Tommy arrived at last, gasping and panting for breath. He sort of bowed to us, he was that bent over from the effort of running so fast. Don McLean started singing about 'bad news on the doorstep.'

'What you wanting, Squeaker?' asked Lion, towering over him like some giant troll or something. We called Tommy 'Squeaker', because that was our rather juvenile name for a fart, and that was what Tommy was; a little fart.

'Had another wank you wanna tell us about, eh?' Lion continued, wrinkling his nose as though sniffing the air around the little lad. I had to bite back a bout of the giggles.

Tommy shook his head and looked embarrassed. He'd once tried to ingratiate himself with us lot by telling us all that he masturbated a lot, and I mean a lot. He bragged that he could do it twelve times in a day. But after he'd told us that we noticed that this weird fishy smell always clung to Tommy and so we all figured that he just left the discharge seeping into his black leggings and underpants that his mam would never wash.

'Tell us what you're here for then you little fuck-wit,' said Twinnie, who looked as though he'd already run out of patience and looked likely to clock him at any given moment.

'Come on Tommy, what's to do?' I said, mockingly putting my arm around him and then scraping my knuckles across the top of his hair – it *wrecks* that, if you do it right. I let him go when I realised that he still hadn't even told us why he'd been running.

On the radio, Don McLean sang 'dirges in the dark' and finally Tommy got his breath back, finally he recovered from my knuckle-dusting. He moved in closer to us, a little smile playing on the corners of his lips. I figured that he had some pretty good information on him for him to be acting so conspiratorial around us. Maybe he thought that with the information he was about to impart, he'd move higher up the ladder or something. Not that there was a ladder. Not that we wouldn't kick it away once he was climbing it...

'You've gotta come with me. Someone's found somethin' at the graveyard off Cutter Street,' he half-whispered, half-trumpeted from the hills, if such a thing were possible. I suppose, in hindsight, what he did was *stage-whispered.*

'Found what?' I said, moving in on him again. Cutter Street was quite close to our house, after all, and was pretty much the epicentre of our graveyard-based operations by that time.

'Probably some of Twinnie's used rubber johnnies,' cracked Lion, who I sensed was still mortally wounded by being whipped at raps. Twinnie shot him a look of disgust but made no comment.

'No... no... they found a skull,' cried Tommy, almost tripping over his words in the effort to get them out so quickly.

We all stood in silence and looked at Tommy Peaker. For only the second time in his life he had centre stage. I could tell that he loved it. The little jig-eared fuck never got any attention at school unless it was the teachers getting at him for something or other or us taking the piss out of him; probably got none at home either. Not while his mum kept entertaining her male associates on a daily basis, only acknowledging him when she wanted him to refill their drinks. Not while his sisters were becoming the local bikes; at some point or other all of us fancied pulling a few wheelies on one of them birds...

'It's real,' he whispered. 'Not like that one that they have up in the biology labs. This one's got, like, all this *stuff* on it... And you should see the teeth. The teeth, man. They're all rotten and everything. Like Burt from the shop...'

'You're not lying are you, Squeaker?' asked Twinnie. And from the way he said it, I could tell that one false move from Tommy now would bring us all crashing down like the deck of cards. One false move and we'd give him a kicking as bad as the one we gave him a year or so back. When he had to be off school for at least two months.

'No word of a lie,' he gasped. He was still a little breathless. Maybe it was the excitement, maybe it was his fabled asthma, I don't know. 'Mark found it – you know Mark don't you?'

Yeah, we all knew Mark, or Sparky Marky as he'd wanted us to call him, back before he realised who we were. When he finally did realise who we were – fucking predatory animals – it was too late for him and the name Manky Marky had stuck. He was another runtish little lad from the year below. The sort that always had green snot running out of one nostril or other until he reached secondary school.

The sort who, in olden days would perhaps not even have survived the first winter. Yeah we all knew Mark. And he knew us.

'Well, we were all playing Running the Gauntlet down at the Cutter Street cemetery. Loads of us. It was a right laugh...'

Running the Gauntlet was a game which, if we'd had any sense about us, we'd have copyrighted when we got the chance. We invented it, see, and although we'd long grown tired of it, it was still played with gay abandon, in some form or other, by groups of kids in virtually every year of our school. If only we could have made a board game version of it and tried to sell it to Waddingtons...

But I'm not sure if Waddingtons would have been interested in our game. I'm not sure that making a kid run over the top of as many graves as he could while everyone else simply threw shit at him – anything they could find – until he finally surrendered, would fit in with their ideals of 'fun for all the family'. I'm not sure if they'd have agreed that it fit the age bracket of eight years up, either. And the game wouldn't have been easy to replicate en masse; it wouldn't have easily translated to other towns and villages or cities, where there weren't the sheer number of graveyards. Where there wasn't a plot of some form or other at the end of every fucking street.

'And?' demanded Twinnie.

'Yeah, don't go pretending you got friends, Peaker; just tell us the details,' said Dick, like a dick.

'Sorry,' said Tommy, flinching involuntarily. He did it so many times these days that it had developed into a kind of nervous tic. 'So anyway; Mark was running the gauntlet and he was doing pretty well at it. Getting pretty close to your record, Bully. And I reckon that's why he was just so desperate to make that last grave, right over at the back of the bone-yard. Barry lobbed this half-brick over at him and Mark just made this mad leap over all that overgrown grass and shit... For a second, we all just stood back and watched and we were thinkin' *he's gonna make it, he's gonna make it* and then Mark came crashing down right on top of the grave. Landed so hard that his leg went right through the topsoil. Landed so hard that he opened up this hole at the top. When we all went over, he already had his arm reached right in there. And when he pulled out the skull, all the younger kids just ran away. And it was pretty scary…'

'So where's the skull now?' I asked.

'Still down there… I came to tell you lot as quick as I could.'

'It better still be there,' warned Twinnie.

On the radio, Don McLean warned that it was a day for dying.

And so, the five of us slipped through the woods that marked the bottom boundary of Newton Mills School. We cut across Church Street lower down, where we were sure that we wouldn't be seen. Almost had to turn back when we saw the familiar sight of Mr. Swann's car pulled up haphazardly against the kerb, but when we saw the smoke inside, we knew we were all right.

We started to get excited as we climbed over the allotment wall and Twinnie started to run. Trampled all over the plot right next to my dad's, but I didn't care. The chase was on. Soon we were all shouting and laughing and generally had a good time like we were the boys in *Stand by Me*. We were off to see part of a body; we knew that this was a major step in our school-of-hard-knocks education. We knew it was an event that would long live in the memory. I suppose I was the Geordie character, trying to eek out meaning from the encounter; Dick and Lion were like Vern Tessio and the other one – the boggle –eyed one… But that was where the comparison fell down. Twinnie was no Chris Chambers. In fact he was more like Ace Merrill; dangerous, unpredictable. A force of nature.

We could see the crowd of kids even as we turned the corner from Hangman's Row and onto Cutter Street. Hoards of them, like the school had burned down again and everyone had been turfed out. Half of them probably had no idea why they were there; the other half were only there 'cos their friends were. We barged through them all, sending snotty-nosed bastards skittling off all over the place. The cocks of the school were here now, and the rules of the game had changed. Soon, the crowd became aware of our presence. Silence started to creep in. Nobody wanted to be the one poor fucker that was picked on for the habitual beating. Nobody wanted to be forced to run the gauntlet; not if we were playing.

We reached the gates; those big black imposing things. Twin gargoyles stared down at us; dared us to go through. And we stared right back at them as we squeezed between the bars. Through the gates, there were only a few stray boys knocking around, and we soon sent them off with a dad-like clip round the ear and warnings not to come back.

We were left alone. Just me, Twinnie, Dick, Lion, Tommy and Manky Mark. Manky Mark who was sitting over in the far corner of the cemetery, holding the skull out in front of him like he was practicing for the school production of *Hamlet.* We picked out our path between the graves and made for him. Everything was under cover of the fallen golden leaves, you could barely tell where path ended and grave began. We could barely tell what we were walking on. A million people in a million other-worlds suddenly shivered involuntarily and asked:

Did someone just step on my grave?

As soon as we reached Sparky, Twinnie took the skull from him. And then he just looked at it as though he didn't really know what to do with it. It was a skull. It was part of a dead human. It had strange fission-marks on the top of it; a big crack on the cheek-bone; big gaping eye sockets; a pronounced forehead. But it didn't *do* anything.

Twinnie started manipulating the jaw; making the rotten teeth clack-clack together.

'I'm coming to get you, Tommy Peaker,' he said in this terrible ghost-voice.

Tommy's bottom lip quivered, but only for a moment. Then he realised that he'd better start running. Twinnie was already almost on him, waving the skull around like it was just another half-brick.

'Get him, Twinnie,' roared Dick.

'Oh for fuck's sake,' muttered Lion.

I kept schtum. Watched Manky Mark's reaction. Was he going to stick up for his 'friend?' Was he going to make any move to put a halt to the inevitable beating that Tommy was going to take? Evidently not. Quietly, he started to walk away from us. He stalked back across that bone-yard and made for the gates. He never once looked back, never once took the time to check whether Tommy was being forced to kiss the skull, never once took the time to check whether Tommy was being forced to take down his pants and allow the skull's rotten teeth to touch his tiny prick.

Which is what was happening. Already the skull had become just another torture-instrument. Already, it was secondary to the main game; making Tommy Peaker's life as miserable as possible in as many inventive ways as possible.

'Here; have a look at this,' said Lion, tapping me on the shoulder. Like me, he'd shunned the torture session. Like me, I think he still had some kind of secret reverence for the graveyard. He still believed that otherworldly things could happen in places like that and that there was some mystery in the world.

He led me over to the grave right in the corner. It was almost hidden by thick bushes but we pushed our way through. It was the grave in which Mark had found the skull. Must have been; there was a massive gaping hole in the middle of it.

'I just stuck my hand in there,' said Lion, as though he wanted a gold star or something. 'There's other bones in there. Dare you to have a go…'

'Nah,' I said. 'Boring.'

'You're chicken-shit,' laughed Lion. 'You don't *wanna* put your hand in there in case something reaches out and grabs you…'

Lion was right. I'd seen that film round at Twinnie's once. He'd rented it from M and S Video Supplies despite clearly being fourteen. It was the one where stray bony hands kept pushing out from the graves and pulling people in with them.

'Give us one of your tabs and I'll do it,' I said. 'I bet you didn't really do it, anyway. Nobody saw you do it so why am I supposed to believe you?'

Lion grinned. Pulled his deck of Dorchester and Grey from his trouser pocket. Held them out to me.

'Dorchester and Grey Lion?' I said, taking one. 'Fuck's sake mate. These are Dot Cotton fags.'

'I know mate. Pinched 'em out me mam's handbag this morning. She'll go ape-shit when she realises…'

I accepted the light. Inhaled the sickly flavour. Realised for the nth time that I absolutely detested the taste of cigarettes, but quite liked the head-rush that they gave me. The extra courage, the extra *fuck-it-all*ness that even holding a ciggie gave me. And then, before I could even give myself a chance to think twice, I bent down and thrust my arm elbow-deep into the hole. Felt live things scurrying away. Felt cold, dead bone. Felt something else which felt like a pulse; like the earth itself was pulsing. And then I think I felt the earth around the hole start to give way. And I think I felt myself being sucked into the hole. And I think I felt like I was drowning or about to be buried alive. To spend the remaining moments of my life with that pulsing thing that was under the earth.

I yanked my arm out sharpish.

Lion whistled through his teeth.

'Fuckin' hell, Bully,' he said. 'I didn't think you'd really do it!'

I grinned; put on this daft old-woman voice: 'I'll do anything for a Dorchester and Grey.'

Lion didn't laugh like I hoped he would. Instead he was staring intently at my arm with an expression which bordered on the horrified.

'What?' I asked.

He didn't say anything.

'What?' I demanded. 'What the fuck you looking at me like that for?'

Again he didn't answer. I looked down at my arm. All of my fingers and most of my wrist was stained this awful purple colour. It was like someone had spilled a whole glass of Ribena over me and I'd just left it.

'Aaaagh,' I screamed. 'Get it off me, get it off me…'

I started chasing Lion around, trying to wipe the mould or the stain or whatever it was off onto his school shirt. Dick and Twinnie must have been alerted by our noise because they were soon over with us, dragging Tommy Peaker behind them by the collar of his shirt. The collar was ripping badly now and there seemed to be a bad cut on his neck, too.

'Where's the skull?' I asked, rubbing a leaf on my arm. The purple was disappearing rapidly now. Almost as quickly as it had come on.

'Dick only went and smashed it off one of the gravestones,' said Twinnie. But he didn't sound too disappointed. 'What's that on your arm?'

Lion was only too happy to tell them, and as he did so, I got this terrifying vision of what was going to happen. I *knew* what they were going to do, probably even before they did.

'Bully stuck his hand into the grave,' said Lion. 'That's dead-body juice all on his arm.'

'Dead body juice is *blood*, Lion,' I corrected him, wearily.

'Whatever. You got all shit on you from sticking your arm in there. And all for a ciggie,' said Lion.

'I did. Let's go back up to school now. If you've smashed-up the skull, there's not really any point being here, is there?'

Twinnie cocked his head and looked at me. I could see his mind working. The wheels of his one-armed bandit spinning round. Soon, they would all come to a stop, and there'd be a payout. And that payout would be paid directly to poor little Tommy Peaker.

'Let's see what happens when we stick Tommy's hand in there,' said Twinnie, finally.

'Yeah!' roared Dick. 'Or why don't we make him put his tiny little cock in there. See if that goes all mouldy like Bully's fingers.'

Twinnie gave him a withering look: 'You can go fiddling about with Tommy's cock if you want. Me, I reckon we stick his head in.'

Lion and Dick grabbed Tommy's kicking legs and held them still. Twinnie still had one hand clamped around the lad's collar and one in his hair. They yanked him up off the ground, making it look very easy. There was nothing to Tommy after all; we'd seen his caved-in chest in PE once, when he was made to exercise in only his shit-encrusted y-fronts; teacher said that he'd heard the 'forgotten kit' excuse too many times to care any more. And Tommy's legs were kinda knock-kneed too. And about the thickness of one of my arms.

There was nothing to him, and he didn't have the strength to fight back. They lifted him up, spun him around a little bit, just to get

211

him nice and dizzy, nice and frantic, and then they lowered him down again, head-first into the rapidly widening hole in the grave. Tommy screamed, but it came out all muffled, like he had a mouthful of grave-dirt inside him or like he was down the bottom of a well, shouting up at us.

They pulled him back up. His whole head was purple, either from all the blood rushing into it after the way they'd held him, or from that other stuff; the stuff that had coated my arm. The stuff that I could still see traces of, underneath my fingernails.

'That's enough now,' I said, or think I said. My head was spinning. It was head loss, but not how I'd ever experienced it before. This was a loss of control that felt like an out-of-body experience. Like I was looking down on the five of us in that leaf-strewn, litter-choked graveyard and there was no way I could step in and alter the course of history. I felt at once old and young, at once dead and at once alive. It was as though the whole universe had collapsed in on itself and was dying.

Nobody paid any attention to me, so I figured that they'd not heard my remonstrations. They were laughing too hard now. Screaming abuse at Tommy Peaker, driven wild by their desire to inflict more agony.

'Look at his face!' yelled Twinnie. 'He's turned into a fucking blackberry.'

'Let's do it again, let's do it again,' shouted Dick.

And for once, they all listened to him, or were already going to do it anyway. So I stood back and watched, as helpless as Manky Mark, as they Dairylea dunked him into the death-juice filled grave. And I swear that I felt the earth move under my feet. It felt like Tommy, the earth which surrounded him, the grass on which we stood, were all being sucked into something down there. We were feeding the appetite for misery of something far larger than ourselves and there was only me that knew it.

They pulled him out again. Now I could no longer make out the features on Tommy's face. It was as though his face wasn't there any more. But still the three of them did not sense that they'd taken it too far. No: something other than themselves was driving them on. They were pawns in some game that was far greater than themselves, the shit-hole school, the decaying town, the mills, *everything.*

They are processing him, a voice in my head told me. *Chewing him up, and spitting him out like he's nothing. Processing him just like they used to with the workers in the mills…*

I stared down into the hole in the grave. Saw something massive moving in there. Saw the hole starting to get bigger again. Big enough to fit a small boy's body in now.

Twinnie saw it too: 'Let's put his whole body down there; see what happens.'

'Turn him all-blackberry,' agreed Dick.

Lion just had this blank look on his face like he was faraway somewhere else, just like I was. But he gripped Tommy Peaker's left leg with a strength that nobody had yet felt the full force of. And Dick grabbed on to the right leg just the same. Twinnie was holding on so hard to Tommy's hair that big chunks of it were starting to fall out now, and the poor lad's collar was no more. The cut on his neck had turned into a wide, gaping gash now, but nobody cared. Only I could see it, I think, underneath all that purpling.

There were no whoops of joy as they lowered the whole of Tommy Peaker into the grave. The burial was conducted with the solemnity that history demanded. Only after, when he was inside, all curled up into a ball, did anyone speak.

'Let's cover him up,' whispered Twinnie. 'Kick some of the dirt back over him. Only for a bit, like. Just to see what happens.'

Everyone readily agreed. Dick started shovelling up great handfuls of muck and chucked it down onto Tommy's prostrate body. Lion kicked more in. Twinnie took off his shoe and started using it like a bucket.

And gradually, they covered him up. Gradually, as the dirt rained down, there was no more of Tommy Peaker to see. And he never screamed once. Perhaps he thought that once this was over with, once we were back in cold, grey reality, we'd all experience some kind of gigantic turnaround, realise what we'd done, and all the bullying would end just like that.

Twinnie levelled off the earth at the top of the grave just as we heard the first of the police sirens. His face blanched. All of our faces blanched.

'I've gotta get out of here,' he said. 'I'm already on my last warning with them fuckers...'

And he was off, leaping over old graves, breaking all known records for running the gauntlet. Soon Dick was careering after him, more clumsy in his progress, but still making up good ground. Lion and I stood over the fresh grave and looked at each other. A massive, unheard scream passed between us. Within it was the agony which said: *what have we done?*

And then I saw the reflection of blue flashing lights on Lion's face. He must have seen them on mine too, because he offered me this completely helpless shrug and then bounced away after them, running faster than I'd ever seen the fat bastard run in any of the football games we'd ever played.

I was left, standing over the grave of Tommy Peaker.

Would he be alive in there? Could he be alive in there? Would there be breathing space in there along with all that mud?

A policeman shouted at me. He was already trying to squeeze himself through the bars of the gate, I saw, but was too fat to fit. Too many years sat on his arse in the Choke, drinking lager along with everyone else in the town. Police and criminals alike.

'Oi!' he shouted again. 'What do you think you're doing in there? This graveyard is private property. You're trespassing. And you're skiving school. Wait there!'

I realised too late that I was running too. Away from Tommy Peaker's grave, away from what we'd done, away from everything. And I knew I'd be running for a long time to come.

We'll go back though, I thought to myself as I ran. We'll go back later and dig him up. Nobody but us will know about Tommy. The police won't find out about what we've done. They'll just think it was kids messing about. They won't even bother to follow up on us... They won't bother going over to the grave right in the corner of the yard. And they certainly won't stop to notice that it looks like fresh dirt has been pushed over the top of it. And Tommy won't call out for help. He knows better than that. He knows better than to invite trouble by grassing. He'll be okay, he'll be okay, he'll be okay...

But he wasn't okay and we all knew that there wasn't any point going back to dig him up.

Chapter Twenty-One

"Satan's spell"

Everything in the graveyard was under cover of the fallen golden leaves from the now bare sentry trees which flanked it; guarded it, even. It hadn't been autumn earlier, and I had absolutely no idea when or how it had changed, but change it had, and we were now in Cutter Street cemetery on the day we'd buried Tommy Peaker alive. Somehow, despite it being a scientific impossibility, I knew we were back there, me and him, and we'd almost reached the end of my journey.

'Right now, your dad is putting the finishing touches on his evening meal,' said Tommy. *'He's pouring the beans out of the little pan that he always uses for soup or beans – never anything else – and onto his toast. He's done the toast under the grill, Bully. He hates toasters, doesn't he? Thinks that they don't do the job properly. And the smell of toast under the grill always reminds him of better times, when there were four of you in that house on Hangman's Row.'*

I knew what Tommy was doing; he was making sure that I knew that he could be in more than one place at the same time. He could occupy two (or more) quite separate periods, one twelve years ago and one now – if there was a now – and he could reach between the folds of the two, and drag back whatever prey he fancied.

'Now he's picking up the tray from the side of the fridge. It's a funny tray that, Bully. It's got a sort of cushion thing underneath so that it's more comfy on your knees. He bought it up at the second hand shop up on the main street, when he couldn't stand sitting at that empty kitchen table any more. Now he sits with only the fucking television for

company, eating his beans on toast and not even noticing what they taste like.

When he finishes his food, he'll think, 'I'll just give myself five minutes' and he'll put the tray on your mother's empty seat and close his eyes for a bit and try to remember what it felt like to have you on his knee, listening to the rhythm of his beating heart. But he can never last the full five minutes. He always feels something nagging at him. He thinks that he'll go to rack and ruin – go purple if you will – if he doesn't get the washing up done.

So he'll slipper his way down that hallway and back into the shabby little kitchen and he'll run a full bowl even though he's only got about three things to wash. And its always the same order he washes it all in; first the cutlery, when the water's boiling hot and it will keep the fake-silver looking sparkling; then the plate which will have traces of bean juice in it; then the wooden spoon he's used to stir the pan; then finally, when the water's already messed-up, he'll wash that stained little pan that he only uses for beans and soup.

It's a sad little life he has now, Bully. I don't think he'd be that gutted if we brought him back here so he could get a proper five-minutes in that nice retirement-grave that I just showed you. Shall I go and get him now, or shall I let him do the washing-up first? I reckon he'd hate it if he left the house messy, don't you? He'd reckon people would think that it was a bad reflection on him, and in some mad roundabout way, on his wife – your mother – even though she's been dead twenty years now.'

'Is there nothing I can do to save him?' I asked, blinking back the tears. My eyes stung. I felt that if I just reached out, I could touch my dad and smell the ripe smell of his Barbour jacket and hear the now haphazard beating of his once strong heart.

'Death is a terrible thing, Bully,' he said. *'But the process of death starts as soon as we are born. From the moment we pop on out into this world, we're rotting away. In Newton Mills, it's even more pronounced, this living-death thing. They call it the purpling. Old Burt told you about the purpling, didn't he? When you went to him with the guilt after you'd been released from hospital after your fall at Grange Heights...*

*And the purpling will never stop here. It's embedded in the very
bedrock of the town in which we live. It's ingrained in the gorge and
flows in the river. It is the very material from which they made the
dome for the library at that fucking school. It's in the beer and in the
drugs and in the Dorchester and Greys. Dorchester and Greys, Bully?
I can't believe you made them your ciggie of choice. What a goddamn
waste…*

*So, in answer to your question; no, there's nothing you can do
to save him. Not in the long term.'*

'In the short term?' I gasped. 'Is there anything I can do in the
short term? Would it help if I went to the police now, or whenever we
are, and confessed to what we've done?'

'I suppose that might have helped, once upon a time,' sighed
Tommy. *'And it would tie up everything ever so nicely. But that time
has now long passed. I'm afraid that I want blood. I want to wring
every last drop of blood out of every last one of you. Thoughts of
revenge are burning holes in me, Bully. You're too polite, or too
scared to comment about my appearance, but really? Look at the
fucking state of me…'*

I looked at him. He was right; he was getting worse and worse
by the minute, as though the oxygen in the air was poison to him. His
face was more skull now. The eyeball that he had so tried to pop back
into the socket had long given up the ghost somewhere along the line.
He was a one-eyed, bone-skinned, walking-talking freak show now, it
seemed.

'What do you want from me?' I yelled, half-standing, grabbing
at his collar.

And suddenly, I saw the fear in Tommy's eyes. The total, utter
goddamn desperate fear that lay within him.

'I don't know,' he whispered. *'I don't know. I just wanted you
to feel how I'd felt for so long…'*

'I do feel that way!' I shouted. I was making a breakthrough, I
could sense it. There was a way that I could turn this all around. There
was a way that I could save myself and make everything right and
make everybody…

Tommy punched my hands off him and shook his head as though trying to clear away the doubts or cobwebs in his head. More of his skin and flesh flew off him. And then he picked me up like a baby in his giant arms and started to carry me off in the direction of the corner of the graveyard. He beat away the thick bushes and revealed my fate to me; the grave in which we'd buried him twelve years ago. And I wasn't even surprised. I'd known this would be my punishment all along. I deserved it.

Tommy sensed my resignation and dropped me on the floor next to the grave. I took in the fact that it looked *exactly* the same as when the three of them had put him in there. He hadn't bothered completely emptying this grave. Just left enough space to fit me in, before he could start shovelling the dirt back over me.

'*Get in,*' he ordered.

I climbed to my feet. For some reason, I was not half-footed any more. I was completely able-bodied. Completely able to walk over to the hole in the grave, dangle my leg over it and then drop myself in.

'*Good; very good,*' said Tommy, clapping his hands together in a terrible imitation of a fourteen-year-old's excitement. One of his thumbs fell off, such was the force he was using. '*Get yourself all the way in there.*'

I still had two hands touching the sides of the hole, but most of me was inside it, feeling the mud compact around me and little slithery things starting to get to know my feet and legs. Starting to take little bites and tasters. Dinner was served for those grave-insects.

'If I do this, will you promise to leave my dad alone?' I asked, taking one last look at Tommy Peaker's face.

'*I will promise, Bully,*' he said. '*But only because I'm tired like you now. If I had more energy I'd go for him, but I'm getting so tired now.*'

As if to emphasise his point, he flopped down onto the floor and sat by the grave cross-legged like we used to sit in assembly. Absently, he started fidgeting, just like he always used to. When he went to pick his nose though, it simply came away in his hands. Then, one of his jug ears slipped off his face and landed in his lap.

'There's not much time,' he said. *'At this rate, I'm not even going to have the strength to bury you. Now can you please get in there?'*

I suppose I could have fought against him. I suppose I could have raged against the dying of the light. But to be honest, death was ready for me, and I was ready for death. And if there was one thing good I could do with my life, it would be to end it all and let Tommy finally have a minute's peace.

'Good. Good,' said Tommy, as I let first one and then the other hand loose from the edges of the hole. As I let myself fall off the precipice and into nothingness. As I fell, as each meaty fistful of earth rained down on me, I remained quiet as the grave. And I empathised at last. I empathised with Tommy and how we'd made him feel. I suppose you could call it an epiphany, but it was too late. Far, far too late.

I was drowning in mud and leaves. Falling into hell or that great maw which was at the epicentre of Newton Mills and everything that ever happened there. I could hardly see anything of the graveyard at all now, let alone Tommy Peaker. But I got the funny feeling that he'd already gone. He'd already disintegrated. And I *knew* he'd gone when the first of the concrete was poured over me. When the graveyard started to become a car park. When my head was finally, after everything, lost.

THE END

Biography

Writing fiction to suspend belief in skint reality is Andy's stock in trade. He has had short stories featured in a wide number of publications, including anthologies (Legend Press's *Eight Rooms*, *Nemonymous 8: Cone Zero & Nemonymous 9: Cern Zoo* from Megazanthus Press, Graveside Tales' *Fried: Fast Food Slow Deaths)* print journals (Sein und Werden, Skrev Press, and Champagne Shivers) and webzines (New Voices in Horror, Pumpkin, The Second Hand, US Short Story Library, and Underground).

He was runner-up in the 2008 Huddersfield Literature Festival creative writing competition, and has been short-listed for the Cinnamon Press short fiction prize and the Mere Literary Festival prize.

Andy has written three other novels; the crime-thriller, *The Magpie Trap,* (published by Youwriteon.com and Legend Press) *When Elephants walk through the Gorbals,* (won third prize in the Luke Bitmead Memorial Bursary) and the dark techno-thriller *Perfect World.*

Andy lives in Leeds, UK with his girlfriend Heidi and his incredibly noisy cat, Eric.

To find out more, visit Andy's website:
www.andykirbythewriter.20m.com